whip up   er

MURDER IS SER

"Like Conan Doyle's London, the Lockridges' New York has a lasting magic. There are taxis waiting at every corner, special little French restaurants, and perfect martinis. Even murder sparkles with big city sophistication. For everyone who remembers New York in the Forties and for everyone who wishes he did."

—*Emma Lathen*

"The versatility of Frances and Richard Lockridge knows almost no bounds."

—*New York Times*

"This husband and wife team is unexcelled in the field of mystery writing when it comes to a completely entertaining crime story."

—*St. Louis Post-Dispatch*

Pam and Jerry North made their first appearance in *The New Yorker* in the 1930s. In 1940, Richard Lockridge's first book-length mystery, *The Norths Meet Murder,* was published. Richard and Frances Lockridge went on to write dozens of Mr. and Mrs. North books, as well as numerous other mysteries. The Norths became the stars of a Broadway play and a movie as well as a long-running radio program and popular television series.

Books by Richard and Frances Lockridge

Death Takes a Bow
The Judge Is Reversed
Murder by the Book
Murder Comes First
Murder in a Hurry
Murder is Served
Murder Within Murder

Published by POCKET BOOKS

MURDER IS SERVED

RICHARD AND FRANCES LOCKRIDGE

PUBLISHED BY POCKET BOOKS NEW YORK

POCKET BOOKS, a division of Simon & Schuster, Inc.
1230 Avenue of the Americas, New York, N.Y. 10020

ISBN: 0-671-47328-X

First Pocket Books printing August, 1983

10 9 8 7 6 5 4 3 2 1

POCKET and colophon are registered trademarks
of Simon & Schuster, Inc.

Printed in the U.S.A.

MURDER
IS
SERVED

1

John Leonard tilted his chair, felt its back engage the eraser trough behind him, removed his glasses and regarded forty-three members of X_{33}, Experimental Psychology, most of whom regarded him. He enquired whether everything was clear to everyone and forty-two men and women looked back at him, as if hoping that he would, in fact, make everything clear. The forty-third looked rather dreamily out a window.

"Good," Leonard told them. "Very good. Then you may as well get about it."

Forty-three students got about it. A young woman in the front row shook her fountain pen, as if to shake thoughts out of it. The young man next to her looked at the ceiling. Three rows back, a girl—undergraduate, as Leonard remembered—put her pencil in her mouth, and, although he could not see them, he could guess that she tied her legs into a knot. Situation normal, Leonard told himself; situation as always was and always would be. He lighted a cigarette. He watched while, one by one, the forty-three began to write in little blue books; he shuddered to think how difficult most of what they wrote would be to read. Situation

7

normal, situation as always. And the two or three who would have the most to say would be the least decipherable.

What would they make of it, he wondered? He wondered what he would make of it if he were one of the forty-three. You came expecting something, you came for an examination. You came, perhaps, with names and dates, with definitions. And you got this—this evasive instruction. Write me a discussion, as long as you like, as short as you like, of the effect of some emotion on human behavior, the effect of hate or fear or love or greed as those things were felt normally by the normal mind. Tell me, from what you have heard here, what you have read during the course, what you have found out during your lives, how one of these emotions colors thought, tilts logic into illogic, makes the abstract into the particular. What would I have made of such a demand? John Leonard wondered. What would Weldon Carey make of it? The young woman looking out of the window? The undergraduate with the tangled legs? What would Peggy make of it? John Leonard, Associate Professor of Psychology, Department of Extension, Dyckman University, corrected himself. Not Peggy—Mrs. Peggy Mott. In this room, at this time—not Peggy. He looked at her. She was writing very rapidly, very intently. The shadows on her face, with her head bent so, made her expression uncharacteristically sombre.

Love would be the emotion of which she wrote, John Leonard suspected. It would be appropriate; if he was not mistaken, it would be something she knew about. Not hate, surely not fear. Fear—or hate or anger—would be what Weldon Carey would know about. Carey had had cause to be afraid, Leonard suspected, to be afraid, to hate. And he seemed always, obscurely, angered. He would, in all probability, write the best discussion of any of them, and the most violent, the most resentful. Probably, as regards me, as of now, his resentment is abstract, Leonard thought, looking at the top of Weldon Carey's head, with the black hair sprawling from it. Carey has enough abstract resentment to go around.

You got a mixed bag these days, Leonard thought, and let his chair drop down again to the floor. This was a mixed bag, even for Extension, even for nowadays. The half-dozen undergraduates, five of them female— that was normal. The housewife from Jackson Heights, she was normal. The middle-aged businessman was normal too, and as essentially inexplicable as always. Why was he there? Why was he giving two evenings a week, from seven-forty until nine, to hear lectures on psychology? Had somebody told him John Leonard would make him a better salesman? Teach him how to approach the boss for a raise? He was always there, he was always inexplicable. The undergraduates, the housewives from Queens, the unexplained businessmen—those were standard, those formed a nucleus. You added the anonymous ones, with no apparent personalities, no recallable names, and you had perhaps two thirds of the class. Then the mixed bag began, the really mixed bag. The Peggy Motts, the angry Weldon Careys, the illusive Cecily Breakwells.

Carey was, Leonard guessed, about thirty. He should, in the normal course, have been done with all this years ago. But not if you took five years out, if somebody took five years out. Five years to be afraid in, to hate in, to build resentment in. God knows, Leonard thought, I'd resent it. I'd resent it like hell. I'd resent me, because I had it soft; I'd resent everyone who had it soft, and everybody who made it hard. I wonder how he'll write it, Leonard thought. I wonder if this sort of thing helps him any?

There were a good many Careys, although most of them did not hate so much, or feel anything so much. Or, if you came to that, think so much. They were part of the mixed bag, these men home from the wars, going back to school as beneficiaries of the "G.I. Bill of Rights." How idiotically people used words, Leonard thought. Why "bill of rights," for God's sake?

He put his cigarette on the floor and stepped on it—and wondered a little how he still got away with smoking, letting the class smoke. The rules forbade. He wondered whether he did not smoke so much in class because the rules forbade. Resentment of rules, there was an emotion for you. He picked up his book, turned so the light fell on it, and began to read. But he was always conscious of the forty-three. Forty-three minds at work, forty-three pens and pencils moving on paper, leaving marks which would, for the most part, be barely decipherable. And of those minds, perhaps half a dozen—be generous, Professor, be generous—perhaps half a dozen which worked well enough to matter. He laid the book down and walked to the window and looked, far down, at the snow-covered street. Carey's mind mattered, he thought; perhaps Peggy Mott's did, although he might think that because of the way her hair fell, because of the wideness of her eyes. The young man in the back row, the balding young man who was now regarding the ceiling with an expression of pleased interest, had a pleasantly quirky mind and the baby undergraduate—Dorothy Brown? Agnes Brownley?—had something. It was too soon to tell what.

That did not add to half a dozen. There would be the dark horse, of course; the unexpected prize which came, out of the anonymous, often as not, on the occasion of a final term paper. All right, Leonard thought, call it five, and figure my own subjective in, my own response to the way hair lies, sleekly, around a pretty head. I'm a hell of a professor, John Leonard thought; a hell of a psychologist. He looked at his watch. They had been at it almost three quarters of an hour. The first fireman was almost due, the speed demon, the lad who could dispose of the emotion of love in half an hour, and correct all his errors thereon in fifteen minutes.

Leonard walked back to the table and sat at it, a long man and a thin one, sprawling. His blond hair, which was thinning only a little, looked as if it had been pawed. His face was long and narrow, with unexpectedly red lips; his forehead was high and domed. Looking at himself, John Leonard too often thought, "My God, you look it. What else would you be?" And next he thought, more moderately, "Why shouldn't I? It's what I am." And then, finally, and almost always, "It's what I want to be." It was absurd to object to looking what you were—an associate professor with thinning hair, working toward full professorship and baldness. And—his mind now running on vaguely—doing what comes naturally, as Ethel Merman had been singing the year before at the Imperial. He began, half-consciously, to hum the tune. But you couldn't hum the Merman's little kick. You couldn't hum any part of the Merman.

The trouble was, Professor Leonard thought, rubbing his hair, that too many things came naturally. Teaching was fine, and sometimes almost exciting, and it came naturally. If the mind were as neat as any classification made it, that would round things off. I am John Leonard, Associate Professor of Psychology. Stop. Full stop. But the mind didn't stop, the inclinations didn't stop. Emotions affected human behavior, and human need. Love and hatred, fear and greed. Greed in my case, most probably, John Leonard thought. Greed for color and light, for things which could be touched and tasted, for the sensations which ran from fingertips, from eyes, from nostrils, from the taste buds of the tongue, into the mind. Sensationalist, Professor Leonard told himself. Sensualist, if it came to that. He smiled, thinking of Professor Handleigh, head of the department, round, jovial, to whom being head of a department came more naturally than anything else. A professor of the old school, Handleigh was, with the cultivated light touch. "Ah, Leonard," Handleigh had said once, coming on his junior, with a girl who was clearly his junior's junior, at André Maillaux's, coming on them late in the evening, when they had brandies in front of them. "Ah, Leonard, so far from the cloister?" he had said, with the air of one who, almost pointedly, does not disapprove. And, subsequently, Professor Handleigh was reported to have told someone that Leonard, brilliant beyond question, was also "something of a rogue." Handleigh, John Leonard thought, ran a personal sanctuary for words far gone in obsolescence. A rogue, indeed! A rogue, forsooth. I could stand a brandy now, Leonard thought; I could stand doing the rest of that evening over again.

He controlled his thought, put his glasses on again, and tilted his book to the light. *Duration of Post-hypnotic Suggestion in Relation to Induced Fatigue.* That was where he was; that was his homework. Then there was movement, the sound of movement, in front of him and he looked up. The first fireman was sliding down his greased pole. He was one of the anonymous ones. He put the blue book on the table in front of Leonard, who murmured, "Your name's on it? Oh, yes. Thank you, Mr. Ah—."

"It was a very interesting course, sir," the anonymous one said. "I feel I got a lot out of it."

"Good," Leonard murmured. "Er—good."

Mr. Ah went away, having broken the ice. Two other students, neither of whom had wanted to be first, stood up simultaneously and advanced, holding blue offerings. Leonard smiled to their vague smiles, checked the presence of their names, began the pile of blue books. When they had left the classroom, he opened the topmost book, looked at the chirography, and shuddered. He put it down and, unconsciously, rubbed his fingers with the tip of his thumb. He hoped that conscience would not, tomorrow, make him fight his way from the beginning of that one to the mist-enshrouded end. A rogue, indeed! He would bet Handleigh, faced with that, would give it three minutes, two paragraphs, and a B minus. And I'll bet I won't, Leonard thought, and sighed. He did not enjoy his conscience.

They came more rapidly then. By eight-forty they were coming one a minute. They had enjoyed the course. They had got a lot out of it. They hoped they could arrange to come back for the spring term. "Yes," Professor Leonard murmured. "Yes. I'm glad. I hope so. Yes." And the pile of blue books grew. A second pile started.

Weldon Carey came forward at eight-fifty. He was not smiling. He seemed to consider Leonard one with the desk, the chair. He did not say that he had profited from the course, or that he hoped to come back for the spring term. He put his book down and turned away.

"Oh—Carey," Leonard said. Carey turned back, did not move back, waited. "How's the new play coming?" Leonard said.

"All right," Carey told him. "All right, I guess." He was not impolite, but he was waiting to go on.

"Good," Leonard said. He smiled faintly, and Carey did not return the smile. "Why did you take this course, by the way?" Leonard said.

Carey did not seem surprised at the question, or much interested in the question.

"Had the time," he said and paused. "You can't tell," he added.

"No," Leonard said. "You can't tell. All right, Carey."

He watched Carey go out. Where would he meet Peggy Mott, Leonard wondered. At the subway kiosk? At the coffee counter in the book shop? Or would he merely wait outside, in the corridor? And where would they go? Professor Leonard looked, almost without volition, at Peggy Mott.

Peggy's head was still bent forward, the light still made shadows on her face. But the shining blondness of her hair reflected the light. She had finished writing, was reading over what she had written. As he watched her she turned the last page, changed a word on it and closed the book. She looked up then and the light fell on her face. She's got the widest eyes, Leonard thought. The *widest* eyes. She was looking toward him, but did not seem to see him, or anything. The shadow which had been on her face seemed still to be in her eyes, although literally it was not. She sat so for a moment, and then she pushed back the hair which had fallen against her right cheek. She stood up. She had her fur jacket over her arm. They were meeting in the corridor, then, Leonard thought, suddenly.

She was rather tall. He wondered if that was a problem to her. It was better for actresses not to be tall; height in women was a casting problem. He watched her move the few feet toward his desk. She walked well; she had learned that part of her business. He wondered whether she could really act. She smiled as she came toward him and she put the examination book on top of the smaller pile. She had written her name in the corner—"P.S. Mott" and "X_{33}," and the date—and then his own name, "Professor Leonard." He looked up at her, taking his glasses off.

"It's been very interesting," she said. "May I come back next term?"

"I'm glad," he said. "Of course."

He felt he was looking at her too intently, that he was embarrassing them both. He looked down at his desk.

"I hope it's all right," she said, seeming to mean her examination paper. She started away and paused after a few steps. "Next term," she said. "If—if nothing happens."

Then she went and opened the classroom door and kept her left hand on the knob, pulling it shut behind her. There was a large dinner ring on the smallest finger. That was all. Well, Leonard thought. So. Professor Leonard resumed his glasses.

He picked up her blue book. She printed. It was an affectation of which, for practical reasons, he strongly approved. He found it easy to read the first few sentences. He turned the page. Then, as he read on, lines formed in his high forehead, and his eyebrows drew together. He shook his head slightly, as if to shake off something, and went on reading. When he finished, he laid the book down carefully on the pile, took his glasses off and began to polish them with a handkerchief, looking at nothing, looking across the two toilers who remained, still writing anxiously, still pouring forth their ideas of hate and love, of greed and fear.

Professor Leonard did not see them, was not even impatient for them to finish. He sat for a moment, polishing his glasses more and more slowly. Then he stood up, still carrying his glasses in his handkerchief, and walked to the window. He looked down into the snow-covered street seven stories below. There were moving figures, indistinguishable, on the cleared sidewalk, and Professor Leonard watched them without thinking about them. He would be damned, Professor Leonard thought; it was, certainly, the damnedest thing. He had not expected anything like this.

2

"—subsidiary rights," Mr. Gerald North said, finishing a sentence. "Make it 'cordially,' Miss Corning, under the circumstances. Now, take one to Miss Wanda Wuerth, and be sure it's u, e, not o, care B and B, dear Miss Wuerth several of our readers have objected that damn that telephone I told them never mind, I'll take it—yes?"

"A Mr. Leonard is calling," the girl at the switchboard said.

"Leonard?" Jerry said.

The switchboard girl was firm.

"A Mr. Leonard," she said. "He says it's important. Wait a minute, please. Yes?" There was a momentary pause. "He says it's Professor Leonard of Dyckman, if that helps," she said. "Just a moment, please." Jerry North reclined against the telephone in his left hand and looked at nothing. "He says you ought to remember," the switchboard said. "He says because it only sold twelve hundred and you lost your—"

"Miss Nelson," Jerry North said, with firmness. "Please. I do remember. Just put Mr. Leonard on."

16

"I have Mr. North for you now," the switchboard said. "Go ahead, please."

"Mr. North?" a new voice said. It was a male voice, modulated, vigorous. "This is John Leonard. You did a book of mine last year and—"

"I remember," Jerry said. "Hello, Leonard. Another book? I'm afraid—"

John Leonard laughed.

"Don't sound so alarmed," Leonard said. "Not that bad, Mr. North. Nothing worse than murder, this time."

"Oh," Jerry said. "What? You mean you've done a mystery? I thought—"

"Not I," Leonard said. "One of my boys and girls. Potentially. Or I'm afraid so. I want advice."

"In that case, I'm afraid our mystery list's full up," Jerry said.

John Leonard made sounds. He said that Mr. North didn't understand. He said he would admit it was difficult.

"It has nothing to do with a book," he said. "That's where we went off. I'm not calling you as a publisher. I really want advice." His voice changed. "It's serious," he said. "I have a feeling it's vital. I think a young woman in one of my classes is working up to kill somebody. I feel I've got to try to do something."

"My God yes," Jerry North said. He looked at Miss Corning, still poised with her shorthand book. She looked merely attentive, obedient, politely detached. "Who?" Jerry said into the telephone.

"—thought of you," Leonard said. "Because you know this detective, know about things like this." Now there was anxiety in his voice. "I tell you," he said, "I'm damn serious, North. I want help. Can I come around and talk to you?"

"Now?" Jerry said.

"Any time," Leonard said. "Better, lunch with me. Can you do that?"

"I suppose so," Jerry said. "Of course, I don't understand this. Why don't you go to the police?"

"You would understand it," Leonard said. "That's the point. The police—no. It's too vague. Too intangible. Perhaps, if you agree, you can take it up with that friend of yours. The chap I met. Winan?"

"Weigand," Jerry said. "Bill Weigand." Jerry had a sudden idea. "I'll have to check something," he said. "A—a tentative engagement for lunch. Can I call you back? Are you at the university?"

"In my office," Leonard said. "Do that. I'll wait." He paused again. "I think it's important," he said then, slowly. "As important as—death." Then he hung up.

Jerry held the telephone receiver off and looked at it and shook his head at it. He looked at Miss Corning, who raised her eyebrows in polite attention and waited.

"The damnedest thing," Jerry said. "Where was I, Miss Corning?"

"—our readers have objected that," Miss Corning said, "to Wanda Wuerth, care Brandt and Brandt." She hung her pencil in the air over the page of her notebook.

"Never mind," Jerry said. He pushed the telephone instrument to her end of the desk and said, "Here."

"Get me Professor John Leonard at Dyckman University, will you?" he said. "Be sure it is Leonard."

"Certainly, Mr. North," Miss Corning said. She repeated her instructions to the switchboard girl. She waited. After a time she said, "Professor Leonard?" Then she looked at Mr. North and he shook his head. "One moment, please," she said to the telephone, and pushed it toward Mr. North. She held a hand over the transmitter end but she did not say anything. She merely nodded.

"Mr. Leonard?" Jerry said and listened. There could be no doubt about the voice; there could be no doubt that there was sudden relief in it. There was even a kind of eagerness.

"North!" John Leonard said. "Good! You can make it?"

Jerry decided then.

"Yes," he said. "Around one o'clock all right? The Oak Room of the Ritz? Meet in the Little Bar?"

"Good," Leonard said. "Anywhere you say."

"See you then," Jerry said. He decided something else. "Wait a minute," he said. "I think I'll try to get my wife to join us. All right with you?"

There was, perhaps, the faintest hesitancy. Then John Leonard said, "Fine, perfect."

"One o'clock, then," Jerry said. He put the telephone back in its cradle and looked at Miss Corning.

"—our readers have objected that," Miss Corning said. "To Miss Wuerth."

"Later," Jerry said. "Will you see if you can get me Mrs. North?" He pushed the telephone toward her. He left his desk and walked to a window. In the street, many stories down, a dwarf Sno-Go was turning a soiled gray pile into a stream of white dust, spraying it into a truck. "Mrs. North," Miss Corning said. He went to his desk in two long steps.

"Pam," he said. "Are you tied up for lunch?"

"Jerry!" Pam said. "How nice. But—yes. Hair, you know. I told you."

"Cancel it," Jerry said. "I want you to—to see a man. A man who thinks he's stumbled on a murder. Or—a potential murder."

"Jerry!" Pam said. "Not you!"

"Of course not me," Jerry said. "A man named—" But Pam North said, "No."

"Getting us into something, I meant," Pam said. "I realized it was another man. I suppose I can, but it looks terrible."

"It?" Jerry said.

"My hair, of course," Pam told him. "And tomorrow's Henri's day off and I'll have to take just anybody. Where?"

"Oh, the Ritz," Jerry said. "One o'clock. The man's name's Leonard. He's a professor at Dyckman. He says a girl in his class is going to kill somebody."

"Good," Pam said. "The Ritz. One o'clock."

There were always a good many people you knew in the Ritz Little Bar. Publishers took authors there to explain why present conditions required shares of subsidiary rights, and authors, softened, sometimes grew meek. Agents took publishers there and extolled authors over scotches; radio writers went there with producers, dutch, and told them sure it would work, see? Jerry North went down the stairs and discovered that he did recognize Professor John Leonard, who was folded in a small chair by a tiny table in the no-man's-land between bar and restaurant. Professor Leonard unfolded himself and made greeting sounds. A look enquired as to the whereabouts of the rest of the Norths.

"We'll wait in the bar," Jerry told him, and led the way. George said, "How're you, Mr. North" and jerked his head toward the nook. Jerry North smiled and nodded to two publishers, noticed that one of them had in tow Helen Langford, and that Miss Langford looked embarrassed on seeing him—and made a note in his mind to check the latest Langford sales figures, to see whether she was worth fighting over. He preceded Leonard into the nook and said, "Well!"

"Late," Pam North told them, incorrectly. "I've been waiting hours." She indicated a half-empty martini glass in front of her. "Hours," she repeated. She slid into the corner and looked up at Professor Leonard. It was a long way up. Jerry North made introducing sounds. Pam looked again at Leonard, who smiled suddenly.

"Yes, Mrs. North," he said. "Don't I?"

"What?" Pam said.

"Look like a professor," Leonard said. "You were thinking that, weren't you?"

"No," Pam said. "Oh no. I didn't have to think about that. I was wondering whether I was right. To save time, I mean."

Jerry North looked at Pam, who was guileless, who appeared guileless. She had on a cherry red dress and a small hat which seemed to have been made out of part of a leopard. She looked at him without a flicker in her eyes.

"I'm afraid—" Leonard began. He looked a little afraid, Jerry thought, like a psychologist who has slipped on something—a semantic, perhaps. He and Pam North ought, Jerry decided, to be rather interesting together. It would be interesting to watch a professional approach to the Pam North mind. At the moment, however, Professor Leonard did not seem to be approaching. Jerry motioned him to sit beside Pam; sat opposite them.

"Cocktails," Pam said, as if it were obvious. "I took a chance and—oh, all right George. But I'm afraid I was wrong."

George had brought in two martinis.

"However," Pam said, "it works out. I'm almost ready for another, and Jerry wants one, and we can send George back for something else. Scotch?"

"To save time," Leonard said. "Oh!" He looked at Pam North, who remained guileless. "Of course," he said. "A martini's all right. Fine. Unless you?"

"Oh, I can wait," Pam said. They drank. And waited.

"Well," John Leonard said, "it's a funny thing. A frightening thing, in a sense." He looked at his cocktail, drank half of it. He turned to look at Pam North.

"Did Mr. North tell you anything?" he asked. Pam nodded, amber earrings nodded.

"A little," she said. "You've stumbled—he said 'stumbled'— on a potential murder. Or murderer?"

Leonard nodded. He said, "Good. A potential murderer. I keep thinking I must be wrong. Then I read it again. I'm not wrong. Do you see?"

Both the Norths looked at him, and both waited.

"The uncertainty," he said. "The feeling it's all—all imagination. My own. That I'm reading things in. It's one of my students, you see. A girl—rather beautiful, in her—oh, her mid-twenties. She's an actress. I don't know how good, how much she's really worked at it. Summer stock, I think, and a few parts in town. She's taking dramatic courses chiefly. Working in the experimental theater, reading plays. We have courses like that, you know. Playwriting, even. I don't know why she's interested in psychology."

"It's reasonable," Pam said. "Understandable."

Leonard said he supposed so. At any rate, she was in one of his classes, listening to lectures on psychology, reading psychological treatises, trying to find out how the mind works.

"The normal mind, you know," Leonard said. "What we call the normal mind. Why it acts as it does. An elementary course, naturally. Designed to give them—oh, an inkling. A little familiarity with terms. I don't know what good it does them."

He paused with that, and finished his drink. Jerry leaned back, caught George's eye at the other end of the open room, and gestured. George nodded.

John Leonard turned his cocktail glass slowly round and round in long, thin fingers.

"Anyway," he said, "I had them write this term paper. In class." He looked at Jerry North. "It's the end of the winter term, you know," he said. "They have to have grades. I have to find out which have been listening, or even thinking. So they write these papers."

"I remember," Jerry said.

Leonard nodded gravely. He said of course. He described the nature of the assignment—to write, to discuss, the way one of the dominating emotions affected the normal mind. The idea being that they would reveal what they had learned, what they had thought.

"They're all kinds, of course," Leonard said. "From kids just twenty to a few middle-aged people. It's an extension course, you see. Naturally, I got a—a variety in the papers. You can imagine it, probably. 'I think love is the most important emotion affecting the normal human mind because it is so universal.' That sort of thing. 'Looking around at the people I see every day, I am afraid that a great deal of human activity is motivated by the emotion of greed.' You can imagine. And some very different. A G.I. named Carey, for example—one of the ones who went through it. Did you ever think very much about fear—just plain, animal fear of being hurt, of being killed? Of—of ceasing to be? Of, as he said, having your guts spilled out? Carey has. A good deal, apparently. He wrote quite a paper."

George brought new drinks. Leonard looked at his in apparent surprise. He started it. He said he was getting off the track.

"Actually," he said, "not so far off. Carey and this girl are obviously seeing a lot of each other. I don't know how much, of course. I would think a—lot." He gave the last word a special emphasis, an intentional importance. He picked up his glass and looked at it, but for a moment did not, to Pam North, seem to see it. Then he did see it and moved it to his lips.

"This girl's named Peggy," he said. "Mrs. Peggy Mott. She wrote about hate. She was one of the few who did." He looked at Pam North. "Actually," he said, "not many people really experience hatred, you know. Annoyance, dislike, disapproval, but not the big thing. Well—this girl, this Peggy Mott—she has experienced it. She is experiencing it. This little essay she wrote, this paper, it was about the real thing. I'd stake—well, that's my business. I'd stake my job on it, my chance for a full professorship. This pretty young woman—she's blond, very pretty smooth hair, very wide eyes—hates somebody so much that she could kill him. And—I think she's *going* to kill him!"

"It's a man, then," Pam said. "Does she—identify him?"

Leonard shook his head.

"Actually," he said, "I only think it's a man. She says 'this person,' 'the one I hate'—that sort of thing. She doesn't write particularly well. It's full of clichés, of obvious words. I don't think she even tried to— well, to write it, to make it sound like an abstraction, like a hypothetical situation. And that's frightening, you know. Abandonment of disguise, of pretense, is a kind of failure to protect one's self, you see. It may indicate a kind of desperation. In a way, it's as if she had given up. I read that into it. I'm supposed to be able to read below the surface, you see." He drank again, and now he looked at Jerry North. "As a matter of fact," he said, rather simply, not with emphasis, "I'm quite good at it. I really know my business."

Jerry North nodded his head.

"Did you bring this paper?" Pam said. "Can we see it?"

"I typed out parts," Leonard said. "It's long, you understand. Long and full of repetitions. It's not all on one pitch, either. She goes off the track, gropes around, mixes obvious stuff with this—this other. I copied out passages—the beginning, sentences here and there. I brought that along."

He took two sheets of typewriter paper, folded lengthwise, out of his coat pocket. He offered them to

Pam who looked at Jerry and, when he nodded, took the sheets.

"She had a title on it," Leonard said. "Printed at the top, rather large, underlined twice, just one word—'Hatred.' The second underlining was heavier than the first. The first paragraph is the way it started, the rest is what I've picked out here and there."

Pam nodded, beginning to read. She read:

"People say hatred isn't very common and that what most people think is hatred is really just dislike. I do not question that that is true of most people. But I know that there are some people whose whole approach to life is governed by hatred; hatred that makes you want to kill, very slowly and so that it hurts a great deal for a long time. I myself have experienced that kind of hatred and I still experience it. It makes everything else seem unimportant. More than anything else I want to kill this person I hate."

Pam finished and looked up. Leonard was watching her.

"That first paragraph was her first paragraph," Leonard said. "I thought she would go on and say what caused this hatred, or even say who had aroused it. She doesn't. As I said, I only think it's a man. Because—"

"Oh yes," Pam said. "Because of the—intensity. You think love is mixed up in it—sex. That it's—built up, somehow, by sexual emotion."

Leonard nodded.

She was not fencing with Leonard now, whatever she had done at first. Jerry noticed that. And, as he thought about her, she looked at him, as she so often did.

"I'll read it aloud," she said. "It goes—"

She read the first paragraph again, aloud. Then she went on:

" 'It can last for months, perhaps even for years,

and merely grow stronger. Other emotions may fade and grow less important. Hatred is like a hunger and grows stronger. . . . Another thing hatred does is to crowd out everything else. It doesn't leave room for anything else.' "

Pam stopped reading and looked at Professor Leonard and then at Jerry North.

"She's studying drama," Pam said to Leonard. "You said that."

Leonard, who had been looking at his empty glass while Pam North read, looked up at her now. He did not raise his head fully; it was as if he looked at her over his glasses, although at the moment he was not wearing glasses.

"I made allowances, Mrs. North," he said. "Say she dramatizes it. Say that, in this relation, she is dramatizing herself to—to anyone who will listen. Take all that into account. And don't get the idea that people who dramatize their emotions in words, in attitudes, don't also dramatize them in action—aren't more likely to dramatize them in action. Don't think that it's really the still waters which run deep. That's the easy, comfortable thought; the reassuring thought."

Pam North continued to look at the thin, gangling man beside her. He takes this seriously, she thought; he takes it hard. I wonder whether he knows how hard he takes it? Such a red mouth he has. But all she said was, "All right," and then she went on reading.

" 'It can begin slowly and be built up by a lot of little things,' " Pam read from the typed words in front of her. " 'Or sometimes, I can imagine, it can come suddenly. There could be a kind of hate at first sight.' "

Pam stopped and looked again at Leonard, and this time he shook his head.

"All right," he said. "Dramatization. Not true of the sane mind. But go on."

" 'The deepest hatred, I think, comes about because of many little things,' " Pam read. " 'Little betrayals, little cruelties. It starts small and grows like a snowball and . . .' "

Jerry interrupted.

"Clichés, you realize," he said to Leonard. " 'Grows like a snowball.' 'Hatred is like hunger.' Clichés of expression, possibly of feeling?"

Leonard answered the question in Jerry's inflection by shaking his head again.

"I said she doesn't write well," he agreed. "She falls into easy verbal forms. Most people do. It doesn't mean anything about—well, the importance of what's being said. In this case, the reality, the intensity, of what she feels." He paused and seemed to consider. "Of course," he said, "I know her, to some extent. I've seen her, heard her talk. Perhaps that makes a difference." He looked at Pam North suddenly. "You think I overstated?" he said. "Took it too seriously? Go on."

" 'It is difficult to explain hatred to a person who has never felt it,' " Pam read. " 'I suppose it would not be difficult, or anyway not so difficult, for a writer. But the words I think of, now that I try to explain why it seems to me the most important emotion a person can feel, do not seem adequate to explain what hatred is like. Most of the words are the same words you would use to write about dislike or annoyance or something like that. There isn't anything to compare it to.' "

Professor Leonard interrupted this time.

"To give a sense of magnitude, I suppose she means," he said. "To express its quality of uniqueness. You see what she means."

"Oh yes," Pam said. She looked back at what she had read. "All at once," she said, "I don't think you took it too seriously. I did at first."

"Oh," Leonard said. "Obviously."

"Anyway," Pam said, and resumed reading:

" 'When a person hates another person, really hates them, it would be in a strange kind of way fulfilling. It would be—' "

"You notice how she shifts there," Leonard pointed out. "She did from time to time all the way through. An unconscious attempt to get back to a general discussion, you know. To avoid betraying herself." He nodded. "At the expense of grammar," he added. "Which is rather significant. She started one way, ended another, as if something took over in the middle of the sentence. The instinct of self-preservation, I think the something was."

Pam nodded, rather abstractedly, and said, "Listen." She read again.

" '—in a strange kind of way fulfilling,' " she read. " 'It would be *satisfying*, more satisfying than anything else.' " Pam interrupted. "The first 'satisfying' is underlined," she said. "It goes on: 'Nobody who has not really hated somebody can understand that—how it fills you up, fills your mind up. As I said, it leaves no room for anything else. But after a while you don't want anything else, because hating is enough, hating is a *complete* emotion.' " Pam looked up again. " 'Complete' is underlined too," she said. She went back to the paper:

" 'Most people think that love is the most important emotion. Perhaps it is, sometimes. But for a person who has been in love, hating—you could almost call it being in hate—is a great deal more important, because hatred occupies you so much more completely. Only a person who has had both experiences can realize that. And I should think that killing the person you hate would be a more satisfying emotional experience than anything else.' "

Pam looked up again.

"She didn't plan to write 'anything else,' did she?" Pam asked.

Leonard shook his head.

"She started another word," he said. "She scratched it out, thoroughly. The censor at work, of course."

"Yes," Pam North said. "I see why you thought it was a man."

Leonard looked at her a moment and then said, in a faintly surprised tone, "Oh."

" 'Such a culmination would have finality, completion,' " Pam read on. " 'It would offer complete discharge, complete release, beyond anything I can imagine. It is possible that, for a person fully what I have called "in hate," the killing of the object of that hatred is the only way to attain that release. Real hatred cannot be sublimated.' "

Pam looked at Leonard again.

"Is that true?" she said.

He raised his thin shoulders, let them drop.

"If she thinks it is," he said. "It could be. You want fixed criteria? No, Mrs. North. There aren't any. It could be true for—for this person. Not for you, not for me. A subjective truth. But subjective convictions can lead to objective actions."

"If a person is sane?" Jerry said, and then Leonard merely looked at him and shrugged again.

"You think she can't be—well, dramatizing? Making it up? Letting a notion run away with her?" That was Pam North. Leonard looked at her, again over the glasses which were not there.

"Of course she can," he said. "She can be doing it for any purpose—to work off something, to make up a story, to see her instructor jump."

"But you think that isn't it?"

"I think she hates somebody and is thinking about killing somebody," Leonard said. "I think she's close to killing somebody. For what it's worth, that's what I think."

"And?" Jerry said.

"Obviously, I want to share the responsibility,"

Leonard said. "That's what motivates me. I want to get out from under, or have somebody under with me. You've had experience."

"Vicarious," Pam said. "What do you think, Jerry?"

They both looked at Jerry North, who said, "Lunch or another drink?"

"No," Pam said. "Answer me."

Jerry smiled at her, rather faintly. He asked whether she had read everything. Pam looked at the paper again and then looked, with an odd expression, at Professor Leonard.

"Except one line," she said. "Some dots and then . . . 'That is why I think hatred is the most important emotion affecting the normal human mind.' Did she really—?"

"End that way?" Leonard said, and nodded. "Yes. Tying it together again, rounding it off. They almost always do. It amounts to a mental tic. I copied it off because—well, it completes the picture, somehow. Don't you think?"

"Peculiarly," Pam said. "Well, Jerry?"

Jerry North spoke slowly.

"It's nebulous," he said. "Intangible. There's nothing for anyone to get hold of." He spoke to Leonard. "You realized that. Otherwise, you could have gone to the police. As it is, they wouldn't listen." He paused. "How could they listen?" he added.

"Not to me," Leonard agreed. "An academic theory, a crackpot scare. Coming from me." He returned Jerry North's look. "This friend of yours," he said. "This police lieutenant. Weigand. He'd listen to you. To both of you."

"Listen," Jerry said. "Certainly. What can he do?"

"Talk to her?" Leonard said. "Watch her? Find out, somehow, who she's talking about and—warn him? I don't know."

Jerry shook his head.

"Listen," he said. "A young woman, with a dramatic temperament, writes a term paper which may indicate she's thinking of murder. She may be pulling your leg. She may be talking out of the top of her head, just working up excitement. She may be experimenting, trying to identify herself with some imaginary person—acting an emotion. She may be just an hysterical young woman. There must be—God—thousands of hysterical young women in New York, threatening to kill their husbands, talking about killing themselves, saying 'I hate you' to their boy friends. You see that?"

Leonard shook his head; he started to get up.

"You're wrong," he said. "I can't prove it. Or—you may be wrong." He was standing now. "My apologies," he said. "I had thought—" He did not seem to think it worth finishing. "Thanks for the drinks," he said, instead.

"No," Jerry said. "Sit down. I realize you're an expert, that your experience and training carry weight. Bill Weigand would realize that. You say she's not just one of thousands of hysterical young women. I see that. Bill would see it. Because you say so, and you know about these things. And still—what's Bill to do?"

Leonard did sit down. He sat down and regarded his still empty glass, but not as if he saw it. After a time he shook his head slowly.

"However," Jerry said, "I will tell him. We'll both tell him. We'll put your case—your fear. It'll worry him. It worries me. I guess it worries Pam. And—if this girl's really going to murder somebody, we won't stop her. Bill won't stop her. There's nothing he can do. He can't arrest her. He can't have her followed around. If he talks to her she'll merely be—well, more careful. If she really means all this." He stopped, suddenly. "Aren't you going to talk to her yourself?" he asked Leonard. "Wouldn't that be a normal step? An expected step?"

Leonard looked at him for several seconds. He looked at Pam, more directly this time. But then he said only, "I don't know. I'll—think about it. It might help." He paused again. "But I still wish you'd tell your friend," he said. "Tell him—tell him anything you like. That I'm a neurotic scholar, disturbed by fantasies. But—tell him. Yes?"

"Oh yes," Pam said. "Oh yes, Professor."

The Weigands had listened. Dorian sat in a big chair with her legs curled under her, and looked into the little fire which darted, needlessly, pleasantly, among the logs in the Norths' fireplace. But she listened. Bill Weigand, dectective lieutenant, attached to the Homicide Squad, sat at one end of a sofa, with Pam North at the other end. Jerry sat beyond Dorian, nearest a chest with bottles on it. The Norths told it together, filling in, amplifying, commenting, and from time to time Bill Weigand nodded. As one of them emphasized a point, Bill looked at the typed sheets which lay on the sofa beside him—lifted them, looked at them, put them down again.

"And," Pam North said, "we've told you."

For a few moments, Bill Weigand said nothing. He looked at his slender wife, curled like a young cat in front of the fire. She seemed to feel his eyes on her, and turned and smiled, but merely waited.

"He knows his business?" Weigand said, then. "This professor of yours? This Leonard?"

Jerry North nodded and said he thought so. He said others thought so, others better trained to form an opinion. "Special readers," he said. "Before we brought out his book. They thought he was good."

"And he takes this seriously," Bill said, as if he were talking to himself.

"Oh yes," Pam said. "He says so."

There was something in her voice. The Weigands and Jerry North looked at her, Dorian twisting in the chair by the fire. Pam looked back at them and seemed a little puzzled. "That's all," she said. "He says he takes it seriously. So I suppose he does."

"And?" Jerry said.

"No 'and,' " Pam told him. "He knows the girl. So it isn't just words on paper. It's words plus the girl."

"Look," Jerry said. "You're arguing. With whom? Why?" He waited. Then he told her to come on.

"Because he knows her," Pam said. "And she's his student. Why didn't he ask her? Why didn't he say, 'Oh, Mrs. Whatever-her-name-is—' "

"Mott," Bill said.

" 'Oh, Mrs. Mott, about this paper of yours. Are you really going to kill somebody you hate? Or is it just fun and games?' Why wouldn't he do that?"

Dorian Weigand looked at her husband and nodded.

"If he was worried," Pam said. "If he took it so seriously. Unless—"

She paused there and, when Jerry's eyebrows invited her to go on, she shook her head.

"That's all I think," she said. "Why? Why come to us? To come to you, Bill? Without talking to her?"

"I haven't the answers," Bill Weigand said. "I haven't anything. How did it sound to you, Jerry?"

Jerry North thought a moment.

"I accept it," he said. "I think I do. It—worries me. And I don't know why he didn't go to the girl. Why, when I suggested it, he seemed—oh, hesitant, doubtful."

Bill Weigand nodded, and said, "Right."

Pam had been looking past Dorian, at the fire.

"Of course," she said, "we didn't see all of it, all she wrote. Just—that." She motioned toward the typed pages. "Excerpts he typed out. He copied from—" Then she stopped again and her eyes widened.

"Of course," she said. "That's what he says. Again. It's what he says."

There was the faintest possible emphasis on the last word. Dorian was the first to pick it up.

"But why?" she said. "Why would he make all this up? What reason would he have?"

"Look," Jerry North said. "We just ask each other questions. The point is, we haven't enough to go on."

Bill Weigand nodded at that.

"Right," he said. "Or—any place to go. If he's worried, if we're worried, if it's all what he says it is, still there's no place to go. You realize that."

They realized it. Their expressions said so, the movement of their heads.

"Not now," Pam said. "Unless—it's part of something else. A beginning of something else. A—a string we're supposed to pull, which pulls a bigger string and then—then something falls down. Like a Goldberg. Which reminds me, shouldn't we let out the cats?" She looked at the others. "String, you know," she said.

Jerry went in and let the cats out of the bedroom. They came in single file, Martini leading, blue eyes round and, somehow, doubtful. The other seal-point came after her and had an anxious, puckered face. The blue-point, which had been so unexpected and still looked so surprised, came last, with her head on one side.

Martini sat down and flicked the end of her tail and the seal-point jumped on it.

"Gin," Pam said. "Watch out. You ought to know how your mother—"

Martini whirled, made a kind of clucking sound in her throat, and bit the ear of the seal-point kitten. The kitten ducked its head and waited for the storm to pass. The blue-point made an odd, irregular leap over her sister and landed on her mother's head. Martini wrapped forepaws around the blue, wrestled the smaller cat to the floor and, apparently, began to devour her. The other kitten, clearly pleased at this development, leaped on Martini's tail again, worrying it happily. The blue-point struggled loose, jumped backward, ran furiously halfway across the living room and stopped, sat down and began to scratch an ear all in one movement.

"There's no doubt," Pam said, "that three cats are a lot to watch. Of course, if she'd had all five, we'd only have had two—her and one. But when there were only two we had to have three. Because they were so fond of each other."

"What?" Bill said, and then said, "Never mind."

"Five kittens we couldn't have kept," Pam said, ignoring the last. "So we'd have given away four. But three is just possible." She looked at the cats, which had merged again and seemed to be engaged in a battle royal. "I guess," she said. "Sherry!" The blue-point had suddenly disentangled herself, rushed across the floor and bumped, at full run, into the leg of a chair. She bounced, sat down and looked dazed.

"She'll knock her brains out," Bill said, judicially.

"It's only because she's so cross-eyed," Pam said. "They both are, but she's cross-eyed *and* one of her eyes goes up. So she never knows, poor baby. Do you, Sherry?"

Sherry got up and advanced toward Pam with a slight lurch. She jumped and came down in Pam's lap.

"Always," Pam said, "she overjumps. I think she sees too far up."

They digested this. The blue-point purred on Pam's lap. Martini lay down on her side and the seal-point kitten began to nurse her. Both the Norths spoke at once, Jerry saying "Gin!" and Pam, "Martini!" Neither cat paid any attention.

"She hasn't had any milk for weeks," Pam said. She looked at the cats. "You'd think they'd know," she said. "Anyway, you'd think the kitten would—miss something. Wouldn't you? But the vet says, so what, everybody's happy, and that it won't go on forever."

Martini stood up suddenly. She backed away from her kitten, crouched, and leaped at it. The two rolled over and over, a swirl of brown ears, of waving brown tails. Then the kitten suddenly shot out of its mother's embrace and dashed madly from the room. Martini bounded in pursuit. They disappeared and the bluepoint on Pam's lap suddenly wailed. She looked up at Pam North, weeping, and then slid from the lap and went after the other two at a gallop. There was a sound from the front of the apartment of something falling. It did not sound like a cat falling; it sounded, as Jerry North pointed out, more like a table.

"So deft," he said. "So catlike. So precise in all movements. Good God!"

Pam was looking at the fire again and she spoke in a different tone.

"About the other," she said. "About the—the hating girl. We just wait?"

"Right," Bill Weigand said. "And probably for nothing."

But to that, nobody said anything.

3

André Maillaux, moving softly, seeing everything, came past the checker's desk and his pleasing plumpness intercepted an invisible ray. The door in front of him opened widely so that if he had been balancing a tray, even the largest tray, there would have been no excuse for accident. André Maillaux was not, to be sure, balancing a tray; it had been upward of fifteen years since André had balanced a tray. Even the lightest tray, occupied by the most special cocktails, prepared under André's own instruction for the most special of guests, was carried after André by another and lesser as André progressed, triumphantly, from service bar to honored table. The tray was held for him while André, with the deftest of fingers, conveyed the glasses, delicately one by one, from napkin-covered chromium to waiting service plates. But now M. Maillaux conveyed only his own pleasing plumpness from kitchen to dining room.

He walked lightly, slowly, his eyes everywhere. A bus boy filling a saltcellar, his back to Maillaux, spilled a few grains on the tablecloth and brushed them away with his fingers. Maillaux spoke from half across the

37

room. The bus boy stiffened and shuddered, and dusted with a napkin where his naked fingers had profaned. Maillaux moved on.

The bus boys wore dinner jackets, black ties. The jackets did not fit so well as to encourage confusion between bus boy and patron. The waiters wore red coats with yellow piping and white ties and were a vastly superior breed. Since they could be confused only with one another, their coats fitted very well indeed and their stiff collars held their chins high. The captains, again, wore dinner jackets, and were to be distinguished from dinner and supper patrons only by a kind of enhanced elegance, a certain air of being in costume. There were gradations in captains and the two who were superior to the others were, by the narrowest of margins, easier in their elegance, wearing it more casually. Now the captains watched the waiters, who laid silver, folded napkins and watched the bus boys. André passed among them, watching everybody. The most superior of the captains stiffened under André's gaze, and watched the waiters with new, more worried, intensity. When André looked at a table, taking in its silver, its napkins, its place plates, the captain responsible looked at it with sudden, acute anxiety and, with a kind of desperation, counted the number of forks displayed, the alignment of the knives. The waiter who had placed the forks, aligned the knives, stiffened under the redoubled scrutiny and wished himself elsewhere, possibly in another trade.

The lesser captains bowed slightly to André Maillaux, and the greater captains bowed also but permitted themselves a gently breathed "M'sieu," one to each. To these, André nodded; he said, "Good morning, Henri" to one and, "Good morning, Armand" to the other. He spoke without accent to his staff, and usually in English. To the patrons, who naturally expected it, he spoke the easier words in French and the others in accented English. André, who was a man of intelligence, precision of mind and well-established instincts, had no difficulty in remembering, and reproducing, the accent he had brought to the United States twenty years before, from Paris. He gave attention to such details, and to others.

William, who was greater than the greatest of the captains, who was only lesser than André, could not have been distinguished from any other good-looking man in his early forties who happened to be wearing striped trousers in a deserted restaurant at eleventhirty in the morning. He was sitting on a stool of the customers' bar, off the foyer, conversing with Hermann, the head bartender, their conversation being partly professional and partly social. Hermann drew himself up slightly when André, near the end of his progression through the dining room, approached the bar. He said, "Good morning, Mr. Maillaux." William slid from the bar stool, his striped trousers instantly assuming the drape of trousers perfectly disciplined by their occupant, and said, "Morning, André."

"That Nick," André said, without preliminary. "He continues to speak Italian to Fritzl. It is possible—it is even probable—that he does so within earshot of the patrons. I am distressed, William."

A shadow of reciprocal distress crossed the face of the maître d'hôtel. William shook his head; he made soft clucking sounds.

"I know," he said. "I have spoken to him. He promises. It appears that he forgets. It is, of course, true that he is Italian, and that Fritzl is Hungarian and—"

"At the Restaurant Maillaux there are no waiters who are Italian," André said. "There are no waiters who are Hungarian. All are French. If they speak among themselves, they speak in French. Many of the patrons can tell when waiters are speaking in French and when in Italian. It is a flaw, William. A serious flaw. It is undermining."

William, who had come from England two years after André had come from France and had an accent in English, French and, when he chose to speak it, German, which was completely unidentifiable, nodded agreement and permitted his face to show pain.

"I have explained," he assured André. "I have said, 'At André's we are all French.' I have said this in English, Italian, German, Polish and even, on occasion, in French. They all know. Even the busses."

"A bus does not speak," André said. "That is understood." The thought of busses appeared to cause him pain. "Not even to another bus," he said. "That I *cannot* permit. You will arrange it, William."

"O.K.," William said. "You're the boss."

"Naturellement," André said. He looked at the slim white-gold watch on his wrist. He compared it with the discreet clock behind the bar. He motioned toward the coatroom.

"He has arrived?" André said.

"Early," William told him. "You said early, Herman?"

"At ten-thirty," Herman said. "A few minutes after. I had just arrived." He nodded. "It is my day to check the bar, you understand," he said. "To prepare my—requisition." He paused momentarily before the last word, and said it with a certain care.

"For lunch also, then," André said. "It is—" Now he hesitated. William looked at him. "Admirable," André finished. "An admirable example."

André looked at his watch again, and noted it was nearing noon.

"Soon," he said, "they will begin. The visitors. The little ones. You will see to them, William. I shall consult."

William merely nodded, this time. Daily, at a few minutes before noon, André presented to William the task of taking care of the "little ones"—the odd people, the tourists, the hesitant explorers of the great

world, the people who thought noon was a time for
lunch at the Restaurant Maillaux in East Fiftieth.
Among them there were none who could merit attention from André Maillaux himself, who could merit
even a glimpse of André Maillaux himself. Even William was beyond their deserts. One of the greater
captains would have done as well. Who were they to
know the difference? There was, however, an issue of
noblesse oblige.

William did not return to the bar stool. He walked to
the head of the three wide steps which descended from
the bar to the main dining room and looked out over
what was, for the time, his domain. The tables were
set; the waiters were waiting, the bus boys were
inconspicuous; the captains, minor, were circulating
slowly; the captains, major, were at their stations,
Henri a little to the right, Armand a little to the left. All
was in readiness. William returned to the foyer, re-
aligned the bar stool which he had imperceptibly disturbed, and looked at the clock behind the bar. It was
now five minutes past noon. The little ones were late;
there had been a time, only three weeks ago, when two
of them had appeared at eleven-thirty. *Noblesse oblige*
had been under strain.

When he left William in command, André Maillaux
crossed the foyer to the cloakroom and disappeared
within it. Cecily Breakwell, the advance guard of the
hat-check girls, was sitting down. She stood up and
said, "Good morning, sir," as she had at about this
hour each day for the past two weeks. André looked at
her and said, "Good morning, my dear," as he had
each day except the first, when he had said, "What is
your name, my dear?" and had not, so far as she could
tell, listened at all to her reply. He was, Cecily
thought, a funny little man. He looked so foreign.

André Maillaux would not have been displeased by
this, nor would he have been surprised. If he did not

look foreign—distantly foreign, foreign at several re-
moves—there would have been a failure in technic,
and that was inconceivable. It took doing, after twenty
years, particularly for a man not physically of a type.
Not tall, to be sure, a little plump, but there it ended.
There nature ended and art began, the delicacy of art.
It had taken skill to find a tailor who could, without
ever overdoing it, without any suggestion of bur-
lesque, give to André's clothes the faintest suggestion
of a Parisian cut—of, in effect, a reformed Parisian
cut. It had taken considerable explanation, a good
many years ago. One of André's minor worries was
that this admirable tailor would not prove of long life,
that the explanation would have some day to be repeated. "The effect," André had said, those years ago,
"the effect, you perceive, it should be that I make
every attempt *not* to appear French, that I pattern
myself—you perceive?—after the Americans. But that
the clothes, these admirable American clothes, unavoidably—you perceive?—take on the appearance of
the boulevards because it is I who wear them." He had
looked at the tailor, almost as if he were a bus boy
undergoing final examination before being graduated,
and had been stern. "It is subtle, no?" André Maillaux, building toward success, had said. "You perceive, yes?"

The tailor had perceived; for fifteen years he had
continued to perceive. "An artist," André thought to
himself each time he ordered new clothes, of that
special dark gray so difficult to obtain, "a fellow
artist." It pleased André to see that others appreciated
this; that his friend the tailor had also prospered.
Perhaps, André had long thought, they might achieve
world fame together—the most admirable tailor, the
greatest restaurateur, of the habitable world. (The
habitable world was not, to André, very large.)

It was no slight trick to remain permanently foreign
in any part of this world, particularly for a man of no

physical idiosyncrasy and with a marked aptitude for languages. The retained accent, the artfully tailored clothes, the barbering, these were essential, but these were only the costuming of the part. "He even walks like a foreigner," Cecily Breakwell thought, watching him recede through the coatroom. "It's funny how you can tell." André would have been pleased had he been able to overhear that thought; here, he would have realized, was a tribute to an art purely personal. The walk, the gestures, the use of the eyes, the inflection of the voice—these were of André, of André only. Even now, after many years, André Maillaux sometimes invented a new gesture, at once Parisian and personally idiosyncratic, to make himself more perfect, more perfect as the impeccable proprietor of the greatest restaurant in the world. There was little of planning, of diligence, of ingenuity, which André Maillaux was not ready, and for that matter, able, to contribute to make that dream a reality.

Cecily Breakwell watched M. Maillaux walk, like a Frenchman, down the length of the cloakroom and leave it by a far door. Cecily sat down again, but almost at once got up. The first of the little ones appeared; she helped him off with his overcoat, took his hat, smiling welcome with all of her small, pert face. You could never tell who might come to the Restaurant Maillaux, or what might be the effect of her charm, her youth, her piquancy, on some guest who was looking for just that, who had almost, perhaps, decided not to produce that delightful little play because nowhere, in no casting office, had he found just the girl, with just the charm, the piquancy, for the leading part. And here, where he would least expect it, he would come upon the girl, drudging with hats and coats as Cinderella drudged at whatever menial tasks Cinderella drudged at. (Cecily was not very precise on this.) And then, Cecily thought (sitting down again, since this did not seem to be the man), he finds out I am really a college girl, just filling in here—between parts, really—and—

"Please, miss," a new patron, who also did not look like a theatrical producer, "I'd like to leave my coat, huh?"

André Maillaux was in the office suite, by that time. The new suite, added to the restaurant during extensive alterations the summer before—the alterations which had expanded, and in so much changed, the Restaurant Maillaux.

Enlargement of the main dining room, conversion of the second-floor dining rooms, had left no place for the offices, just when the offices, also, needed enlargement. That had been solved by renting the premises next door, in which a dress shop had just failed. The show windows had been painted over and the forepart of the space was used now for storage. In the rear, the offices of André Maillaux, Inc., had been partitioned off. Various passages connected the offices with the restaurant itself, all of them inconspicuous. The one through the coatroom led into the receptionist's offices, which also could be reached from the street, through a passage beside the storeroom, without entering the restaurant itself. M. Maillaux emerged into the reception room and said, "Good morning, my dear" to Gladdis Quinn, who said, "Good morning, mess-sere," a form of address at which M. Maillaux no longer winced. Now he merely nodded toward one of the doors opening off the reception room, and raised his eyebrows. Miss Gladdis Quinn nodded also, and smiled.

André went, with quick, light steps, to the door, opened it without knocking and, as he opened it, spoke cheerfully:

"Mon cher Tony," he said. "I come to—"

Then, abruptly, he broke off. Then, in a tone Gladdis Quinn had never heard him use, in a voice suddenly higher in pitch, strangely loud, M. Maillaux said:

"My God!" Almost at once he said, in a voice nearer his own, *"Mon dieu!"* Then he went through the door he had opened and Gladdis Quinn, without thinking about it, got up from her desk by the switchboard and hurried, almost ran, behind him. When she got to the door and looked into the room M. Maillaux had entered, she screamed.

The man sitting at the desk was dead. He was very bloodily dead, collapsed forward on his desk. The top of the desk seemed to be almost covered with his blood. There was a knife sticking out of his neck on the left side, so that only the black wooden handle showed. She saw all this, looking past M. Maillaux, who was standing near the desk, a little to one side, and seemed to be swaying slowly. He looked around at her and his eyes were wide and seemed to be popping out.

"It is murder!" he said, and his voice was high and shrill. "Someone have killed my friend!"

Pamela North hooked her leopard jacket close about her, shivered in anticipation, and emerged from Charles' into Sixth Avenue. She began to beat her way south and to know the familiar resentment against an unnatural phenomenon. On the east side of Sixth Avenue between Tenth Street and the south side of Eighth Street, the winter wind always blows against you. It does not matter which way you go, uptown or down, the wind is in your face. A northwest wind is in your face, a northeast wind takes your breath away, a wind from the south buffets you head-on although you are walking with it. It had, Pam thought resentfully, something to do with the old Jefferson Market Courthouse. Pam looked at the courthouse with animosity. She looked up at the clock on its tower. The clock informed her, smugly, that it was twenty minutes after ten. Pam had looked at the clock in Charles' as she walked under it, coming out, and knew that it was actually about ten minutes after two. The wind blew dust in her face and her eyes watered. She put her head down, held on to the leopard-skin hat, and burrowed through.

She passed two newsstands and, blurrily, saw big headlines on afternoon newspapers. She felt the instinctive alarm which large headlines inevitably arouse in city dwellers of the atomic age and, at Eighth Street, stopped, braced against the wind and bought a copy of the *Sun*. (Jerry could read Sokolsky when he got home, so discharging in a single burst, against a worthy object, all the pent-up animosity of the day.) The *Sun's* headline said: "A. J. Mott Found Slain at Office Desk." So, Pam thought, tucking the newspaper under her arm, that's all. No atoms today. She fought on against the wind.

When she reached the apartment, she tossed the newspaper on one of the beds and left it there while she put her face back on, while she told Martha to have steak for dinner, but to call up for it instead of going out and while she said hello to Martini and the kittens, Gin and Sherry (which was gradually being translated into Chérie). Martini climbed on her lap and looked devotedly into her face, stroking her chin with a soft paw, and the kittens, excited by her return, dashed from the living room into the bedroom. It was only when Pam heard them tearing paper that she remembered to wonder who had been killed in an eight-column line. She went into the bedroom. Sherry had burrowed under the newspaper and Gin was scratching her way through it toward her sister. Pam rescued the newspaper, dropped the kittens on the floor and read the headline again: "A. J. Mott Found Slain at Office Desk." She ignored the banks of the headline and read the beginning of the story:

"Anthony J. Mott, II, son of the president of the Greystone Bank and Trust Company, and himself widely known as a financier, was stabbed to death today as he sat at his desk in the office of André

Maillaux, Inc., operators of the restaurant of that name at—East Fiftieth Street. Mott recently purchased a controlling interest in the restaurant company.

"The body was found shortly after noon by M. Maillaux, founder of the restaurant and one of its chief owners. He had gone to consult with his associate on routine matters.

"M. Maillaux opened the door of Mott's office and, as he did so, called a greeting to him, according to a receptionist in the office. But the greeting was stopped on his lips by the sight of Mott's body. It was sprawled across the desk and bleeding had been profuse. The knife with which the financier had been killed was still in the wound, in the left side of the neck. According to the police, the weapon was one of the restaurant's steak knives.

"Death had—"

Pam North interrupted herself. She went out into the living room and through it to the kitchen, carrying the newspaper in her hand.

"Oh, Martha," Mrs. North said, "on second thought, I think we'd rather have fried chicken tonight; if you'd just as soon?"

"Yasum," Martha said, politely. She was making a cake and had no time for discussion. Pam returned to the living room, scooped up a kitten for company, and returned to the news account.

"Death had taken place within the past hour or hour and a half, according to a representative of the Medical Examiner's Office, who said also that Mott must have lost consciousness within seconds after he was stabbed.

"According to the receptionist, Gladys Quin, 23, of—East 180th Street, the Bronx, Mott, who was about 37 and lived at—Park Avenue, had entered his office some time after 10 o'clock this morning. So far as she knew, he had had no visitors until Maillaux entered his office shortly after noon. According to the police, however, there are two other exits from Mott's private office, both leading to corridors from which either the street or the main dining room of the restaurant can be reached. It is assumed that the assailant used one of these methods to enter and leave the office.

"Similar exits exist from Maillaux's office, giving any assailant a wide choice of avenues, the police say.

"Deputy Chief Inspector Artemus J. O'Malley, in charge of Manhattan detectives, is in personal charge of the investigation. He is being assisted by precinct detectives and detectives of the Homicide Squad under Acting Captain William Weigand. Inspector O'Malley said—"

Pam stopped at that point, because one of the cats, presumably Gin, who had been on top, had removed the rest of the column, together with several adjacent columns. So far as Pam could tell, after a search of the bedroom, Gin had then eaten it.

Thus prevented from sharing Inspector O'Malley's thoughts, Pam North looked to see which kitten she had scooped and, finding it Gin, told the little cat that it should be ashamed to eat Inspector O'Malley. "Indigestible," Pam told the small cat, which looked at her in surprise and then began to purr loudly. It then looked around, found that it had been deserted by its mother and sister, and began to wail, also loudly. "Funny little thing," Pam said, letting it go. "I—"

And then, belatedly, it struck her. Mott. Anthony J. Mott, II—but that would be *Tony* Mott! *The* Tony Mott! The night club Tony Mott, the play backer, the marrying Tony Mott—in short, the entirely fabulous Tony Mott. No wonder he required an eight-column line to do justice to this last, still fabulous, front-page appearance. Well, Pam thought inadequately, well, for heaven's sake! I was thinking about him only—when was it? Something reminded me of Tony Mott only the other— And then, for the second time, she was struck, remembering. And she reached for the telephone.

The telephone on Jerry North's desk rang, he said "Sorry" to an author important enough to bring him back to the office after lunch on Saturday, and "Yes?" into the telephone. He said, "Put him on" and heard the modulated, slightly professional voice of Professor John Leonard. The modulation seemed a little hurried and Leonard said, "North! It's gone. Out of my office."

Jerry North, who was used to having things come at him suddenly, said "What?" only once. Then he said, "You mean the paper the girl wrote? The thing we were talking about?"

"Of course," Leonard said. "The blue book. It was on my desk, I went to lunch, it was gone. Just like that."

"You've looked?" Jerry said.

"I've looked. It's gone." Leonard gave that a moment to sink in. "It's the damnedest thing," he said. "Have you got the copy I made? Did you show it to this Weigand?"

"I did," Jerry said. "He kept it, I think."

"How did he feel about it?"

"About as I thought he would," Jerry said. "That it was—funny. Disturbing. That he couldn't do anything. Do you think the girl took it?"

Leonard said that anybody might have taken it. Registration for the spring term had begun, the Extension offices were crowded. It was impossible to tell where everybody went; impossible to lock up the offices of individual faculty members since most of the offices were shared by several professors and so constantly in use. "And crowded," Leonard said. "Several people standing around in each office, rushing in and out. You know."

"Was the girl there?" Jerry asked.

"Probably," Leonard said. "The girl, her boy friend—anybody. Anybody could have walked in, student or not. It's—it's like the concourse of Grand Central, for all the check there is. What do we do now?"

"I don't know," Jerry said. "I'll tell Weigand. But I don't know what we do. Was it by itself?"

"The blue book? Yes. I'd held it out. I was going to talk to her about it, you know. When I got a chance." He sighed. "If ever," he added.

"I'll tell Weigand," Jerry repeated. "I don't know what he can do."

"It's a funny thing," Leonard said. "Disturbing."

"Yes," Jerry said. There was a short pause.

"Well, all right," Leonard said. "I don't know what we can do, either. But it's a funny thing."

Jerry let Leonard repeat himself, promised to let him know what Weigand said, hung up. I don't know if it's as funny as all that, he thought, and turned to the writer, who leaned forward and gave full attention.

"As I said," Jerry told him, "we like it. We want to bring it out. There are one or two points—"

The telephone rang again.

"Damn," Jerry said. "Sorry." He picked up the telephone and said, "Miss Nelson! Please don't put anybody on for—oh." He waited a second and said, "Hello, Pam?"

"Jerry!" Pam North said. "Did you see it? But I can tell you didn't or you wouldn't just be sitting there."

"I'm—" Jerry said. "What?"

"It happened," Pam said. "It's in the papers. She did do something."

Jerry ran the fingers of one hand through his hair.

"Pam," he said. "Look, darling. I'm talking to a writer about a—"

"With a steak knife, apparently," Pam said. "The one in the professor's class."

"Look," Jerry said. "What steak knife? In what professor's class? You mean Leonard's?"

"Of course," Pam said. "Not the steak knife. That was in—well, that was in Mr. Mott. Her husband. Don't you see? The one she hated." Pam sighed. "Jerry," she said. "Don't you *ever* read the papers?"

"Mott?" Jerry said. "Look, Pam—what are you talking about. Forget the papers a minute."

"Mott," Pam said, very carefully. "Tony Mott. *The* Tony Mott. You know. He was killed in a restaurant he owned. Somebody stuck a steak knife in him. Don't you remember the name of the girl?"

"Good God!" Jerry said.

"Of course," Pam said. "What do we do?"

"Look," Jerry said. "Bill won't miss it. Only—I was just talking to Leonard. The paper she wrote. He says it's gone. Apparently somebody took it—stole it, really, from his desk. He wanted me to tell Bill."

"Did you?"

"Look," Jerry said. "I haven't had a chance yet. I just finished talking to him and you—"

"Anyway, he's out on it," Pam said. "I tried to get him, to be sure he saw it was the same Mrs. Mott. He and Mullins both. Jerry, we've got to *do* something. I mean, Professor Leonard won't tell Bill about the paper's being stolen. He'll leave it to you. And she did it so that it wouldn't be evidence of—of her state of mind. Because now she can deny that she ever hated Mr. Mott and—"

"Pam," Jerry said. "Pam! Wait a minute! To start with, we don't even know there's any connection. Suppose her name is Mrs. Mott. Suppose Tony Mott is killed. We don't know—"

"Maybe you don't," Pam said. "I do. Of course it is. She is *the* Mrs. Mott. And so she hated him and—at least, I should think anybody married to Tony Mott would have hated him, from the things he did—"

"Pam," Jerry said. "You don't know this."

"It's obvious."

Jerry hesitated a moment.

"It's likely," he said. "I'll admit that."

"And we have to find Bill and be sure he hasn't forgotten the girl's name and tell him about the blue book. You see that?"

Jerry paused a little longer. Before him he could see it all again—the nervous strain, the dashing about, the probability that somebody would get hurt in the end.

"I'm afraid so," he said. "All right—I'll try to get in touch with Bill. But Pam—you stay home. Don't—"

"Oh," Pam said. "I'm not home, Jerry. I'm downstairs, in a booth."

Jerry North said, "Oh."

"Will you come down?" Pam said. "Or shall I come up? Because I think we ought to *go* to Bill's office. You know how they are on the telephone. Because if we don't say it's important, they don't pay any attention, and if we say it is, there's always—well, do you want to explain it to the inspector? From the beginning?"

"I—" Jerry began, and gave it up. "I'll be down," he said. "I suppose we have to. Only—" He let that hang; the string of hesitation, of hope, frayed and broke. "I'll be down," he said.

He cradled the telephone and looked at the waiting writer without seeing him. Then he did see him.

"Look, Ken," said Jerry to the author, "I guess we've about finished, haven't we? That was an urgent call and—"

4

She had left as soon as she knew he was dead. She had almost run at first but then, before she went out into the street, she had paused and taken deep breaths—one, two, three—until her nerves were quieter, until she could walk, bent a little against the wind, her fur coat hugging her slim body closely, the cold stinging her face, and show nothing. That had been all, at first, she did not know for how long. It had been enough. Merely walking away had been enough, fighting the wind, feeling that with each step it was farther behind her, that she was getting away from it. But it did not remain enough. It was too lonely, and it was too terrifying to be alone.

She had tried to get Weldon, but the landlady had said he was not in, that she did not know where he was, that she did not know when he would be in. Peggy Mott had come out of the telephone booth and stood for a moment holding the door of the booth, as if for support—as if she did not want to leave the shelter of the booth. She thought that Weldon probably would be at Dyckman, arranging his classes for the next term and, at first, she thought she would go there and find him and tell him what had happened. Only probably, by now, he knew what had happened; probably everybody knew what had happened. The radio would have told. "We interrupt this program for a news bulletin." Or would it be that important? And the newspapers would have told. Because by that time, they would surely have found Tony.

She started toward the subway and then turned away, and walked with the wind behind her down a street. She realized she was walking east on Forty-second Street, and realized that she must, earlier, have walked blindly west, always against the wind, without knowing where she went or why, and then have turned and walked south, finally, toward the subway and then, when she decided not to go to Dyckman after all, east again. She could not go to Dyckman, because they would be expecting her there, looking for her there. She did not doubt they would be looking for her; that would be part of the plan.

She came to the Grand Central and had walked into it before she realized that they would be looking for her there, too. They always looked, watched, in railroad stations—in railroad stations, at ferries, at bus terminals, because flight led through such places. She had read about that; she had thought how frightening it would be to be trying to run away and to run to first one hole, and find it blocked, and then to another, and another, and to find them all blocked. She had seen a rat do that once, in a place she was staying when she had an engagement in a summer theater, and the rat had seemed to have many holes and all of them had been blocked by the people who were chasing the rat. The rat had run by her in its flight and it had been squealing and she had covered her face and made a kind of moaning sound, but not because she was afraid of the rat, although she was. She had shared the rat's fear, had moaned with its fear. She moaned now; there was a kind of whimper in her mind.

But she thought it would make them recognize her if she turned, halfway down the ramp into Grand Central, and went back to Forty-second Street. So she went on, a slender girl, rather over the average height, with very wide eyes, set wide apart in her head. And she walked as she had trained herself to walk, erect, not letting her body sway, keeping her head up. People looked at her, as they always did, and she did not let herself look away. She walked into the upper level concourse and across it, toward the Lexington Avenue side, moving among the people, showing nothing. But there was still a whimper of fear in her mind.

That must have been, she thought now, looking at the dimly lighted clock, almost two hours ago. She had left the office before noon, she thought—a minute or two before noon. She had arrived earlier than she planned, earlier than she had been supposed to, and she had stayed only minutes. Two or three, she thought—three or four. Then she had almost run down the corridor and then walked along the street, and somehow an hour had disappeared, because she was sure that it had been around one o'clock when she had come to the newsreel theater in the Grand Central and had gone into it. She had been there since, and she did not have any other plans.

She had not seen, coherently, anything on the screen. She had realized that people were laughing around her, at a cartoon, but when she looked at the screen the moving light on it meant nothing. Once some people around her had hissed when a man on the screen was speaking, and others had applauded. She realized that that had happened several times, as the continuous sequence on the screen repeated itself. And sometimes she had looked at the screen, trying to make it arrest her attention, but she had never been able to watch, or to listen, for more than a moment.

But it was not that she was thinking, thinking coherently, planning. She tried that, too. But her mind kept slipping away, slipping away to the rat running from hole to closed-up hole, to the telephone ringing in her apartment and Tony's voice telling her to come, to blood on the desk and the rat, and the blood, and her hatred, and to what she had written. And to Weldon, who seemed now hopelessly beyond her reach. Now it was almost three o'clock, and she had been in the newsreel theater for something like two hours, and a man on the screen was sitting at a table and speaking in a language she did not understand. The man seemed to be angry, and once he pounded on the table.

They would know now about what she had written, as well as about Tony. They would know that she had been there, because that would not have been forgotten in the planning. They would be looking for her, they would be stopping up the holes.

She tried to remember just what she had written, and found she could not. How much did I say, she thought; how much did I tell? Can they tell from what I wrote who I was thinking of, who I was hating? That I was hating a man whose blood was on a desk, in whose neck there was a knife? That I was talking—to myself, to no one—about killing a man who has been killed? What did I write, and why did I write at all? To free myself, to discharge myself? To—to share the feeling, somehow, with someone else? With Mr. Leonard, who looked at me so often; who looked at me that way?

Almost at once, after she had turned the blue book in, she had wished that she had not written what she had. She had been embarrassed when she thought of it and it had not helped when Weldon, being told of what she had done, had said, "For God's sake, Peg!" in a voice of angry unbelief. She had told him in the elevator and, but only after she had spoken, had realized that others in the class were in the car and could hear her—that Cecily was there, and Randall Cooper and the older woman who thought, who could be felt thinking, that Peggy Mott used a make-up too smooth, too finished, for a college classroom, or for any place.

"I wrote about hatred, Wel," she had said. "How I hated—you know. About how much fun it would be to stick a knife in him and twist it." And then Weldon, suddenly angry, had said, "For God's sake, Peg!" Everybody would remember what she had said; even Weldon would be forced to admit she had said it. And Cecily would not need to be forced.

The audience around Peggy Mott laughed because a cartooned wolf had been blown through a roof and was using its ears in a futile effort to fly above a cloud.

"Right, Mullins," Lieutenant William Weigand said. "Let them in." Mullins said, "O.K., Loot."

"And Mullins," Bill Weigand said, "quit calling this place the Male Ox, huh?"

"O.K., Loot," Mullins said. "It's spelled that way, just about. Why do they spell it that way, then?"

Bill merely shook his head.

"Let 'em in, Sergeant," he said.

Bill had taken over André Maillaux's office. They came in; they filled it. They had press cards in their hats and some of them were in a great hurry. In the office they all started to talk. Those who were not asking questions told those who were to stow it, and give the lieutenant a chance. They quieted and waited.

"I can't give you much you haven't got," Bill said. "Somebody stuck a knife in Tony Mott, severed an artery and he died with his blood all over his desk. You know about Mott. We don't know who did it. It was done, apparently, a few minutes before noon—the M.E.'s guess—by somebody who stood in front of him and used his right hand or stood behind him and either used his left hand or a backhand. Nothing about the wound to indicate which. Mott was sitting down—or standing in front of his chair, and slumped into it—apparently didn't suspect anything. Maillaux found the body a little after noon. According to the girl in the office, at the switchboard, nobody went past her after Mott came in until Maillaux went to the door, called 'Hiyah, Tony' or something as he opened it and then yelled when he saw the body. There are a couple of other doors—one to his office, one to a corridor, so that doesn't prove much.''

"Fingerprints?" the *World-Telegram* wanted to know.

Weigand shook his head.

"Wiped," he said. "The knife, that is. There are a lot of prints in the office, of course. Mott's. Maillaux's. A good many unidentified, of course. Mott's on the telephone—and Maillaux's, because he used it to telephone us. Unfortunate, but he doesn't seem to have covered anything except Mott's own. Mott used the telephone a couple of times, taking incoming calls. He didn't make any calls himself."

"What about the knife?" the *Herald Tribune* wanted to know. "We got it it was a steak knife."

"Right," Bill said. "Wooden-handled, thin, sharp blade. The name of the restaurant stenciled on it—burned in."

"They never gave me a knife like that," the *Sun* said. "I ate here a few times. Steak, too. Just an ordinary, pretty sharp knife."

"Right," Bill said. "An improvement. New knives. Mott had ordered them himself, if you want a little irony. They came in yesterday, somebody took one in to Mott to look at, apparently Mott left it on his desk, handy for somebody."

"Is that particularly ironical?" the *Times* asked.

Weigand shrugged. "Up to you boys," he said. "I've seen you go further. However—"

"And you're getting nowhere, I gather?" That was the *Journal-American,* sounding cross. Bill Weigand was unperturbed.

"Do you?" he said. "I presume we'll get somewhere. We usually do, you know. We haven't locked anybody up yet, if that's what you mean." He looked at his watch. "It happened about three hours ago," he told them. "There's been a lot to do. A lot's been done."

"Suspects?" the *Journal-American* said, still cross. "Who're your suspects?"

"No comment," Weigand told him, and smiled.

"No suspects," the *Journal-American* said. "You admit it."

Bill merely shrugged at that.

"That's the way I play it," the *Journal-American* said, and looked around at the others. "How about you guys?"

"What the hell?" the *Post* said. "What's biting you, Schmidt? You can't lay it on the Commies."

"The trouble with you pinks is that you don't—" Schmidt began, and was urged to skip it. Weigand waited, smiling faintly, indicating that it was not his fight.

"How did Mott fit into this deal?" the *Times* said, waving around. "The set-up?"

"What we know I can tell you," Weigand said. "Last spring—late last winter, perhaps—Maillaux needed money. You know the kind of place it has always been? Very dignified, very expensive, very good food, a little—well, dingy? Very special place, for people interested in special food. Well, Maillaux indicates there weren't enough of them, at the prices he had to charge nowadays. So he looked around for money and there's where Mott came in. Arranged to have Maillaux's incorporated, took over a lot of the stock, put in a lot of money—"

"How much stock?" That was the *Sun*.

"Control," Weigand said. "Maillaux had the rest— and complete control of the kitchen, according to his story. Mott took over brightening the place up. They closed down last summer—July and August—and did a job. You can see the job."

"Have," the *Sun* said. "Very elegant. Did it work?"

"In increasing patronage?" Bill said. "Yes, apparently. Got the kind of people Mott wanted—the 21 crowd. Mott got interested and began to stick around, welcoming people. Giving it class. People came to see the place, to be welcomed by Mott, to see if Walter Winchell was around."

"And God, how the money rolled in," the *Herald Tribune* suggested.

Bill Weigand said he supposed so.

"And now what?" the *Sun* said. "What happens to the place?"

Bill shrugged again.

"Nothing, so far as I see," he said. "Mott's heirs inherit his stock, Maillaux keeps his, the place goes on. Of course, Mott doesn't greet his friends any more."

"Maillaux doesn't get it?" That was the *Post*.

"I haven't seen the will," Weigand said. "We're checking. Maillaux doesn't expect it, he says. No insurance in favor of the corporation, or anything like that."

"Well, who?" The *Post* was insistent.

"We haven't seen the will," Weigand told him. "I believe Mott was still married to the last one. You can always look her up, and ask."

"I did," the *Times* said. "He was."

"Right," Bill said. "Then she gets part of everything, of course. Including this place."

"And about thirty millions more," the *Sun* said.

Weigand said he wouldn't know.

"I would," the *Sun* said. "About thirty millions."

"That's a nice piece of change," the Associated Press reporter said, thoughtfully. "A very nice piece of change."

Nobody challenged this.

"That's the way I play it," the *Journal-American* said. "Who profits?"

"Not from us you don't," Bill told him. "Not from the police."

"This babe," the *Journal-American* said morosely. "This latest Mrs. Mott. This last Mrs. Mott. What does she have to say?"

"She hasn't been questioned," Bill said. "She wasn't at Mott's apartment."

"Look," the *Times* said. "I'm not going along with Smitty here. But they were separated. Why would she be at Mott's apartment?"

They all looked at Bill Weigand and waited. Bill said merely, "Were they?"

"At least," the *Journal-American* said, "you've got a pick-up order out for her? Or hadn't you thought of it?" His tone indicated that he did not suppose Weigand had thought of it.

Bill was patient. He shook his head, and smiled.

"We expect to talk to her," he said. "Obviously. We're not worried about finding her."

"No?" the *Journal-American* said. "No?"

Bill Weigand let it go.

"That's all we've got at the moment," he said. "All clear?"

"All you've got for us," the *Herald Tribune* said, without animosity. Bill smiled again and said, "Right, if you prefer." He smiled a little more widely. "Of course," he said, "if you aren't satisfied, you can always talk to Inspector O'Malley. He's in charge, you know."

The *Times* said "Ha." Nobody else said anything. The *Times* as became his confidence—and the fact that he could pick up anything he needed from the afternoons anyway—said, "Be seeing you," generally, and left. The *News, Mirror* and *Herald Tribune* left after him. The afternoons eyed one another with some suspicion and went in a body. They would hang around, after telephoning; the services would hang around. The mornings would return. It was, Bill realized, going to be a major circus.

Bill sat alone in the office, drumming gently on the desk top with the fingers of his right hand. He wished they would pick up Mrs. Mott, Mrs. Peggy Simmons Mott. He wished it very much. She was not at her apartment, which was a long way, in blocks and other things which counted more, from Mott's apartment. She was not, so far as they could determine, at Dyckman University. There was nothing to indicate that either fact had significance; there was nothing to indicate that she was in flight. It was also technically true that there was no pick-up order out for her. But she would find it difficult to get out of the city by train or plane or bus—difficult but not impossible. Bill Weigand had no illusions about that.

He reached for the telephone and stopped with his hand on it when Mullins came to the door.

"This Meiau wants to see you," he said.

Bill blinked a moment and then said, "Oh."

"All right," Bill said. "Let him in. And—Mullins."

Mullins waited.

"Maybe it will be simpler if you just stick to Male Ox," Bill said. "At least I'll know."

"O.K., Loot," Mullins said. "I'll bring in Male Ox."

M. Maillaux was round and clean; he had a round, clean face and small, plump hands, with tapering fingers. He walked lightly on small feet, although he was not a light man. His clothes did not look quite like ordinary clothes. M. Maillaux walked to the wrong side of his own desk, looked down at Lieutenant Weigand and said he had been thinking.

"Sit down, Maillaux," Bill said. "Yes?" ___

Maillaux sat down.

"You suspect me, yes?" he said. "That is what I have been thinking. It is inevitable, you perceive."

"What makes you think so?" Bill asked him.

Maillaux shrugged. He was very French. It was in his expression, his movements and his accent, as it was in the dark gray suit he wore. But it was nowhere emphasized.

"I am an associate," he said. "You perceive? I have found his body. I could have gone to his office from here, from the kitchen. To me the knife is available. It is inevitable that I should be the suspect."

Bill Weigand nodded. He agreed there was something in what Mr. Maillaux said.

"The circumstances," Maillaux said. "You perceive?"

"I perceive," Bill Weigand said, to his own surprise. "Why do you insist on this, M. Maillaux? Do you want to convince me?"

Maillaux regarded his pointed fingers and shook his head.

"We are intelligent men," he said. "Of experience, no? It is merely that I wish you should perceive my understanding of the circumstances. You perceive?"

"I per—right," Bill said, catching himself. "But I presume these circumstances are misleading? You did not kill your—is 'partner' the word?"

M. Maillaux looked at Bill Weigand intently. He looked almost as if he were about to cry.

"More," he said. "But much more. My friend, my good friend. My rescuer. You perceive?" Maillaux suddenly put his fingers against his forehead, shielding his face. He as suddenly removed them. "It is a catastrophe," he said. "But a catastrophe. Maillaux has been destroyed."

"Why?" Bill said. "You did well enough before. I've heard of Maillaux for a good many years."

"But obviously," Maillaux said. "Who has not? Of

the old Maillaux, the *grande cuisine,* who had not heard? But who came? You perceive?"

Bill Weigand said he had always gathered that a good many people came. Maillaux spread his hands.

"But yes," he said. "Of a type, certainly. I do not deny. The quiet ones, the elders. For the food, yes, for the wine, certainly. Those were great, you perceive. But not the famous people—the Winchell, the Lyons, what you call the café society. For Tony, they came. They were the friends of Tony. For lunch they came, for the dinner, afterward for the drinks. You perceive?"

"And the money rolled in?" Bill said.

Maillaux put together the thumb and second finger of each hand. He snapped them in the air, almost soundlessly.

"And how!" he said, unexpectedly. He looked surprised at himself. "Of a certainty," he said. He shrugged. He looked at Weigand and raised his eyebrows. "I am a business man, you perceive," he said. "That I do not deny, Lieutenant. For me the good Tony was a very important friend. You perceive?"

"I agree you seem to lose by his death," Bill Weigand admitted.

Maillaux's round face became as tragic as its contours allowed.

"But everything!" he said. "But all! It is a catastrophe!"

"And you had no—well, personal animosity against Mr. Mott?" Bill said. "No dislike? No rivalry, say?"

Maillaux looked astonished. He shook his head with energy.

"But we were friends," he said. "We were associates. Would I permit myself—?"

"Perhaps not," Bill said.

"In addition, there was no cause," Maillaux said. "For the girls I do not compete, you perceive? It is not that I—however—I am of an age, no?"

Bill Weigand was not entirely convinced, but he did not argue. He did not think that M. Maillaux had quarreled with Tony Mott over a girl.

"Right," Bill said. "As long as you didn't kill him, don't worry."

"But," Maillaux said, and looked very worried, "I find the body? Yes?"

Bill sighed faintly.

"Even so," he said. "Even so, Mr. Maillaux. If you had no reason—yes?"

The last was to Mullins, who had reappeared at the door.

"There's a girl," Mullins said. "The hat-check girl. She wants to tell you something. She keeps saying she has to leave and—"

"All right," Bill said. "Let her in, Sergeant." Maillaux started to get up. "Stay if you don't mind," Bill said. He smiled. "Sobering influence," he said, remembering the hat-check girl. Cecily Breakwell floated in. She was a little flushed and seemed excited. She saw Maillaux and did sober.

"Lieutenant!" she said. "I have to tell you—"

She was pretty, quick, consciously (Bill Weigand thought) piquant. She seemed to poise, temporarily, in front of the desk. Bill stood up, indicated a chair. She poised, temporarily, in the chair.

"It's dreadful," she said. "Really dreadful. To think of Mr. Mott—"

"Yes," Bill said. "You wanted to tell me—?"

"She hated him," Cecily Breakwell said. The words seemed to scamper out of her small, pretty mouth. "I have to tell you. I didn't want to but I said to myself, 'Cecily, you have to tell the police, you really have to' because it isn't anything that they would—"

She stopped and looked at Bill Weigand with her lips slightly parted. She looked at Maillaux.

"I'm terribly afraid I'm excited," she said. "Terribly excited. It's nerving myself to it, you know. Because

Peggy is so sweet, really. I keep telling myself she couldn't have meant what she wrote. About hating Mr. Mott, you know. About wanting to kill him. But that's what she did write, for Professor Leonard's class in psychology. In the term paper, you know."

"Peggy," Bill said. "That would be Mrs. Mott?"

"Oh yes," Cecily said. "They were separated, you know, and she hated him. And when we had to write this paper about emotions, she wrote about how she hated him. I sit next to her, you know, and I couldn't help glancing at her paper and it was dreadful. Frightening, you know, because it sounded so much as if she meant it."

"This paper," Weigand said. "A kind of an examination?"

"Oh yes," Cecily said. "For the term grade, you know."

"She wrote about hating Mr. Mott? By name? I mean, she mentioned who it was she hated?"

Cecily looked for a moment as if she were thinking.

"Oh I think so," she said. "I'm almost sure. And anyway, I knew, of course. And then in the elevator she said something about it to Mr. Carey—about what she'd written, you know—and then looked as if she wished she hadn't. Mr. Carey said, 'For God's sake' or something like that and was very angry at her."

"Mr. Carey?"

"Weldon Carey," the girl said. "They see a lot of each other, you know. Mr. Carey and Peggy. I think they're in love, you know."

Bill Weigand said he saw.

"About this paper," he said. "You just read snatches, I suppose? Just sentences here and there?"

"Oh yes," the girl said. "I had to write my own, you know. I wrote about—well, about love."

"Did anybody else see what she'd written, do you think?"

"Oh, I don't think so. We write on the arms of the

chairs, you know, and I was right next. Of course, Professor Leonard saw it. That's what she wrote it for."

"Of course," Weigand said. "I realize that."

"Maybe it doesn't mean anything," Cecily said. "It was just writing, you know. But it sounded so—so real. As if she really wanted to kill Mr. Mott. And then, somebody did. And in the elevator she mentioned a knife, that she wanted to kill him with a knife. A lot of us heard her. And he was killed with a knife, so I said to myself, 'Cecily, whatever you think you've got—' "

"Right," Bill said. "You couldn't do anything else. Thank you, Miss Breakwell."

"Oh, I hope I was right," Cecily Breakwell said. "I felt I had to."

"Of course," Bill said. "Thank you, Miss Breakwell."

She went, piquantly, to the door and through it. Bill Weigand found that both he and Maillaux were looking after her.

"A type," Maillaux said. "She would like to be an actress, no?"

"Probably," Weigand said. "Do you know Mrs. Mott?"

"But yes," Maillaux said. "She was with Tony last winter. Before we became associates. She is beautiful, that one. *Charmante!*"

"Did she hate Mott?"

Maillaux shrugged. It was more elaborate than his previous shrugging.

"I am not aware," he said. "Together they were charming, you perceive? One does not enquire."

He was being very correct, Bill thought. He was not so sure that Maillaux was being as illuminating as he might be. There was a suggestion of the conventional about Maillaux's correctness. It was possible that the suggestion was there by intention.

And then Mullins opened the door again, but this time Pam North was visible beside him and he did not need to say, as he did say, "Mr. and Mrs. North, Lieutenant."

"Bill," Pam said. "Mr. Leonard says it's stolen. The blue book. From his desk and—" She saw Maillaux and stopped. Maillaux was standing. Weigand introduced Maillaux and the Norths. Pam laughed suddenly, lightly, and said she was sorry.

"But," she said, "do you know that Mullins calls you Mr. Male Ox, Mr. Maillaux?"

Maillaux looked at her with round, puzzled eyes.

"Only," Pam said, and now she was speaking to Jerry rather than to the others, "isn't that a contradiction in terms, really? Because aren't oxen—"

"Yes, dear," Jerry said. "I've always understood so."

M. Maillaux, Bill Weigand thought, looked more puzzled, more disturbed, than he had at any time. It was, Bill thought, an appropriate tribute to Pamela North.

Bill Weigand said, "Thanks, Mr. Maillaux" and Maillaux went out, walking lightly. Bill listened, then, while Jerry told of his talk with Professor Leonard, of the report that the blue book, containing its hymn of hate, had disappeared from an office desk. He listened while Pam explained that they had started for Bill's office, thought better of it, and come to the restaurant. "Because," Pam said, "it seemed important. Is it?"

Bill looked at them a moment, lightly drumming on the desk. Then he said, "Apparently."

"If she mentioned her husband by name, obviously," Pam said. "If she said, 'I'm going to kill Tony Mott.' Did she? The professor says she didn't."

"Even if she didn't," Bill said. "It's still interesting. Still—incriminating. And the girl who was sitting next to her in class thinks—isn't sure, but thinks—she did mention Mott."

"Which makes Mr. Leonard a liar," Pam pointed out. "Why would he be?"

Bill shrugged at that, and Pam answered it herself.

"If he was trying to protect her," Pam said. "Then he might. He might even, I suppose, bring the whole thing up as a way of protecting her, but not say she had mentioned Mott because if anything happened to Mott it would be—well, too direct. Maybe he thought we could do something to stop her—you could, Bill—but didn't want to tell us too much in case we couldn't."

They digested that. Bill said, "Maybe."

"But where would it get anyone?" Jerry said. "Because Leonard had read it, and copied part of it." He paused. "He says," he added.

"Right," Bill told him. "He says. She denies it, say, and in the absence of the paper itself, we take our choice. The jury takes its choice on a point of veracity. Even this Cecily Breakwell—the girl next to her—only saw a few words, heard a few words in an elevator. That could be explained away. The paper itself couldn't. Produce it, show it to a jury, point out 'This girl said one day she hated a man enough to kill him. The next day he was killed' and you've got something. Say, 'That's what people tell us—a professor who lost the paper, an excitable hat-check girl who remembered it only *afterward*'—well, you see the difference. If she killed Mott, she's better off with that essay of hers in a fire somewhere."

"Even if she didn't, if you come to that," Pam said. "Only—"

She stopped and they looked at her and waited.

"Actually," she said, "the theft of the essay *makes* it important. Whether she mentioned Mott or not. It—it directs attention. Doesn't it? Suppose somebody else, not the girl at all, *wanted* to direct attention. Or even suppose—" She stopped again, but continued more quickly. "Suppose there wasn't really any essay—I mean, not one that said what we think it did, and suppose it wasn't really stolen. Is Mr. Leonard a nice man, Jerry?"

"Good God," Jerry said. "I don't know."

"Anyway," Pam said, "it's something to think about."

Bill Weigand was nodding, but he seemed to be listening with only half his mind and, looking at him, Pam said suddenly that she was sorry. He shook his head, then.

"No," he said. "But we can think anything. Guess anything." He looked at them. "We need the girl. The girl herself. Maybe she can prove she was somewhere else."

"Do you think she can?" Jerry asked and Bill Weigand shook his head. "No," he said. "Oh no."

The dim-faced clock showed a quarter of four. Once again the cartooned wolf flapped desperately, using its ears as wings, above a cloud. Once more the people around her laughed.

There is no good in sitting here, she thought. I am waiting for nothing, waiting to be found, to be caught. I can't sit here always, so it does not really matter when I leave.

Her thoughts, more coherent now, circled, seeking a way. I need help, she thought. And then, almost as if it were the same thought, I need Weldon. He will know something to do. I have to find Weldon. He will be very angry, he will almost hate me, but he will help.

She left the newsreel theater and found a telephone booth. She waited, hearing the sound of ringing, and then the woman's voice. "Mr. Carey?" the girl said. "Mr. Weldon Carey, please."

"Not here," the woman said.

"Do you have any idea—" Peggy Mott began, but the woman cut her short.

"Not here," the woman said. "Don't know where he is." Then the woman hung up.

Dyckman was the best place; he would be there, waiting, angry at waiting, angry at the line and at the others in it. Suddenly she knew he would be there.

She started across the station concourse, looking ahead through her wide eyes, not seeing people looking at her, refusing to see people looking at her. She expected each moment that someone would say, "There she is! There's the one they're looking for!" and she walked with a kind of stiffness, being afraid. But no one did say that, no one reached out and took hold of her arm. She went through the subway turnstile, sat in the shuttle train, took the West Side express uptown. It was a little after four when she climbed stairs to the street level and began to walk, the blustering wind behind her, the two blocks to the Extension Building at Dyckman University.

Bill Weigand was not surprised. Always they were seen; the world had too many eyes. They thought they were unnoticed—sometimes they thought the night was empty, sometimes they thought a crowd made them anonymous. But always, somewhere, there were eyes. So Bill Weigand was not surprised when it came. He had been waiting for it.

"Right," he said to Mullins. "Let her in."

She came in mink, which slipped to the back of the chair behind her and dragged one sleeve on the carpet. She was very blond and very slender, but her breasts were vigorous against the hugging black wool of her dress. Her mouth was very red and very perfect and she had large, round eyes. Her dress was cut in a deep, narrow V and she leaned forward toward Bill Weigand, her left elbow on a crossed knee, her left hand, with fingers curled, just touching her throat beneath her chin. She was Elaine Britton, and she had just read about the terrible thing—the terrible, terrible thing.

"Tony!" she said. "I couldn't believe it. Not Tony."

Bill Weigand waited.

"We were—friends," she said. "You've heard?" She looked up at Bill, her very large blue eyes apparently moist. "We had hoped—" She put her hand gracefully to her smooth forehead, bending a little more forward. She kept it there for perhaps thirty seconds. She raised her head and looked at Bill Weigand. Her eyes were apparently no more moist than they had been. "To have it end this way!" she said. "You'll forgive me, Inspector?"

Bill made small sounds, indicating he understood, forgave, shared her sadness. He knew that she knew his rank, and did not remind her.

"To think that I saw her!" Elaine Britton said, and there was a hopeless sigh in her voice. "That I might have—" Again she rested her forehead against the curling fingers of her left hand. This time she was more briefly submerged. She looked at Bill and shook her head, mourning a lost opportunity.

"You're sure it was she?" Bill said. "I've only what you told Sergeant Stein on the telephone, so far."

"I had to telephone," she said. "You realize that, don't you, Inspector? It isn't that I want to hurt anyone. I can't bear to hurt anyone." She looked at him earnestly. "Really," she said. "Really I can't."

Bill appreciated her hesitancy, her tender-heartedness, her unwillingness to hurt. He applauded her triumph over these obstacles, her decision to help the law. She listened, nodding a little.

"I knew you'd see," she said. "You'd understand. Poor, dear Peggy. Of course I didn't see—"

"No," Bill said. "I realize that. Tell me just what you did see, Mrs. Britton."

"I was coming here, you know," she said. "To see Tony. There was a truck in front of the new service entrance—in front here, you know? So the cab driver couldn't ´stop where I told him, and stopped at the restaurant entrance instead. I was walking down, toward the private entrance."

"When was this?"

"A little before noon," she said. "I telephoned Tony and said I'd try to make it by noon and—oh, Tony! Tony!"

The pretty blond head bowed again on the curling fingers, with their perfect, reddened nails. Bill Weigand made appropriate sounds.

"I mustn't," she said. "I must just go on, mustn't I? As if—as if it were someone else?"

"If you can," Bill said.

"A little before noon," she said. There was a large diamond on her left hand; it sparkled into Bill Weigand's eyes. "I was—oh, a few steps away and I saw her. She was going into the private entrance. I knew, of course, she was going to see—Tony. She—I'm afraid she was desperate, poor darling. You know what I mean, Inspector?"

Bill shook his head.

"She tried so hard," Elaine Britton said. "So desperately hard, poor darling. Tony used to tell me and we were both so sorry for her. But when you don't love somebody you can't make yourself, can you? That's what Tony used to say. 'If I don't love her any more, I can't make myself, can I, Tootsie?' And of course he couldn't, could he?"

"No," Bill said. "Oh no." He passed his right hand across his forehead, unconsciously.

"But she just couldn't seem to understand that it was all over," Elaine Britton said. "Poor darling Peggy. That Tony—that Tony was in love with someone else, and it was all over. So hard to realize, isn't it?"

"Yes," Bill said. "Oh yes."

"Well," Elaine Britton said, "where was I? Oh yes—I was a few feet away and she could have seen me, but she was looking straight ahead, the way she always does, you know, and going into the private entrance. So of course I knew she was going to see Tony.''

"And—?"

"Of course I wasn't going to butt in," Elaine Britton said. "It would have been too—too harrowing, don't you see? Poor, dear Peggy and—and little me barging in? It would have been so dreadful for her, because she couldn't help knowing—seeing—"

She bent her head again.

"So I just waved to the taxicab—the same taxicab, actually—which was just starting up and went on and kept my appointment. The one I was going to break just to see Tony. And then, when I telephoned Tony, he—he—" This time her slender shoulders shook under the hugging sheer wool dress. They seemed to invite patting, but Bill did not accept the invitation. There was a few seconds' pause, which seemed oddly awkward, and then she looked up again. Her eyes were perhaps a shade more moist.

"And that's all," she said.

"You are certain that this was Peggy Mott? Mr. Mott's wife? You'd testify to that? You couldn't have been mistaken?"

She uncrossed her knees, sat straight and looked at him through eyes which no longer seemed quite so large, nor at all moist.

"You bet I can," she said. "Try me, darling. Just put me on the stand, Lieutenant. I know that—I know Peggy Simmons when I see her."

She stood up and, unexpectedly, seemed to sway a little.

"Tony!" she said, in a low, caressing voice. "Oh—darling. Darling!"

Bill came around from behind the desk and helped her on with her minks. She started for the door. She stopped.

"My address—" she began.

"Just give it to the sergeant, please," Bill said. "We'll be in touch with you."

"And my telephone number?" Elaine Britton said.

"Right," Bill told her. "Give it to the sergeant."

She went, then. She left fragrance behind. The ventilators took it out.

Bill waited a minute or two and called Mullins. Mullins came, looked at the lieutenant and said, "Boy, oh boy."

"Right," Bill said. "You got her address. And telephone number?"

"Yes *sir*," Mullins said, and was advised to be himself.

"About that one I want to know everything," Bill said. "Where she came from, what she does, who pays her rent, what her friends think of her, who she—"

"O.K., Loot," Mullins said. "I get it."

"Specifically," Bill told him, "where she was a little after noon today, and how long she stayed there. And whether she was going to be, or *thought* she was going to be, the next Mrs. Tony Mott."

"O.K., Loot," Mullins said. "We'll turn her inside out." He considered this. "Which would be a pity," he added. "On account of her outside—"

"Right," Weigand said. "I noticed, Sergeant."

"Sure," Mullins said.

"All right," Bill said. "Let's see this guy, William. The maî—the guy who stands in the foyer and pulls them in."

"O.K., Loot," Mullins said.

5

Saturday, 4:05 P.M. to 8:45 P.M.

"The simplest way to look at it," Pam North had said
as they waited in the foyer of the Restaurant Maillaux
for the doorman to get them a cab, "is that we pointed,
and that you can't just point and then sit back. You
have responsibilities."

"I wonder if that's really the simplest—" Jerry
began then and interrupted himself. "All right, Pam,"
he said, "I know what you mean."

"Obviously," Pam North said. "It's as clear as
anything."

"What you don't consider is that it was Leonard
who pointed," Jerry said. "Not us."

"Through us," Pam pointed out. "He pointed and
we—we relayed it."

Jerry had said that he was not arguing. He had said
that his office ought to know he would not be back,
and had found a telephone booth. The doorman had
said, "The taxicab, madame" and Pam had said, "In a
minute, tell him," and a very slender, blond young
woman came in from the street and said, to no one in
particular, "Br-r-r!" She was wearing mink, a great
deal of mink. Too much mink, really, Pam North

76

thought. The blond young woman looked at Pam North appraisingly, could be seen thinking, "Oh, leopard," and looked away again. She looked around, saw William, immaculately idle, and said, "Oh, William. Isn't André here?"

"No," William said. "I'm sorry, Mrs. Britton. He went to the bank, I think."

The bank's closed, Pam North thought.

"Most banks are closed on Saturday," the mink said.

"The bank," William said. "A lawyer. I do not know, Mrs. Britton. You wished to see him, particularly?"

"It'll keep," the mink said. "After I see the cops, maybe. Where're the cops?"

Mullins answered that one, coming out through the coatroom. He looked at Pam, said, "I thought you'd gone, Mrs. North," and looked at William, who was waiting to speak. "O.K.?" Mullins said, to William. William said, "This lady was asking for you, Sergeant. It's Mrs. Britton." He looked at the mink. "Mrs. Elaine Britton," he amplified. Mullins said, "Yeah, we've been expecting you, Mrs. Britton. The lieutenant wants to see you."

The mink took one more look at the leopard, marking it down with a glance. She preceded Mullins through the coatroom, apparently knowing the way. Mullins looked back over his shoulder at Pam and made a fleeting grimace which might, Pam thought, mean anything. She made a face in return, which meant "Watch it, Sergeant" and Jerry came out of the telephone booth saying, "All right, Pam. He get a cab?"

They had gone to the cab, then, and when they were in it, had said "Dyckman University" to the driver and lighted cigarettes, Pam had said, "Who is Elaine Britton, do you suppose? All covered with mink."

"What?" Jerry North said.

"Mink," Pam said. "I didn't count because it was leopard." She looked down at her jacket. "Of course," she said, "mink is mink. You can't get away from it."

"You can, my dear," Jerry assured her. "Unless manufacturing costs—"

"I know," Pam said. "Who is she, do you suppose? Apparently Bill sent for her."

"Darling," Jerry said. "How would I know?"

"To me she looked like one of Tony Mott's girls," Pam said. "Not that I ever saw any of them. Maybe it's just the mink."

"Maybe," Jerry said. "What do we say when we see Leonard?"

" 'Look, Professor, come clean,' " Pam told him. "In effect. What precisely did the paper say, and try to remember more of it. Did it specify Tony Mott? Did he know she was Tony Mott's wife? Is he in love with her himself and did he kill Mott because she still loved Mott and he was jealous? Leonard, I mean. And—"

"Pam!" Jerry said. "You're not going to ask Leonard if he killed Tony Mott and tried to throw the blame on the girl because of whom he killed him?"

"Relatives," Pam said. " 'Hims' and 'hes.' " She paused. "And 'whoms,' for that matter," she said. "It doesn't sound very orderly, does it? Maybe he had another reason to kill Mott."

"Maybe he didn't kill Mott," Jerry suggested.

"Of course, if you're going to be negativistic," Pam said. "Did you notice how that girl stuck out? I mean—"

Jerry said he knew what she meant. He pointed out that he had not seen that girl, presuming they were talking about an Elaine Britton.

"Probably just as well," Pam said. "I wouldn't trust her."

"Trust me," Jerry said, and put an arm around her.

"Within reason," Pam told him. "But it would be nice if she did it."

Jerry asked her how many murderers she wanted. She said the mink would do, fine, but they still had to think of Leonard. They thought of Leonard.

"Where at Dyckman?" the taxicab driver said, interrupting them. They were stopped by a red light, and he was turned to face them. He looked at them with doubt. "You want to register?" he said.

"Thank you," Pam North said. "No."

"People older than you do," the driver said. "Yesterday I drove a man up there must have been fifty." He nodded. "Coincidence," he said. "Makes you think, if you know what I mean. Here I been driving a cab two years—three years come next summer. So, up to yesterday did I go anywhere near Dyckman University? Then I drive this party up there and now I'm driving you two." He shook his head. "Makes you think," he said.

"It's a small world," Jerry told him.

"That's what I say," the driver said. "What about these Russians, now? What do you think?"

"The light's changed," Pam said. "It isn't red any more."

"Say," the driver said, "that's a good one, lady. That's a good one." He started the cab. "Where at Dyckman?" he repeated.

"Extension Building," Jerry told him.

"Like this party yesterday," the driver said. "It sure makes you think."

He became, apparently, lost in the thoughts thus forced upon him. They went up the West Side Highway, swung right at 125th Street, continued up Broadway, turned right again and stopped. The Norths got out, paid and tipped. The wind took them, swept them into wide doors. A young man sitting at a desk marked "Information" told them they were wrong. This was the building, yes. But this was not a means of ingress. "The Dyckman Academic Theater, this is," the young man said. "To get to the Extension offices you go out and around. Around to the right's shorter. Go in the students' entrance and climb the stairs."

"There must be a way through," Pam said. "It's cold out there."

"Passages," the young man said. "Subterranean. Full of old desks. And, anyway, I can't let you. Against regulations. The regulations say out and around."

They went out and around. They walked with the wind behind them beside the tall building, which might have been any tall building. "No ivy," Pam said, her teeth chattering. They found a wrong door, locked, and then the right one. They went into a corridor and faced a flight of stairs. "Even universities smell like schools," Pam said. "It makes you think."

"It's a small world," Jerry assured her.

A stenciled hand pointed up the stairs toward "Offices of University Extension." They started up. The first flight was only half a flight, ending in a landing, with double doors on the left and corridors leading off on the right. They started across the landing toward the next flight of stairs and stopped halfway, opposite the double doors, which were marked "Exit Only." There was a sound coming from behind the doors; a human sound. It was a voice, it was a wordless moan.

"Oh," Pam said. "No!"

The moan came again.

"Oh," Pam said. "Somebody's—"

Jerry North was already pulling at one of the double doors. It opened toward him. Just inside a man was lying, face down. Beyond him, the seats of an empty theater stretched away, around and down toward a stage. The man moaned again. It was a kind of "oh, oh, oh," slurred into a single, continuing sound. Pam North held to the door and Jerry knelt beside the man. Jerry touched him and then looked at his hands. There was blood on them. "Oh," the man said. "Ohohohoh." Gently, carefully, Jerry turned him a little so they could see his face. The eyes were closed.

It was a familiar face. It was John Leonard's face. Jerry pulled at his coat, opening it. The shirt was red around the left shoulder. More blood was seeping into the shirt from a wound under it.

The movement seemed to arouse Leonard. His eyes opened slowly and he looked up at Jerry North.

"Lie still," Jerry said. "You'll be all right. You've been hurt."

"Knife," Leonard said. "A knife. Wasn't it?"

"I don't know," Jerry said. "How do you feel?"

Leonard started to get up.

"No," Jerry said. "You'd better lie still. We'll get somebody."

"I feel all right," Leonard said. "It just—stings. I remember, now. He had a knife—whoever it was had a knife. I was—" Leonard could look down, now, at the blood on his shirt. He closed his eyes suddenly and let himself slip back onto the floor. "Makes me faint," he said. "Always did. Since I was a boy. One of those things, I guess."

But his voice sounded stronger.

"I'll get somebody," Pam said. "Where?"

"Through the theater," Leonard said. "There'll be somebody at the information desk in the lobby. Have him call the Medical Office. Only I don't think it's anything. Just the blood."

Pam went, her heels clicking on concrete. She came out on the other side and the young man at the information desk said, "Hey, you're lost again. I told you—" and then stopped when Pam spoke, talking fast.

She was back only minutes when a doctor came. Jerry had taken his own coat, rolled it, slipped it under Leonard's head. Leonard did not seem in much pain, and his voice was quite strong. But he kept his eyes closed. "The blood," he said. "I don't want to pass out again."

It took the doctor only minutes. And the wound was nothing, almost nothing. A slash by a knife, not much below the skin, nicking the muscle in the upper part of the left side of Leonard's chest. The bleeding was slow; gauze and adhesive tape covered it, seemed almost to stop it.

"You're all right," the doctor said. "You can get up, now. We'll fix you up at the office." He looked at Leonard, who sat up. "Not that you weren't lucky," he said. "What happened?"

It did not become entirely clear, then or for some time later, what had happened. Re-bandaged, his left arm in a sling, Professor Leonard told the Norths, and the doctor, what he thought had happened.

He had been at his desk, advising students, at about twenty minutes after four. A friend had telephoned him from the book store and suggested he take a breather and come over for coffee at the fountain. Leonard had agreed. He had finished with a student, told the next that he would be back in a quarter of an hour, and gone out of the office and down the stairs toward the street. When he had reached the double doors of the exit from the theater he had noticed that one of them was partly open and had decided to cut through the theater auditorium.

He had opened the door further, stepped through and almost at once felt a slashing pain in his chest. It was dim inside the doors but there was enough light for him to see that his coat was cut and then, in an instant, to see blood coming out of a wound. He had more heard than seen someone starting to run across the auditorium and had started in pursuit. And then, apparently, he had fainted and fallen.

He had seen the back only of the running figure, and that through the swirls of darkness which began to converge on his mind when he saw blood seeping through his shirt. He started to shrug his shoulders, winced with the pain, and said he couldn't even tell whether it was a man or a woman.

"You say you started after him," Pam said. "But you were just inside the doors when we found you. Against them, almost. And they were closed."

Professor Leonard shook his head. He managed to smile faintly. He suggested he might have come to, partially, tried to reach the doors, fainted again against them. "I don't know," he said.

"This man who called you," Pam said. "This friend—"

"Paul," Leonard said. "Paul Weinberg. In the philosophy department. My God, do you suppose he's still waiting?"

A telephone call answered that question. Professor Weinberg was not waiting in the book store. He was in his office. He had been in his office all afternoon. He had not been at any time at the book store. And he had not called his friend and colleague, Professor John Leonard. He had been too busy even to think of it.

"Well," Leonard said. "Well. Think of that. So it was—intentional. Planned." He passed his free hand through his thin blond hair, in a gesture which made Pam North think of Jerry. He looked at Jerry North, then at Pam. "Who?" he said. "Why?"

Neither of them could answer that.

"Maybe Bill can," Pam said. "Lieutenant Weigand. Eventually."

"Tell me again," Weldon Carey said. His voice was rough, he sounded angry. "Tell me again. Make it better if you can."

She told him again. She had got a telephone call from Tony Mott, asking her to come to his office. "From my husband," she said. "My dear husband." Weldon Carey told her to skip that. "Skip the whole line," he said. His voice was still rough. But he reached out across the table and covered one of her hands with his.

"You got this call," he said. "You're sure it was Mott?"

"I thought so," Peggy Mott said. "It sounded all right."

"Go on," Carey said. "Tell me again."

She had gone to the office, getting there perhaps five minutes before her appointment with Mott. She had gone in the back way, as she had done before, as he suggested she do. She had knocked, thought she heard him speak—she was not certain now that she had heard anything—and had opened the door. "I was keyed up," she said. "I thought—I hoped—"

"All right," Carey said. "I know. Go ahead, Peg."

"He was lying there," she said. "He'd—he'd fallen forward across his desk. There was—was blood all over the desk."

"He was dead?" Carey said.

"I thought so," the girl said. She began to shake; he could feel the movement in her hand. "I thought so."

"You didn't touch him?"

"Oh, no! No!"

"And you went out. Did you run?"

"I think I walked."

"You didn't tell anybody? Go for help?"

"I was afraid. Oh, don't you see? Don't you see, Weldon? I was afraid."

"You found him, you don't know whether he was dead, you didn't call anybody. Sure I know. It's what I'd have done, or anybody. But you'll be talking to cops, Peg. Don't you see? You'll be talking to cops."

She kept on shivering. Her wide eyes were fixed.

"It was that way," she said. "What shall I do?"

They were in a booth, in a little restaurant near Fourth Street. There were cocktails in front of both of them. He finished his in a kind of fury.

"Drink your drink," he said. "For God's sake—drink your drink."

She took the glass, raised it to her lips, set it down again as if she had forgotten why she lifted it. Her eyes were fixed; she was not using them to see with. Damn those eyes, Weldon Carey thought. Damn those beautiful eyes. Oh, lady, but you're lovely! He was furious at her, trapped by her loveliness; resentful of her loveliness. Good God, Weldon Carey thought, haven't I had enough of the big things? Can't I just have the little, easy things? The pleasant, trivial things? Do I have to beat my brains out all my life?

He was a dark, angry man. His black hair was disordered and there was a kind of fury in his black eyes. He leaned a little toward the girl; even seated, his whole body had a kind of thrusting, forward movement. Now he snapped his fingers, holding his hand up in front of her face.

"Drink your drink, I said," he told her. "Drink your drink, Peg. Drink it!"

The girl's eyes came back.

"Why do you bother?" she asked him, and her voice was suddenly quiet. "It's hard on you—wrong for you. You ought—"

"Shut up," Weldon Carey said. "Shut up, Peg." He made her eyes meet his. "Don't be a fool, Peg," he said. "Don't be a fool, darling," he paused. "Darling," he said again, very slowly, very carefully, as if it were a word which held some special magic.

"Start over," he said then. "Drink your drink." He waited, making her conscious that he was waiting. She lifted the glass again, and this time she drank from it. She put it down and looked at him, and now she smiled.

"It's a mess, Weldon," she said. "Maybe I'm a mess. Tony—and all."

"Quit it," he said. "That doesn't count. *We're* not a mess."

"In a mess," she said. "You could—" She saw his face darken. "All right," she said. "I won't say it again."

"Don't," he said. "Not any time."

"The only thing is," she said, "I love you. For what good it is."

"You'd better," he told her. "You'd damn well better."

She looked at him, and again she smiled and now he smiled too. His smile was not grudging, it changed his face for an instant. Then his smile went, and he shook his head.

"This is a funny love scene," she said. "It wouldn't play."

He did not seem to hear her, or he took what she said as an exit line from a situation.

"The cops won't believe you," he said, forcing them back. "It's an old line. Dead before you got there. And you didn't call them. They'll laugh at you."

"You believe me," she said. She waited an instant. "You do believe me?"

"I'm not a cop," he said. "My believing doesn't count." He smiled, very briefly. "Anyway," he said, "I've got to believe you. Nobody else does, you know. Nobody in the world. And—nobody will."

"Then?" she said.

"Two things," he said. "Take all the time we can grab. Maybe there'll be a break. Don't volunteer. The old rule. We'll make them find us. That's the first thing. If they do—when they do—none of this. You understand? You weren't there. You don't know anything." He looked at her, hard. "You'll do that?" he asked. "Dumb up? Most people talk themselves into holes. What you don't say won't hurt you."

"Somebody will have seen me," she said. "They'll prove I was there."

"Do you know somebody saw you?"

"No."

"Probably no one did. It would be straight bad luck if anyone did. Unless—" He stopped suddenly. She waited and then said, "Yes?"

"Unless somebody arranged the whole thing," he said. "Unless somebody is framing you, using you."

"No," she said. "I don't believe that. It's just—bad luck. Just a mess."

"We'll play it that way," he said. His voice was not assured. "We'll bet it's that way. If we're wrong, we'll find out, soon enough." He stopped and looked across the table at her, leaning forward, thrusting forward. "You'll play it this way?" he said.

"Yes." She looked at him. She nodded.

"All right," he said. "Finish your drink. Then we'll have another and eat." He shook his head quickly. "Don't say it," he warned. "You'll eat. And like it. See?" His inflection put the last word in quotation marks. He was obviously, heavily, the tough guy.

"Okay, boss," she said. She lifted her drink again and he leaned forward, looking at her. For an instant they were fixed so, violent darkness against pale quiet. Then, deliberately he turned and raised two fingers to the bartender, pointed down with two fingers at their glasses.

It was then a few minutes after eight.

It was eight-fifteen by the clock over the door at Charles'. The Norths and Weigand sat around a corner of the bar, Pam in the middle, and Gus set a fresh glass, heaped with ice, in front of each of them. He retired a little way down the bar and poured gin and vermouth into a mixing glass. They watched with anticipation. Gus returned, emptied ice from the glasses and filled them with colorless martinis. He waited while they tasted, was satisfied with their expressions, and moved a little way down the bar.

"So," Bill said, "they patched him up and you talked to him. Right?"

"Not much patching," Jerry North said. "Not much of a wound."

"Which is funny," Pam said. "Isn't it? Do people faint when they see blood? I mean, if there's some reason not to faint. I should think he'd have chased first and then fainted."

Bill Weigand shrugged at that one. Presumably people did faint at the sight of blood—some people.

"Usually their own blood, probably," Pam said. "However, that's what he says. Alternatively—"

She stopped and took a sip from her glass.

"Alternatively?" Jerry said.

"He could have faked it," Pam said. "As he could have faked the paper—"

Bill shook his head.

"No," he said. "That's corroborated. By this girl in the class. Cecily Breakwell."

"Who only read snatches," Pam pointed out. "So he—the professor—could really put in almost anything he wanted to. And then, of course, he would have to have it stolen, because he couldn't really produce it."

They both looked at her.

"Why?" they said, almost at once.

"He's attracted to her," Pam said.

"So he frames her," Jerry pointed out. "Really, Pam!"

"I know," Pam said. "I haven't got it all worked out. There's a man named Carey in it somewhere and—wait a minute. You know he said she went around with him, Jerry?"

Jerry North said, "What?"

"Leonard said Peggy Mott went around with this man Carey," Pam said. "It was perfectly clear before. Now suppose Leonard's in love with Mrs. Mott. All right?"

"All right," Jerry said. "All right with you, Bill?"

"Professor Leonard is in love with Mrs. Mott," Bill said, gravely. Pam said both of them made her tired.

She suggested that Bill do his own supposing, if he didn't like hers. Bill merely smiled.

"All right," Pam said. "Leonard's in love with Mrs. Mott. So, to make her—well, available—he kills Mr. Mott. But *then* he finds out that she's really in love with this Carey and that makes him mad—makes Leonard mad, Jerry—and so he decides to frame her with the murder. So he makes up part of this paper she wrote and then pretends the paper is stolen and then pretends he was attacked and—"

"Why?" Jerry said.

Pam finished her drink quickly and looked very alert.

"In the first place," she said, "the person with an obvious motive for stealing the paper is Mrs. Mott. Right?"

"Right," Bill said.

"So that's settled," Pam North said. "Now, just stealing the paper wouldn't be enough, because Leonard had read it and could tell you, Bill, what was in it, so the logical thing to do is to kill Leonard. Put yourself in her place. Wouldn't you—"

"Wait a minute," Jerry said. "No, in the first place. And, in the second place, whose side are you on? You started out with Leonard and now you're putting yourself in the girl's place and what do you come up with? Attempted murder."

"That's what we're supposed to think," Pam said. "That's what Leonard wants us to think. I thought that was clear all along."

But now, suddenly, she looked doubtful, and now she looked at Bill Weigand. The gravity with which he nodded was, this time, not assumed.

"Right, Pam," he said. "You've come up on the wrong side."

Pam looked at Jerry and he, in turn, nodded. He said he was afraid so.

"And remember," he said. "Leonard sticks to it

that the paper didn't mention Mott, directly or indirectly. If he'd made it up—or made part of it up—he'd make it as incriminating as he could."

Pam North said "hmmmm." She finished her drink.

"Of course," she said, "there is that." She did not sound happy about it. She turned to Bill. "You think it was the girl?"

"Everything fits, that way," he said. "No twisting. No forcing. She was married to Mott and separated from him; if he dies she comes into a lot of money. She hated him, by her own admission. She was there by this other girl's story. Elaine Britton's."

"The mink's," Pam said. "But the mink also said that Peggy Mott loved Mott and was trying to get him back. Didn't you say she said that?"

"Right," Bill said. "Listen, Pam. I'll grant Mrs. Britton has a knife out for Mrs. Mott. I'll grant that, in wanting to give us a motive and not knowing the situation—not knowing there was reason to think Mrs. Mott hated her husband—the Britton girl went off at a tangent. But the significant part of her story probably is true. I think she did see Mrs. Mott go into the building. Don't you?"

Pam thought; she was reluctant.

"I'd rather not," she said. "I'd hate to believe the mink. Still—"

"Still, you do," Jerry told her.

"I guess so," Pam said. "Still—that doesn't mean—"

"Pam," Bill said. "Come off it. Whose side are you on?"

"It's just that there's too much against her," Pam said. "It's too—neat. It's too convincing."

Jerry North ran a hand through his hair.

"Look, Pam," he said, "it's convincing that two and two make four. It's neat—simple. Also, they do."

"People aren't like arithmetic," Pam said. She looked at Jerry. "You can't add up people. There wouldn't be any—well, any *fun* left. Sometimes, Jerry, you talk just like a man."

"I—" Jerry said. He finished his drink and looked anxiously at Gus, who responded by advancing. Gus raised his eyebrows.

"Not for me," Pam said. "Two plus two indeed!"

They compromised by going to a table first and having drinks brought them there. Pam was quiet for a time and then she looked at Jerry and smiled.

"I suppose you're right," she said. She looked at Bill Weigand. "Both of you," she said.

Bill nodded, apparently at his soup. He said he was afraid they were. He said that, if it was any consolation to Pam, he doubted whether they would make first degree stick, as against Peggy Mott.

"Unless she makes it hard for herself," he said. "We bring her in. She says she wasn't there. We prove she was there. Then she says Mott was dead when she got there."

"And you prove he wasn't?" Pam said. "How?"

"We raise the probability," Bill said. "If we have to. But about then, if she's wise, she gives it up—says she was there, saw a knife, that everything went black, that he had been brutal to her—as probably, in his way, he had been—that she doesn't remember what happened next. She's probably good looking, maybe beautiful. She is sad and sweet on the witness stand, she has a good lawyer. The jury breaks into tears. It gives her—"

"All right," Pam said. "I get the idea. Then all you have to do is to get her?"

"I think so," Bill said.

"Inspector O'Malley will be happy," Pam said, innocently. "It's all so—obvious."

Bill Weigand looked momentarily unhappy.

"Even so," he said.

"Except getting her," Pam pointed out.

Bill smiled this time. He got up, still smiling, and

said he had to telephone. He returned very quickly, still smiling. He sat down again and said he was glad Pam had reminded him. She looked at him with suspicion.

"To pass along the word she's probably with this Carey," Bill said, contentedly. "This Carey you told me about, Pam."

6

She had eaten nothing, or almost nothing. He had watched her not eating, watched her pushing food around her plate, sometimes trying to eat. Her mouth would be dry inside; she would be chewing food and it would be turning to dry flavorlessness, to something you would choke on if you swallowed. It could be that way when you were afraid, and there was nothing much you could do about it. There was always some time when you were afraid, and this was her time. You couldn't swallow the first time, if that was the way it hit you.

She could drink her coffee, black, acrid from long roasting, tasting as if it had been burned. She drank slowly, but she drank, looking over her cup at nothing. He wished he knew what she was thinking, planning. Conversation had drifted away from them after they finished their second drink; he had eaten and she had played at eating almost silently. He could not think of the words to get conversation started again, and at the same time felt anxiety that the silence would let her start thinking and making plans without him. He thought now that it had. He pushed his cup away and,

93

responsive to the movement, she put her own cup down and looked at him and waited.

"We can't stay here, Peg," he said. "We've got to get moving."

"That's it," she said. "That's just it. You can't stay anywhere. I found that out. After while you have to go some place else, but you can't stay there, either." She shook her head. "There's no use running, Weldon," she said.

It made him angry again; he leaned forward again.

"You don't know what you're talking about," he said, and his voice was harsh. "They're tough, Peg. Good God, you don't know about tough guys—about being locked up, not able to go where you want to, being pressed down and closed in on. You can't take it, I tell you."

"Sooner or later," she said. "You know that, Weldon."

He said that was just it. That was just what they didn't know. Perhaps they would find somebody else, maybe even the right one. Then she would never have to go through it.

"You don't understand," he said, and tried to force her to understand with the intentness of his gaze, the demand of his voice. "They'll hammer at you, over and over. They'll—put you in a hole you can't get out of. They'll beat your head down. Listen, Peg—you don't get over it. Not all over it. Not ever." He paused. "Damn it," he said, "you think I don't know what I'm talking about. I've told you. About the Jap camp. About what it did to guys. I've told you a little."

She said that this would be different. He gestured, angrily, rejecting a difference.

"The difference won't count," he said. "I know you, Peg. It would do something to you. It would break you up inside."

He looked at her and saw fear in her wide eyes.

"You're afraid now," he said. "You know I'm right. Give yourself time." He pressed it. "Look," he said, "we'll get a lawyer. He'll go with you, stand by you. If we have to. Tomorrow. Monday. I'm not asking you to keep on running, always. Just not to beat your brains out."

"Where can we go?" she said. "Anywhere we go—"

"God," he said. "It's a big city. They're not everywhere. We'll find a place—a little hotel or—wait a minute!" He broke off as he thought of something. "I know a guy down here," he said. "An all-right guy. He's got a place—a hell of a big place. Used to be a loft floor, and he's living in one end of it. We can stay there."

She shook her head. She said they were not looking for him.

"For all you know, they are," he said. "Who does she know? Who does she see? A guy named Carey, somebody tells them. So they stake out Carey." He shook his head. "You don't know them," he said. "What did you think? That they just stood on corners and waited for people to go by?"

"Only if I'm with you," she said. "If I'm not they don't want you."

"You think," he said. "That's what you think."

She seemed to give in suddenly. She said, "All right."

"I'll call this guy up," he said. "See if it's O.K. See if he's got a crowd. If he has we'll wait somewhere—go to a movie, maybe—until the crowd's gone." He looked at her, trying to read her eyes. "O.K.?" he said.

"All right," she said. "Call him up, then."

He went quickly, before she changed her mind. The booth was at the far end of the restaurant, wedged in between the wall and the corner of the bar. He had to

look up the number in dim light, close the booth door
so that the light would go on and he could see to dial.
He hurried all he could, and anxiety hurried into his
mind. He was afraid to leave her there; he had never
known her the way she was now.

"It's all right," he started to tell her, with a nod of
the head, with the words formed on his lips, when he
came out of the telephone booth and looked down the
restaurant toward their table. He saw it was no use,
because the table was empty. He began to swear, and
one of the bartenders laughed at him.

"Walked out on you, Mac," the bartender said.
"Soon as you ducked in there, she ducked out there."
He motioned toward the door leading to the street.
"You have to tie 'em down, Mac. Only way is to tie
them down."

Weldon Carey turned on him, all black fury. The
bartender's eyes widened.

"Take it easy, chum," he said. "Take it easy."

"Look," Carey said. "Did anybody—come for her?
You know."

"Nobody, Mac," the bartender said. "She just
waited and walked out. Nobody dragged her."

Carey began to run toward the door. He went up
three steps to the street, and looked up and down it. It
was lighted, noisy. In the restaurant next door somebody was hammering a piano and people were singing;
the sounds came out through the closed doors. The
wind whipped down the street, but there were people
on the sidewalk. They were mostly young, and in
pairs. There was one group of six, two girls and four
men, who were standing in a kind of huddle, and
talking loudly to each other. One of the girls made a
pretense of striking at one of the men and he jumped
back, overdoing it, over-amused. A sailor and a girl
diagonally across the street, aiming toward the restaurant Weldon Carey had just left. The sailor had his arm
around the girl's waist, holding her close to him.

Then, up at the corner, on the square, a taxicab started up, cold gears strident. Carey found himself running toward the corner, trying to overtake the taxicab. He reached Washington Square South and could see the taxicab, just released by a changing light, starting up again a block away, going east. He hesitated for a moment, about to run after it, hopelessly. Then a cab came from the direction of Sixth Avenue and he waved at it, and had the door open before the cab stopped.

"Catch that guy for me," Carey said to the driver. The driver started up, and half turned.

"Girl trouble, Mac?" he said.

"Sure," Carey said. "She's going home mad." He found a bill, thrust it toward the driver. "Got to fix it up with her," he said, and managed something a little like a smile.

They caught up with the other taxicab at Fourteenth Street and University Place. Its passengers were a sharp-faced man and a girl, embraced. Carey's cab took him back to Washington Square. He was swearing, under his breath, hopelessly. She was going to walk into it.

She had not planned it; until she saw Weldon go into the telephone booth, she had not known what she was going to do. She had only known, all through the evening, that she had been wrong in getting him into it; that he had had enough, that war rawness still acerbated his nerves, that she couldn't load this on him. It had been weakness which had made her hunt him out, weakness and fear which was like a child's fear. She had groped for a hand she knew, was sure of. But it had been cowardly and unfair.

If she went away from him, went on her own, they could not do anything to Weldon. He had not had any part in it, except to know her and, now, to try to help her. But if he ran with her, tried to help her hide, he

would be in it, and in the end hurt by it. You took
enough advantage of people you loved without that.

She went out into McDougal Street and walked
toward the square, the wind trying to push her back.
There was a cab at the corner, its motor turning over
slowly, but she shook her head when the driver looked
at her. She didn't need a cab, she thought, for what she
was going to do. There would be a policeman at Eighth
Street and Sixth; there almost always was. She would
go up to him, she would say, "You're looking for me.
I'm Peggy Mott." Then it would be over, and Weldon
wouldn't be in it, wouldn't be hurt by it.

The northwest wind was more furious, more bitter,
as she walked down Fourth Street toward Sixth. It
snatched at her breath. Once she had to turn, back
against the wind, to catch her breath. When she was
breathing again she turned back and went into it, her
head down, the wind tearing at her skirt, rounding it
close against her long legs. The cold and the wind
seemed to blow tears into her eyes, and she walked
along, head down, and thought she was crying.

It was farther to Eighth Street, against the wind,
than she had thought and when she reached the corner
she did not see the policeman she expected. And she
was shivering uncontrollably. A drug store on the
corner was open and she went into it, and the warmth
was almost choking after the cold outside. She sat
down at the counter and ordered coffee and when it
came drank it, scalding hot and black.

There was a man two seats from her who was,
simultaneously, drinking coffee, listening to a kind of
miniature juke box on the counter, and reading the
early edition of the *Daily News*. She could see the
front page headline and it said: "Tony Mott Slain, Wife
Sought." Below the headline the rest of the page was a
picture, as nearly as she could make out, of Tony's
office. She thought it was a picture of Tony sprawled

across his desk, but she could not make it out clearly because of the angle at which the man held the paper.

Then he opened the paper, and the whole of the third page was devoted to Tony's murder. " 'Playboy' Tony Mott Stabbed at Desk," the top headline read. "Police Seek Pretty Wife for Questioning." There were two pictures occupying a large part of the page. One was of Tony, as he had been alive. The other was of her. She knew the picture; it had been taken for publicity when she was in summer stock, before Tony started pulling those wires of his.

Then, seeing it printed so, knowing it was real, she began to tremble again, so that she could hardly lift the cup to drink what remained of the coffee. She bent her head, and knew that she was bending her head to hide her face—and knew that she was now, again, only afraid. She was afraid as the rat had been afraid when it found all its holes blocked; she was unreasoningly, mortally afraid. And she knew that she could not, as she had thought she could, walk up to a policeman and say, "You are looking for me. I am Peggy Mott." She could have done it before she saw the newspaper, but now she could not do it. There had been some kind of a film over reality, over terror, and seeing the headlines in the newspaper, seeing her picture in the newspaper, had torn the film away. She felt that she was crouching at the counter, that she could leave it only to run, wildly; that there was nothing she could do but run, as the rat had run.

All the rest had been unreal, the subterfuge of the mind. Her decision not to involve Weldon, her determination to give herself up and face it—those had been the mind's pretense, the mind's boasting that it controlled. But the nerves controlled, the shrinking muscles, the flinching skin. Fear controlled. She must run and, first, she must find Weldon again. It was as if Weldon Carey, the existence of Weldon Carey, were a small fire somewhere in a world of ice; a fire she had insanely quitted, to which, if she were to keep on living, she must return.

Mechanically, she paid for the coffee and found her way out of the drug store. On the street she got, as quickly as she could, away from the corner, where light spilled out through the windows of restaurants and lunch counters. Walking uptown, she found she was keeping as closely as she could to the walls of buildings, except when there were windows with the light streaming out. She walked for a time with no purpose, thanking the harsh wind which gave her an excuse to keep her head bent and her face hidden; thanking the cold which kept most people off the streets and made the few there were walk, as she walked, with heads bent, their minds only on the goal of warmth.

She thought of Weldon Carey, of his dark, violent, angry strength, and the thought warmed her a little. Then, thinking of him, she became uncertain, losing faith. She had walked out on him; she had promised to do something and, as soon as his back was turned, had broken the promise. It did not matter why she had done this, and now she became uncertain even of her own motives. Consciously, she had left the restaurant to keep Weldon out of it. But she began to wonder now whether there had not been also in her mind, below the surface, a desire to escape the compulsion of his strength, to get away from his force, his possessiveness. That, probably, would be what he would think, and he might well decide not to bother with her. Wash his hands of her. He'll wash his hands of me, she thought and she had, in the kind of subdued hysteria which gripped her, an oddly clear picture of Weldon's doing just that: somehow physically washing his hands of her.

The absurdity of that picture overbalanced her mood and brought back a kind of sanity; made it possible for her to say to herself, "Peg, you're a fool. You're dramatizing." Because, she found, she could dramatize even this. The thing to do was to find Weldon again. That was the first thing. Nothing I could do, she thought, would really make him quit bothering with me.

But it was hard to decide how to get into touch with Weldon. He would have left the restaurant after he found she was gone; left it in fury, in that somehow plunging way of his. Where would he have gone then? To look for her? That was probable; it was probable that, at this moment, he was walking some wind-torn street in the Village looking for her, walking with his head bent against the wind, as hers was, but looking up at women he passed, looking for her.

She began to look up, now, and for a moment was absurdly sure that she would see him coming down Sixth Avenue. But that mood, that childlike confidence that things were going to come right, lasted only until the first man was not Weldon Carey. Then the mood broke. There was no reason to think she would meet Weldon if she walked aimlessly against the cold wind. There was every reason to think she would, in the end, meet somebody who would recognize her.

If he did not find her, she decided, Weldon would go to her place to wait for her. Then she realized he could not do that, because that was the one place they would certainly be guarding. That hole, of all holes, would be stopped. Their points of contact were not many; she had more with half a dozen people—Sardi's, when the others had the money; the drug store at Forty-fifth Street; even the Astor lobby or, more often, the Algonquin. But she did not meet Weldon Carey at any of those places, nor did she know where he went or what he did when they were not together. The existence of the friend downtown, with the flat which had been a loft floor, had come as a surprise, had been almost an incongruity. Perhaps, when she had run, he had gone there. But that was no good, because she did not know where it was. Her place, his place, the University—it came down to those. And the hole was stopped at her place, in East Forty-eighth Street. And the University, this late on Saturday night, would be closed, she thought. If it were not closed, it would be another hole they would watch.

She was at Fourteenth Street when she decided that there was only one useful thing to do. She would go to Weldon's room, far uptown, beyond even the University, and wait for him there. What he had said about a watch on that place, too, she did not really believe. It would be too preposterous, too efficient. There was no reason to think they even knew of Weldon.

She went down into the subway at Fourteenth Street and got on the first uptown train. It was a Queens express, and at Fiftieth Street she changed for a Washington Heights train. She bought a *Daily News* as she changed and sat with the paper in front of her face, reading about herself—seeing herself look out at her from the page.

The story was more circumspect than the headlines. It told of Tony's murder; it said:

"According to Deputy Chief Inspector Artemus O'Malley, in charge of Manhattan detectives, the police expect to question Mott's estranged wife to determine whether she can throw any light on the crime. Mrs. Mott, formerly Peggy Simmons, a youthful actress, has been living apart from her playboy husband for some months. It has been rumored that she planned to divorce him.

"So far as the police know, however, she will now inherit a major portion of Mott's very large estate. Regardless of any other disposition he may have made, her dower rights would net her many millions.

"According to friends of Mott, he opposed her stage career and it has been suggested that he used his considerable influence in theatrical circles to interrupt it. She had an important part in last season's 'Come and Get It' and played last summer on the barn circuit. She has not been in any production this year.

"Mrs. Mott has not been at her East Forty-eighth Street apartment since the murder, according to Inspector O'Malley, and—"

She read on, read innocuous statement after innocuous statement; felt, rather than understood, the technic which made juxtaposition serve the purpose of allegation. She wondered who those "friends of Mott" might be—those eager, damning, almost accurate tellers of tales. (Tony would have told those "friends." She could almost hear him. "Let her walk out. Let her try it on her own. I said to her—") He had been an ordinary man; that had been the trouble. With all the money he had, with all that money gave him, with all his skill in money's use, he had still been an ordinary man, saying ordinary things, showing more than usual spite when he was annoyed. It was money made the spite effective, hurting, not any special quality in the man. He had not even been a first-rate heel, this Tony Mott of whom, now, everyone was making so much. He had had millions of dollars and used them irresponsibly. That was all you could say of him.

She sat remembering Tony, no longer reading. Three years ago, when she met him, she had not thought any of these things. She had not seen that he was ordinariness stuffed with money. It had taken a year of marriage—no, be honest, Peg. A year of marriage had produced distaste which had become a kind of creeping thing, and contempt, and anger. But it had not really produced knowledge. It had only been in the past few months when, to these things, she had added evaluation of Tony Mott. And that had been because of Weldon Carey; of his and her long conversations, of which Mott was only now and then the center. Weldon, without—at first—knowing Mott, knowing what Mott could do, had known the kind of man Mott was, and had helped her to know it. Weldon had been angry at Mott, as he was angry at so many things, but the anger had been—again at first—abstract. It was when they both found out what Mott was doing to them, how he had extended activities which at first included only her so that they affected Weldon, because of her, that Weldon Carey's anger became personal. And still it had been, at bottom, all so very ordinary.

You took a vain man, a man of small acid vanities, and interfered with him, "crossed him." "Crossed in love," except that, with Tony Mott, it was ridiculous to talk of love. She had been merely a pet who disobeyed him, and was to be taught that nobody disobeyed Tony Mott. She had not even been important to him in love-making, let alone love. (She doubted, now, whether any woman had been very important to Tony, even in that most primary capacity.) She had been merely a possession, turned wilful, challenging the Mott vanity, and hence to be disciplined. And Weldon, when Mott found out, had been merely an associate in disobedience. Perhaps he had hardly been that. Weldon, when Mott found out about them, had become, to Mott, not another person but a mere extension of her insubordination. Weldon had become, in a sense, an action of hers, something she wanted to do. And therefore he had become something to be eliminated.

She had brought Weldon trouble. She was bringing him more. She was bringing it to him as fast as turning subway wheels could take it, and her. And, thinking of Weldon, her mind outstripped the turning wheels. She thought what she would tell him. It was not important, any more, that she was sorry. It was not even true that she was sorry. It was not, except superficially, anything she had done. It was something which had happened; it was as much something which had happened to him as it was something which had happened to her. They were in it together. Up to our necks, she thought. It gives us a kind of—a kind of unity, a kind of inseparability. She was hurrying to the fire Weldon was, but she was part of the fire. Part of the fire was in her.

I never felt this way before, she thought. It was never this way before.

She kept her face bent toward the paper, but she did not read it. She merely waited reunion.

When she got out of the train, finally, and climbed up the stairs to the street, the wind caught her. But this time the wind was behind her as she went toward the house in which Weldon lived. The wind hurried her, so that she was almost running.

She was certain, now, that this was right. Weldon would be at the room, waiting for her. They could not have missed on this. He would have found her gone, he would have understood, known that she would, when she had time to think, want to be with him. So he would have gone uptown to his room and would be waiting for her there.

It was several blocks from the subway to the house, and the wind blew her all the way. It blew her into the door of the old apartment building, which was almost a tenement, and up the stairs to the third floor. She had always hated the place, as Weldon hated it. Weldon's room, rented from a gray couple who had a flat too big for them, was featureless, and, through thin walls, you could hear the gray couple breathing heavily. But now she could not get up the stairs fast enough.

She rang the bell and, almost at once, the door opened. She was so sure it would be opened by Weldon that she almost spoke his name before she saw that the man was neither Weldon nor the gray landlord. It was a man of medium height, slender, dark, with a sensitive, expressive face. At the moment he looked a little regretful about something. She looked at him an instant and, because he was so little what she had expected, did not at first realize what had happened. Even his words came as a surprise, as something deeply inappropriate.

"Mrs. Mott," Detective Sergeant Stein said, not as a question. "We've been waiting for you." He looked beyond her. "Though we did think Mr. Carey would be with you," he added. There was nothing in what he said, or in his attitude, to make her go so cold.

The summarized dossiers had gone through channels, and returned through channels. Inspector O'Malley had had them and had marked a cross in red pencil in the corner of one, representing the O'Malley choice. Looking at it, Bill Weigand nodded slowly to himself. He was afraid so. He was afraid he was going to have to agree with the inspector. It seemed a pity. Dorian would not like it; O'Malley represented all that Dorian, in long experience, had found unlikable about policemen. Having spent some years persuading Dorian, largely by example, that there were policemen and policemen, Bill was doubly reluctant to identify himself with O'Malley. Bill thought of Dorian, and wished he had more regular hours. Nine to five would be pleasant, he thought; or ten to four, if you came to that. She would be waiting for him now, at home, making idle sketches, reading in bed, perhaps fallen asleep over her book. It looked as if she would have a long wait. He hoped that she would not have fallen asleep with a cigarette lighted—and suddenly, hoping she would not, he became certain she had.

"Damn," he said to himself, but there was nothing for it. He picked up the telephone, gave a number to the switchboard, waited while the instrument buzzed rhythmically in his ear. Then Dorian's voice sounded sleepy.

"Bill," she said, "aren't you ever coming home?"

He told her that God knew. He asked her if she was all right.

"Of course," she said. "Why ever not, darling? Is it that Mott case?"

He said it was.

"I should think that would come under the heading good riddance," Dorian said.

So, apparently, might too many people, he told her. There was a tiny pause.

"I just got to thinking about you," he said.

Dorian said she knew. She said it in a soft voice.

"Actually, I got afraid you'd go to sleep with a lighted cigarette," Bill said. "That's the fool thing I thought."

"That's all right," Dorian said. "It wasn't a fool thing. I won't."

"I know," Bill said. "It was a fool thing, all the same."

"Come home when you can," Dorian said, after another tiny pause. "I'll be careful about cigarettes."

"Right," Bill said. He said good night.

"Good night, Bill," she said, and there was the little click of a replaced receiver. It was idiotic that Bill could feel invigorated, renewed, by such trivial words. Doting, Bill thought; all right, why not? He was pleased that he could think of no answer, and returned to the dossiers.

They were terse, boiled down. The one on top was typed, "CAREY, Weldon." It continued:

"Age 31; associate Peggy Mott, degree of intimacy not established; met her about a year ago at Dyckman University, where both taking courses; often together. Enlisted Marine Corps 1942; discharged master sergeant December 1945; served Pac. theater, including Okinawa; described as writer; now student under GI bill; born Louisville, Ky., son Weldon and Mary Carey. Had play accepted prod. current season, but producer abandoned. Reason given, difficulty casting. Rumor expected backing not forthcoming. Peggy Simmons (Mott) announced in publicity for lead at one time. Carey's M.C. record good; no police record."

It boiled down a life, certainly. It boiled down an investigation and a good many hours of diligence; a good many questions asked, a good many telegrams sent and answered (and answered promptly, for a wonder), a good many cards turned over in a good many indices. It was not apparent precisely where any of it fitted in. Weigand looked at the card without seeing it; the fingers of his right hand tapped in rhythm, softly, on his desk. It was interesting. It had no red cross in the corner. Bill Weigand turned it over and looked at the next.

"MAILLAUX, André: 56; born Paris, son Pierre and Hortense M, worked waiter, bus boy, captain in restaurant owned by father and uncle. (Maillaux family in restaurant business several generations, branch family same business Switzerland; Restaurant Maillaux Paris of high rank); André to U.S. 1926, nat. cit.; founded present restaurant 1928, family investing; apparently very successful and place well-known but spring this year took in Mott who—" Bill Weigand skimmed. He knew about that. "—does not inherit Mott's interest; no insurance favor corp. on Mott; found body and made report; Maillaux unmarried, recently no record women; lives over restaurant; reported strict employer but generally fair; no police record. (Note: Some indication Maillaux married in France before here; check under way.)"

O'Malley had made no notations on Maillaux's card. Bill Weigand made none. He went on:

"LEONARD, John: 47; PhD, Col; associate prof. psychology, Dyck., born Albany; major AUS, assigned Washington; inactivated (at request Dyck.) Jan. 1945; unmarried; author several books related psychology; well regarded Dyck; said to have large acquaintance non-academic circles, particularly theater, writing; understood to have considerable private income; former habitué Maillaux's restaurant; no evidence whether acquainted Mott, but sometimes moved similar circs.; report seen several times with Mrs. Mott away from univ. (checking further); (Note to WW: most recent book published by North Books, G. North president); one charge reckless driving (1940) sus. sen.; no other police record."

That really boiled it down, Bill Weigand suspected. The sybaritic professor, responsive—as professors are supposed not to be—to pretty girls in classes. Hence Peggy Mott? The point deserved to be checked further. But things happened to lives when criminal investigations opened them unexpectedly. Little things, trivial things, forgotten things, were broken from context, given misleading importance. "Reckless driving," for example; reckless driving was what a traffic patrolman wanted to call it, possible passing a red light. "Habitué Maillaux's restaurant" was interesting, under the circumstances. But hundreds might have been called that, and it would have meant nothing. You had to watch things like that, Bill Weigand said, and sighed, and thought there were a good many things a policeman had to watch. There was no notation from O'Malley here, either. But Weigand looked at the card rather longer than he had at the others, and drummed a little more sharply on the desk. Then he put the card aside and examined that of Elaine Britton— "BRITTON, Elaine":

Britton, Elaine, was an "actress," the word in quotation marks on the card. Bill smiled faintly. She was "about 27" and born South Bend, Ind. He continued:

"One engagement, chorus line, 1940, no record other theatrical engagement; photographer's model, 1941-1942; married Percy Britton, retired coal dealer, 1943; divorced 1943, with alimony; has since lived at apparent rate not justified by amt. alimony; associated

Tony Mott for about a year, described herself as his 'fiancée' although he married P.S. Mott; early career in NY being checked; report once associate Morton Shepp, conv. 1938, op. gamb. res.; then thought used name Nell Schmidt; known professional Elaine Oliver prior marriage Britton; statement as to birthplace made by her application model agency, not verified; if Nell Schmidt (as above) questioned after arrest Shepp, not printed, no charge. No other police record."

So that was Pam North's "mink." She sounded it. Bill Weigand picked up the telephone and asked for Mullins. He had Mullins in the office within minutes. He tossed the card to Mullins, who read it and looked at the lieutenant and said, "Yeah. I thought so."

"What else?" Bill said.

"She lives on Central Park West," Mullins said. "Swank. In a way. You know what I mean."

"Right," Bill said. "And—?"

"She left there about eleven-thirty this morning," Mullins said. "What she did before that I wouldn't know. She—"

"Friday night?" Bill said.

"Went to a show," Mullins told him. "Went to Leon and Eddie's with a crowd. Mott was in the crowd. Mott took her home."

"And?"

Mullins looked at Bill Weigand. He let his shoulders rise and let them fall.

"Nobody signs in," he said. "Nobody signs out. I wouldn't know, Loot. She was alone this morning when she came out. After two o'clock, the doorman's off and there's just a guy who sort of hangs around. You know. The elevator goes on self-operating." He looked at Bill Weigand thoughtfully. "We can ask her," he said. "Want we should?"

"Later," Bill told him. "If we want to know. Go ahead."

"Got a cab, drove to the restaurant," Mullins said.

"Nobody saw her go in, so maybe it's the way she said. She did get the same cab a coupla minutes later and went to Maxine's. You know—this place the girls go? Bubble baths."

"Really?" Bill Weigand said. "Who told you?"

"There was a play about it once," Mullins said. "The girl took a bubble bath. And they walked up walls."

"Oh," Bill said. "Yes. Right. And?"

"She stayed there," Mullins said. "That's what they say, anyway. Had the works, I guess. Bub—"

Bill told Mullins not to let his mind dwell. Mullins looked at him sadly and said, "O.K., Loot." He said, "But you can't blame a guy, Loot."

"Right," Bill said. "No blame. And?"

"After the—sometime around three-thirty she was drying off, or something—sitting around. They had a radio. And the news about Mott came over. She threw a fit."

"What kind of a fit?"

"Yelled, carried on," Mullins said. "Started to faint and so forth. Then she called us, and came around. That's as far as we took it. O.K.?"

"The cab driver," Weigand said. "The one who took her to the restaurant—to the Male Ox. And took her on from there. How long does he make it?"

"That she was there? Not over a coupla minutes. He waited for a truck to get out of the way, started to pull out and she hailed him again. Not time to go in and kill a guy. Not the way he tells it."

"He's O.K.? The driver?"

"He's an all-right boy, s'far's we know," Mullins said.

"And he's pretty sure?"

"Yeah."

Bill Weigand drummed lightly on the desk.

"It's too bad, in a way," he said. "Pam won't be pleased."

"Look," Mullins said, "does Mrs. North think it was this babe?"

Weigand shrugged. He said a better word would be "hope."

"These women," Mullins said. He brightened. "Hey," he said, "that was the name of that play. *These Women.* Some dame wrote it."

"*The Women,*" Bill said. "Yes."

"Quite a play," Mullins said. "There was this girl and in one scene she took one of these bub—"

"Right," Bill said. "I saw it, Sergeant. I know what you mean."

"There was a hell of a lot of bubbles, though," Mullins said. He was silent a moment, remembering. "This time," he said, "it's the Mott dame, I guess. Don't you, Loot?"

"O'Malley does," Bill told him.

"Still and all," Mullins said, reasonably, "she was there, this other girl says. She scrammed out. She hated the guy. She gets the guy's money. She's running around with a Red."

"Mullins!" Weigand said. "Where'd you get that, for God's sake?"

"The *Journal,*" Mullins said. "It says she's running around with a notorious Red who writes plays."

"For God's sake," Bill said. He tossed Weldon Carey's card to Mullins, who read it. "Well?" Bill said.

"O.K., Loot," Mullins agreed. "It don't show here."

"I suppose the *Journal* suggests Carey got orders from Moscow to kill Mott," Bill Weigand said. "Does it say why?"

"No," Mullins said. "It don't go that far."

"Yet," Bill said. He sighed. "However—" he said.

"The point is, where's the girl?" Mullins said.

It was indeed, Weigand agreed. It certainly was. He

picked up the girl's card, identified by O'Malley's forceful red crossmark.

"MOTT, Margaret (known as Peggy) Simmons; 24, actress." There were no quotation marks around the word this time. "Born New Rochelle; daughter James and Florence Simmons, both deceased; father a lawyer, practiced in New Rochelle; grad. Barnard, Washburn School Dramatic Art; part last year in 'Come and Get It' and good notices; summer stock until August, when let out; no engagements this year; married Mott November, 1946; left him August, 1947; no legal action; no reports of men since except CAREY, Weldon (see report) and possibly LEONARD, John; attended Saturday morning classes Dyckman U., extension, last year and returned this, studying dramatic subjects chiefly. Association with Leonard reported winter 1947, informant thinks not serious; association Carey began about April; apparently met in classes; she then still living in Mott apartment; saw Carey more frequently after returned to city from stock engagement and left Mott; (newspaper hint Mott interfered with career; not substantiated but checking; reason dismissal summer stock company being checked this connection); attitude toward Mott variously reported, some agreement she was bitter at him, but reasons not known; inherits residue Mott's estate under will made immediately after marriage and not changed; missing since murder and pick-up out; attached photo being distributed."

Bill Weigand read the card twice; wondered what, unintentionally, by the mere fact of mention or omission, it overemphasized or, conversely, mitigated. He looked at the photograph, and Mullins looked at it over his shoulder. Mullins whistled.

Bill looked at the picture and nodded slowly, acknowledging the whistle and its justification. She was very lovely, he thought. The eyes, particularly, were inescapable. They were wide apart; a little more, Weigand thought, and they would have been too wide apart. But now the exaggeration was piquant, challenging. And the eyes themselves were unusually wide—or long—from inner to outer corners. The photograph was obviously theatrical, and this wideness of eyes might well have been accentuated by lighting, by make-up. But, with neither, the effect could hardly be less than unusual. The face explained why Mott had married Peggy Simmons. It did not explain why she had married him. Money? The hope he would use his influence for her in the theater? The desire to share the glitter around him? Bill Weigand did not consider seriously that she might have been in love with him. It did not occur to him that Mott had been lovable.

There ought to be little trouble in picking up a girl with a face like that. It was odd that they had not picked her up already. It was inevitable that they would soon, but Bill had never worried about that. Unless something had happened to her, which was not indicated, they would bring her along.

There was one more dossier, this one brief. Bill Weigand picked up the card.

"BREAKWELL, Cecily; 20; born Joplin, Missouri; in NY since last spring; stage aspirant but has had no parts; taking courses at Dyckman; working hat-check girl André Maillaux; only apparent involvement report to WW re statements by Mrs. Mott; social life largely with other students Dyckman; no police—"

The telephone rang and Mullins picked it up. He said, "Yeah? O.*K.*" and turned to Bill Weigand.

"They've got her," Mullins said. "She showed up at this Carey's place. She's outside."

"Right," Bill said. "Get her in."

He finished Cecily Breakwell's brief dossier, and laid it with the others. He sat facing the door, looking over his desk. His fingers tapped quickly on the top of the desk.

It hadn't been make-up, Bill Weigand thought first, looking at the rather tall girl who came through the door—a tall, slender girl who, even now, walked with her shoulders up and, again now, with her head up; a tall blond girl with eyes set far apart, strangely long eyes. She was as lovely as her picture; there was something almost startling about her appearance. And now, Bill saw, she was very much afraid.

7

Saturday, 10:50 P.M. to Sunday, 1:15 A.M.

The man who had brought her down from Dyckman in the police car had said very little after he had said they had been waiting for her, that they had expected Weldon Carey to be with her. He had not touched her, there had been in his words and his actions hardly any suggestion that she was a prisoner. He had said, "If you're ready, Mrs. Mott?" and had walked behind her to the car. It had been a large, dark car, like any other large, dark car, and going downtown they had not seemed to hurry. Only once, as if its patience had worn thin, did the car snarl at an intersection, and then traffic parted and the car went through.

The man had said he was Detective Sergeant Stein. He had said that Lieutenant Weigand had some questions he thought she might be able to answer. After that he had sat beside her in the back seat of the car and said nothing, although now and then he had looked at her and there had been interest, speculation, in his thin sensitive face. He did not look in the least as she had supposed "they" would look. The man driving the car had been, like the one beside her, in civilian clothes, and he had said nothing at all, except "O.K., Sergeant," when Stein said to him, "Downtown." The man driving had looked at her, a little as if he expected to remember what she looked like, but there had not been anything hostile, or anything frightening, in his expression. But she had been very frightened; it was almost as if the lack of anything overt in the actions of these two men had made her more frightened than she would have been if they had acted in the way she had vaguely supposed policemen did act. As they were, they seemed too sure, too unresentful, above everything else, too impersonal.

They had not, as she had expected, gone down to police headquarters. They had taken her to an unpretentious building in the West Twenties, and upstairs into a room where there was one man at a desk. Sergeant Stein had nodded to this man, and, without anything being said, he had picked up a telephone and, with no preliminary, said, "Mrs. Mott's here, Sergeant." There had been a momentary pause, then, and the man at the desk had said "O.K." and nodded to Stein and gone back to reading what appeared to be a legal document. Then Stein had moved to another door and motioned her to go through it, and then had stepped, only politely, not menacingly, behind her.

The new room was smaller than the other and when she entered she was facing a man sitting at a desk, looking up at her. As she came in he stood up and nodded and said, confirmingly, "Mrs. Mott." There was another man, behind him and to one side, who was sitting on the sill of a window which apparently opened on a narrow court, because, very close beyond it, there was another lighted window. The man who had been sitting on the sill stood up when the other did, but said nothing.

The man now standing behind his desk was, again, not what she had expected. He was around forty, she thought and about average height or a little more; he had a thin face, like Sergeant Stein, but the planes of his face were firmer. His voice was low and rather pleasant when he spoke to her, but it, also, had a kind of impersonality.

"I'm Lieutenant William Weigand, Mrs. Mott," he said. "We have some questions we'd like to ask you. About the death of your husband." He looked at her a moment. "I'm one of the officers detailed to investigate his death, you understand," he said. "There are certain things we have to try to find out about."

She tried to speak, but the words seemed to stick in her throat. She merely nodded. He did not seem surprised at this.

"All right, Stein," he said, over her, to the man behind her. "Did you have dinner?" The man behind her did not speak, but apparently he shook his head. "Better get it," Lieutenant Weigand said. "By then we may know more."

She heard the movements of Stein, going out. He closed the door.

"Sit down, Mrs. Mott," the man behind the desk said. "Have a cigarette if you like. This may take a little time. Oh—Mullins." The other man in the room took a step forward. "This is Sergeant Mullins, Mrs. Mott," the lieutenant said. "He'll make notes of what you tell us." Sergeant Mullins, a bigger man, with a face which seemed to have weathered red, nodded.

She did not immediately sit, and while she stood Lieutenant Weigand continued to stand. She started to speak, swallowed, managed to speak. The voice did not sound to her like her voice.

"Am I arrested?" she said, and had to swallow again. "Charged with—with killing Tony?"

The lieutenant seemed surprised.

"Why no," he said. "We wanted to ask you some questions. You didn't—appear. So we had to send for you."

"Do I have to answer questions, then?"

He seemed to expect this.

"No," he said. He smiled faintly. "Did you think we were going to beat information out of you, Mrs. Mott? Try to? But—are you afraid to answer questions? For any reason?" He looked at her. "Sit down, please," he said. The command was in his voice, not in the form of the sentence. She sat down.

"Are you afraid of what we may ask?" he repeated.

She shook her head. Her neck was oddly stiff.

"Right," the lieutenant said. He sat down, too. He was unhurried and seemed calm, but she noticed that the fingers of his right hand, which lay on the desk, tapped out a little, soundless rhythm.

"Were you afraid we would charge you with killing your husband?" The man behind the desk spoke rather quickly. "Is that why you didn't go home? Or—get in touch with anyone? Except Mr. Carey?"

"I didn't kill him," she said.

"But you were afraid we'd think you had?"

"I—I suppose so."

"Why?" The word was sudden, unadorned, and for the first time the voice was really demanding.

"I—I don't know."

"Were you there? When he was killed?"

The answer came very quickly, and she knew it came too quickly. But she could not stop herself; could not keep herself from saying "No" hurriedly, defensively. She thought, spoken so, it became equivalent to "yes." But the man behind the desk did not seem to notice this.

"Then why?" he said. "Why did you hide?" He looked at her, very straightly. "You did hide, didn't you? Try to keep away from the police? Because the natural thing would have been to go home, when you heard about your husband's death. Or to go to the restaurant. To try to—well, do anything you could to help. Don't you agree, Mrs. Mott? It was because you were afraid, wasn't it?"

"I suppose so," she said again.

"Then—why? You weren't there, you say. You didn't kill him. Do you know who did? Is that it?"

"No."

"Then—why? Why, Mrs. Mott?"

She had not expected it to come so quickly, or to come this way. She had thought she would have time. But now, although it was not entirely clear how it had happened, she was already trapped. She had thought there would be time; she had thought it would be, again, running from hole to hole, with fear mounting, hopelessly mounting, but always against it the faint half-hope of escape. She felt a kind of blackness closing about her, and tried to fight it off.

"Why were you afraid?" the man across the desk said, and his voice was insistent. "What was there to be afraid of? You weren't there. You didn't kill him. You don't know who killed him. Why? Why, Mrs. Mott?"

"I—" she said. "We were separated. We hadn't got along. I was afraid—"

"No," the man behind the desk said. "Oh no, Mrs. Mott. That wouldn't make you afraid."

She tried to think, she tried to pull it together. She took a deep breath, and thought that the deep breath in itself was a kind of confession.

"I don't know," she said. "I really don't know. I—I was excited and upset. I just wanted time." She met his eyes. "I wasn't really afraid," she said. "I don't know why I said I was. I just wanted time."

"For what? What did you need time for?"

She had run a little way, toward light she thought was shining through a chink. But there was no light there, really. Why? Why? Why? She hardly knew, for the moment, whether the man across the desk—the police lieutenant—was saying "Why?" or whether the word was forming itself over and over in her mind. She tried to remember; for an instant she could not even answer to herself. Then she remembered.

"Was it because you hated him?" Lieutenant Weigand said. "Was that why? You had threatened him?"

"No. Oh no!"

"But you did hate him?"

"I—no, I didn't hate him."

"Do you know anybody who did?"

No, her mind said. Oh, *no!* "No," she said.

"Did Mr. Carey?"

She had not expected that; she had not even been afraid of that. But now she was afraid.

"Of course not," she said. "Mr. Carey hardly knew him."

"No?" Weigand said. "No? Right. Because of you, then? Because of something Mott had done to you? That Carey knew about? That made him go after Mott?"

"No."

"Carey is a friend of yours, isn't he? A—devoted friend?"

"We go around together. I—yes, of course we're friends." (Oh Weldon! Oh, my dear!)

"More than friends? Was Carey jealous? Afraid you'd go back to Mott?"

"He knew I wouldn't."

"Because he knew you were in love with him? With Carey?"

"I—I don't—" She did not finish. She could not make herself finish.

"Was that why you were afraid, Mrs. Mott? Afraid it was Mr. Carey who killed your husband?"

"No. I said I wasn't afraid."

"You said both things," Weigand told her. "That you were. That you weren't. But you were, of course." He waited a moment. "Mrs. Mott," he said, "you're not doing well. You know that, don't you? It's a little thing, surely. Why were you afraid? That's all I want to know."

Bill Weigand waited. All I want to know—oh no, not by a lot. Not by half. Have I stumbled on something, Bill Weigand wondered. This about Carey? Were they both in it?

"Go on," he said. "Why were you afraid?"

"I wasn't. I wanted time."

She would stick to that, for the moment.

"Right," he said. "You wanted time. You won't say what you wanted time for." He shook his head. "I'm sorry about this, Mrs. Mott," he said. "I suppose you could clear everything up, naturally. However—"

He waited a moment, watching her. She was afraid; she was very much afraid. And he had caught her off guard. But now, for the moment, she would stick on this issue. He shifted.

"You say you didn't hate your husband, Mrs. Mott?" he said. He waited for the inevitable "Of course not." It came.

"You wrote a paper at Dyckman yesterday?" he said. "An examination paper?"

He watched her eyes, her very long, very beautiful eyes. They fixed for an instant, as the mind behind them tried to set itself for this new thing.

"Yes," she said. The pause had been only momentary.

"About hatred," he said. "About hating your husband. Wasn't that it?"

"Not Tony," she said. "Not anyone. It was—just general. Part of the course. I imagined how it would feel and—well, just made it up."

She seems surer about that, Bill thought. It could be true. Or—she could be getting back on balance. That wasn't what he wanted.

"Right," he said. "It was all abstract, theoretical. It—"

"You can read it," she said. "It wasn't about Tony. You can ask Professor Leonard."

Oh no, pretty lady, Bill Weigand thought. Too quick there. That was a mistake, Mrs. Peggy Mott.

"Can I?" he said. "You think I can?"

"Of course."

"Then you don't know the paper was stolen? You don't know that somebody tried to kill Leonard? So we couldn't talk to him?"

He watched her eyes; saw them fix again. But this time he was not so sure.

"Oh *no!*" she said. "*No!*"

"Somebody stole the paper," Weigand said. "Somebody stabbed Leonard."

She believed it, all right—if she had not already known it. And it seemed to Bill Weigand, watching her, that there was more fear now in her eyes—in the blankness of her eyes—in the way her hands twisted together—than there had been at any time before. And Bill Weigand was surprised to find that this made him a little regretful, as if he had, unconsciously, been wishing she could get herself out of it. It must be merely because it was O'Malley who was so sure, Bill thought; he would have to watch that tendency in himself.

"I don't know anything about it," she said. The strain was in her voice.

"Who does?" Weigand said. "Who else? Think, Mrs. Mott. Who else would have any reason?"

He watched that hit her. He waited. Her voice was very low, now, when she answered.

"I don't know," she said. "I—I don't understand."

It wasn't good, Bill thought.

"You're not helping us, Mrs. Mott," he said. "You want to help us, don't you? However you felt about your husband?"

"I didn't take the paper," she said. "I—I didn't hurt Mr. Leonard. Is he—is he going to be all right?"

"Perhaps," Bill told her. He shook his head. "Don't you see where it puts us, Mrs. Mott?" he asked, and his voice was reasonable, enquiring. "You can't suggest anyone else, or any reason for anyone else. But if you did express hatred for your husband in the paper—you may not have named him, of course, but it must have been clear—then you would want to get the paper, wouldn't you? Want to fix it so we couldn't talk to Leonard, who'd read it?" He shook his head. "How would you explain it, Mrs. Mott?"

"I didn't," she said. "That's all I know. I don't know who did."

"Carey? Your friend Carey?"

"No. Oh, no!"

"Who?"

"I tell you—I tell you I don't know!"

Bill Weigand shook his head again.

"I can't believe that, Mrs. Mott," he said. "I'm sorry. However—"

She was not looking at him, now. She was looking down at her hands, twisting in her lap. She gave the odd expression that she was really looking carefully at her hands. She's afraid her eyes will give her away, Bill thought. It was about time.

"Now," he said, "you say you weren't at your husband's office today? Not there at the time he was killed?"

She did not look up. She merely nodded. Weigand stood up, he moved around the desk and half sat on it, looking down at her.

"Now, Mrs. Mott," he said. "I'm going to have to tell you that—"

And then the telephone rang. Bill Weigand was nearest, and scooped it up. He listened, speaking little, and his face set; he looked down at the girl sitting in front of him, and his eyes and his face were hard.

Then, into the telephone, he said, "Right. We were late."

He recradled the telephone and sat for an instant looking down at the girl. She did not look up at first; then she did, and fear came into her eyes anew as she saw his face. It ought to, Bill Weigand thought; you ought to be afraid, Mrs. Mott.

Then, with a gesture of his head, he summoned Mullins and went toward the door, with Mullins after him. In the room outside, Bill jerked his head back toward the door of his office.

"She stays there," he said. "And, get one of the girls with her. She might—"

He did not finish, being already through the door to the corridor. He was moving very fast. He's sore, Mullins thought. The Loot's sore as hell, this time.

It was only when they were out in the corridor, going toward the street, that Bill Weigand told Mullins what had happened. Then Mullins swore.

Police cars were tucked against the curb in front of a tall, narrow apartment house on Central Park West. Mullins tucked the squad car in among them, switched off its blinking red lights. There were two large, long apartments on each floor of the house and there was no trouble in finding the right one. The door was open, light streamed out, the foyer and the living room seemed crowded. A uniformed patrolman on duty at the outer door did not know Bill Weigand and Mullins; Mullins made the introduction curt. The precinct detective lieutenant knew Bill and, seeing him, seemed relieved. The precinct lieutenant was round and comfortable, free of ambition and of jealousy.

"Yours?" he asked Bill, and there was a note of hope in his voice.

"Right," Bill said. "I'm afraid so, George."

"The boys are working out on it," George said. "The M.E.'s been."

"And?"

"Dead," George told him. "Dead for hours."

"Literally?"

"So the doc says. Let's see, now it's eleven forty-five." He looked at his watch again. "Forty-six," he said. "The doc looked at her—oh, say fifteen minutes ago. He said he'd guess. You know 'em."

Bill knew them.

"Nothing definite, wait 'til we cut it up, when did she eat—that sort of thing. Then he guessed. Dead at least five hours, probably not more than six and a half. Gives a nice wide hole to duck into, of course. For the M.E."

"Before six-thirty, then," Bill said. "Not before five. Right."

"Looks as if she was dressing to go out somewhere," George said. "Not that that helps a lot."

A flash bulb went off in the room beyond the living room; another bulb went off. George O'Hanlon said that ought to be about the size of it. They went toward the other room and police photographers were packing their camera cases.

Elaine Britton had fallen back on the satin cover of her bed when she was stabbed below the left breast. Blood had soaked the thin negligee she had worn, had soaked the satin coverlet, had soaked into the bed. It appeared that she had been standing beside the bed, had fallen when she was struck and had died where she fell. There was no expression on the face; the pretty mouth was open and the round eyes stared up at nothing on the ceiling. She was even thinner than Bill Weigand had thought when he talked to her that afternoon.

"No knife?" Bill said to Lieutenant O'Hanlon. "But it was a knife?"

"That's right," O'Hanlon said. "Pulled out and taken along. But it was a knife all right. See what I mean about her getting ready to go out?"

He motioned toward the bed. Near the foot, a black evening dress lay flat on the pale yellow satin, lay as if it had been placed there carefully. The blood had not quite reached it.

Bill Weigand did not touch the woman's body. There was no need; it had been touched enough, would be touched more. There was fresh make-up on the face which had been pretty, fresh red on the lips. The reddened lips were startling, unreal, against the face, now. The blond hair was disordered against the yellow satin. But she had fallen backward and the front part of the hair did not seem to have been disturbed. Bill thought she had finished arranging it when she was stabbed to death. There would have been final touches, little rearrangements, after she put on the black dress.

An evening dress, but not at five o'clock. The later hour became the more probable. She was dressing, starting to dress. She had been to the beauty shop that afternoon; undoubtedly had her hair done; there would have been little for her to do except freshen make-up. (He looked at the slender body. Why had she needed to walk up walls? But now it didn't matter.) She had been dressing, or perhaps lying down, resting, before she dressed. Presumably she had been expecting somebody to pick her up; she had been wearing the thin negligee or, when someone came— the murderer came—she had put it on. She had gone to the door— Or had she left the door unlatched, and merely called "Come in" when someone rang the bell. (Come in and kill me.)

"Was the door locked when she was found?" he asked O'Hanlon. O'Hanlon nodded. "By the way," Bill said, "who found her?"

Her maid had found her. The maid was a colored girl named Agnes—Agnes Connors. Agnes had had the afternoon off, come back a little after ten, opened the door with her key and had been surprised to find all the lights on, including those in Elaine Britton's bedroom. The bedroom door was open and the girl had called, "Mrs. Britton?" When there was no answer, she had investigated. Then she had called the police, not using the telephone extension in the bedroom, picking up the one in the foyer with a handkerchief around it.

"A bright young woman," O'Hanlon said. "You want to talk to her?"

"Should I?" Weigand asked. "Is there any reason?"

O'Hanlon did not think they had missed anything.

"Neither do I," Bill said. "Let her go home. We can always have her back."

The door had been locked. "Snap lock, I suppose?" Bill said, and O'Hanlon nodded. Then Elaine Britton had put on her robe—over nothing, evidently—gone to the door, let the visitor in and—and then? The best guess was she had left the visitor in the living room and gone back to the bedroom to finish dressing. The best guess was the visitor had followed her there, and stabbed her—and gone, pulling the outside door to behind him. Only it wasn't behind *him,* Bill thought. He was becoming pretty sure of that. Everything pointed one way, O'Malley's way, toward the girl back in Weigand's office. Even the little things—even that Elaine Britton might have been more willing, slightly clad as she was, to open the door to a woman. (Not that this would have weighed very heavily with her, probably.) He looked down at the body once more, thought of Pam North's name for her. Poor little mink. Poor, bright-eyed, eager little mink.

He went back to the living room and O'Hanlon went with him. The fingerprint men were at work there. There was plenty of work, but Bill Weigand doubted much would come of it. There would be prints enough—of Elaine Britton, or her maid, of any casual guests who might have come since the room was last polished by Agnes Connors. It was too bad, Bill thought, that there was so seldom a telltale glass, marked with lipstick, laden with revealing prints; so seldom a cigarette of peculiar brand. Murderers were inconsiderate.

"Right," Bill said to O'Hanlon, and stood at the door. "It seems to fit, George. I don't think you'll be bothered with it much, or long. Send the dope along."

"Good," George O'Hanlon said. "Fine by me. The Mott job?"

"It looks like it," Bill said. He summoned Mullins with a movement of his head. The elevator took them to the street. Mullins backed the police car from the curb, flicked on its flickering lights. Mullins said it was too damn bad. Bill agreed with him. They went, fast, downtown.

He had gone abruptly, with the look on his face which frightened her. She had not needed to be told that she was to wait there in the little office, that she would be stopped if she tried to leave it. She sat where she was, looking at nothing, remembering the look on Lieutenant Weigand's face, trying to understand why, seeing it, she had been again so frightened. She thought, finally, that he had looked as if he had, finally, weighed everything and reached a verdict—a verdict against her.

She had been alone for only about five minutes. Then a woman, middle-aged, in a blue uniform, had come in and stood looking at her. After looking at her for several seconds, the woman had said, "Good evening, Mrs. Mott," in a voice without animosity. The woman continued to look at her, after she had spoken, with bright curious eyes. She went over and sat on the window sill where the larger detective had sat before.

"Thought you'd want company," she said, at length, unhurriedly. "You're to wait, you know, dearie. The lieutenant tell you?"

Peg Mott shook her head, slowly. Her eyes were opened wide.

"Did something happen?" she said. "Did they—find out something?"

"Now, dearie," the woman in the uniform said, "you'll find out, won't you? Just take it easy for a while." She nodded, agreeing with herself. "While you can," she said.

"What—?" Peg Mott began, but the woman shook her head and there was clearly no use in finishing. The bright, curious eyes stayed on her.

"You're pretty, aren't you?" the woman said. "That's what does it, I guess. Being pretty."

There was a kind of rather dreadful impersonality in the woman's tone. It was as if she were talking about somebody who had been; as if she were giving a verdict—again a verdict!—on something which was finished.

"You ought to have a nice cup of coffee," the woman said, after another pause. "A nice cup of coffee would help, you know. You want to send out for some?"

Peg Mott shook her head.

"Now, dearie," the woman said. "I could do with a nice cup of coffee myself. What do you say, dearie? While we wait?"

"All right," Peg said. "Oh—all right!"

"Now, dearie," the woman said, and shook her head. "Just take it easy." She nodded again, again in agreement with herself. "Just don't borrow trouble," she said. "We'll just have a nice cup of coffee and a cigarette. You got cigarettes?"

Dumbly, Peg nodded. Dumbly, she watched while the woman went to the door of the room, said, "We'd like some coffee, Mac," to someone in the other room. It was almost ten minutes before the coffee came, in thick white cups, and dumbly Peg Mott paid for it. It was milky, sweetened, but it was hot; it softened, a little, the chill around her mind. She drank slowly, carefully, paying attention to what she did, so that she would not have to look at the woman, would not give the woman a chance to talk. She thought about lifting the cup, about putting her lips to the rim of the cup, about swallowing, making each of these actions a separate, separately willed, action. She did not know how long she took to drink the cup of milky coffee, but the coffee was only tepid when she finished. The woman in uniform had finished hers long before, and now was looking at Peg Mott, with the same bright, curious, impersonal eyes.

"Feel better, dearie?" she said, when Peg looked up. "Nothing like a nice cup of coffee. You got a cigarette, dearie?"

Peg produced cigarettes and the woman crossed the room and took one. Peg lighted one for herself and sat smoking, looking at nothing. Then she heard movement in the next room, and voices, and saw the policewoman cross quickly to the desk and snub out her cigarette in a tray. The woman looked at her and smiled and nodded.

"On duty," she said. "Not supposed to smoke. We'll just forget it, won't we dearie?" Then she went to the door and opened it and said, "All right, Lieutenant," to a question which must have been conveyed by an expression, by lifted eyebrows. Then Lieutenant Weigand came in, with the larger man behind him. Weigand went to his desk and sat behind it and, after a moment, spoke to her. His voice was level, without expression.

"I'll have to tell you, now, that you had better get a lawyer, Mrs. Mott," he said. "Do you want to telephone?"

She shook her head. She shook it slowly, as if the movement were an effort.

"I didn't do anything," she said. "I don't need—"

"No, Mrs. Mott," Weigand said. "I'm afraid it won't work."

"Please," she said. "What's happened?"

He looked at her, for a long moment.

"Right," he said, "if that's the way you want it. Sergeant Mullins will take it down, you know. You'll be asked to sign it. It can be used. You understand that?"

"I didn't do anything," she said. She seemed to cling to it.

"Remember," he said, "I told you to get a lawyer. The sergeant heard me. You know that? You'll try to back out of it later, you know."

"No," she said. "What was it?"

"You knew a Mrs. Britton. An Elaine Britton?"

She wet her lips. She nodded.

"Right," Weigand said. "Now, I'll tell you this. You say you weren't at your husband's office at noon today. You still say that?"

She nodded again.

"But," Weigand said, "Mrs. Britton saw you go into the office—into the building, anyway. And—you knew she had. You saw her. Right?"

"No. Oh, no. I—I—"

"You're lying, Mrs. Mott. You went into the office. You may have quarreled with your husband. You may have planned it from the start. You killed him."

She did not speak this time. She merely shook her head, slowly, as if she would never finish shaking it, as if she had forgotten she was shaking it. There was a kind of hopelessness in the movement.

"Then," Weigand said, and now he leaned forward at the desk, getting closer to her, making the words bite, "then, Mrs. Mott, you remembered that Mrs. Britton had seen you going into the building. That made two dangers—Leonard, Mrs. Britton. You tried to get Leonard."

She still shook her head. She seemed voiceless.

"And—you did get Elaine Britton. This afternoon—early this evening. Which was it, Mrs. Mott?"

She stopped shaking her head, now. She looked up at him, her long eyes wide open, fixed. She's afraid now, Weigand thought. It's terror, now.

"Between five and six-thirty," he said. "Between five and six-thirty, Mrs. Mott, you went to Elaine Britton's apartment. She let you in and went back to her bedroom. You followed her. You—used a knife! Again, Mrs. Mott. Your husband—Leonard—Elaine Britton. Why? Why did you start all this? The money? Because you hated him? Because—"

"No!" she said, and suddenly she stood up. "No! No!" She turned, as if to run for the door.

"Stop," Weigand said. "It's no use. You know it's no use."

"I wasn't near her apartment," the girl said, and suddenly turned to face him. "You can't prove I was there. I—I don't even know where she lived. Was that—was that where you went? Did you just find out?"

"Does that matter?" Weigand said, and his voice was level again, patient in a monotone. "You killed her."

"I wasn't there. Not near there."

He shook his head.

"And you say you don't know where she lived," he pointed out. "How do you know you weren't near there?"

"Central Park West," she said. "Somewhere on Central Park West. I knew that. I wasn't there. I was miles away—up by the University. Don't you see?"

"Lies," Weigand said. "More lies. Prove it. Who were you with? Who can—" He saw her face. "You see," he said, "it's no go. You see that."

"I went up to Dyckman. I—I was trying to find

somebody. That was about four-thirty. Then, about five, I hadn't found this—"

"Weldon Carey," Weigand said. "Name him, Mrs. Mott."

"Weldon," she said. "I telephoned his place. The—the place your man found me."

"Go on."

"About five, I think," she said. "He wasn't there. I waited and tried again in about fifteen minutes. He still wasn't there. Then—then I didn't want to stay at the University and—"

"Because you knew we were looking for you, wanted to pick you up. Go on."

"I went to a movie. Some movie. On Broadway, I think. Way up on Broadway—miles from the park. You see?"

"No. But go on."

"Because it was warm and—and—"

"A place to hide," Weigand said. "I know. Go on."

"I kept calling Weldon. Every few minutes I'd go out and try again. I had to go out to the lobby and—"

"Never mind. Don't make up details. Go on."

"It's true. It's what happened. I had to see him, talk to him. Then—it was almost seven—he was home. Then—then we agreed to meet. Downtown, in the Village. At about seven-thirty. Don't you see?"

"What? What is there to see, Mrs. Mott? Look at it yourself. The time's open. Or do you say you talked to somebody, that somebody will remember you? Do you say that?"

She shook her head again, slowly, still, but not so automatically.

"I don't know. There was a girl there. Directing people, saying where there were seats. She might remember. I asked her where the telephone was. The first time. She might remember."

Bill Weigand shook his head.

"No," he said, "I don't think she'll remember."

"You'll ask her? Find out?"

"Right," Bill said. "Naturally." He did not tell her why it would be natural; that the police would have to protect themselves against some future defense; against a girl at a movie theater who suddenly remembered, at a trial. "We'll ask her," he said.

"As a matter of form," the girl said. "Not to find out. You don't want to find out!"

"To find out," Weigand said. "As we found out about your being at your husband's office. As we'll find out you were at the University earlier, when Leonard was hurt. Not as a matter of form, Mrs. Mott." He paused and looked at her and gave it time. "As we found out you were at your husband's office," he repeated. "Why do you lie, Mrs. Mott? Can't you see we know?"

Now again, the girl's eyes went blank. She might as well say it, Weigand thought. Why doesn't she say it?

She reached out and took the back of the chair, holding it, leaning a little on it.

"Sit down," he told her. "Sit down, Mrs. Mott." She sat down, mechanically, as if compelled.

"Tell me," he said. "Get it over with, Mrs. Mott. This doesn't do you any good. Tell me."

She seemed about to speak. Then the office door opened.

Bill Weigand glared at it. He glared at Detective Sergeant Stein, coming through it.

"I thought—" Bill began, and stopped. He knew Stein. And, if there was damage, it was done.

"You'll want to see this," Stein said, and crossed to the desk. He put a folded sheet of paper on the desk and waited. Bill Weigand read what was written on the paper, looked up quickly and said, "Outside?"

"Outside," Stein said. He smiled faintly. "Very angry. Very—" He let a shrug finish.

Bill Weigand looked at the girl, who was looking at him. Her expression had changed; it was as if she had been able to read through the back of the note Stein had handed him. If she had been about to give it up when Stein came in, she wasn't now. For a moment, Bill Weigand held the slip of paper, looked from it to the girl, to Stein, hesitated.

"Right," he said then, "let's have him in."

"I thought you might," Stein said. He went out. Weldon Carey came in; he was hatless and his black hair was violent—violent as his face. He wore a dark overcoat with the collar turned up. He was furious at all of them, and he went first to the girl. She had turned as he entered, started to get up, relaxed in the chair again as he crossed the room toward her. His movements had an odd, violent thrust to them.

"All right," he said, and his voice was angry, too. "All right. What've they done to you?"

The girl merely shook her head.

"Bloody cops," Carey said. "I told you. Didn't I?" He turned on Weigand. "You," he said. "Can't you leave her alone?"

Bill Weigand leaned back in his chair. He met Carey's angry eyes.

"No," he said. "How can we?" His voice was level, uninflected. "She killed her husband, Mr. Carey. Don't you know that?"

"Prove it," Carey told him. "She wasn't there."

"You know that?"

"I—you're damn right. I know it. Because I—"

Weigand was shaking his head; he was almost laughing. He told Carey not to be heroic, not to be a damn fool.

"Heroic hell," Carey said. "Neither of us was there."

"Oh yes," Weigand said. "She was. She was about to tell me so, Mr. Carey. Weren't you, Mrs. Mott?"

Carey turned from Weigand. He glared down at the girl. She looked up at him, and then, as if she had reached a decision, she shook her head.

"No," she said. "It's no good, Weldon. They know I was there. Somebody—" She hesitated and looked at Weigand. "Somebody saw me," she said. "Elaine, they say. She said she saw me. And—" She stopped and looked again at Bill Weigand.

"And Elaine Britton was killed this afternoon," Weigand said. He was leaning back, his eyes half closed, waiting. He did not amplify it, or need to. Carey was at the desk, opposite Weigand, both hands gripping the desk, leaning forward. He thrust himself at Weigand.

"Not Peg!" he said. He was almost shouting in the little room. "You can't make it Peg!"

"I didn't make it anybody," Bill said. He motioned toward the girl. "She made it. She's a killer, Carey." He nodded. "Not to look at," he said, "but she's a killer. She was there."

Carey continued to lean toward Bill Weigand, trying to beat him down with eyes. Bill merely nodded, slowly.

Then, with an abrupt movement, Carey went back to the girl. He put his hands on her shoulders and looked down at her, and she turned her face up to him.

"Tell him, Peg," Carey said.

Bill Weigand did not say anything. He merely waited. The girl looked at him.

"I was there," she said, and spoke clearly, methodically. "He was dead when I got there. He telephoned me to come at noon and when I got there he was dead. Across his desk. I don't know anything else."

"He didn't telephone you," Weigand said. He shook his head. "I told you we find out. He didn't make any call, you see. There's a switchboard, Mrs. Mott. When do you say he called you?"

"About eleven."

It was no good, Bill told her. Mott had been in his office from about ten-thirty on. He had made no telephone calls; he had received two.

"You telephoned him," Weigand said. "Told him you had to see him. Went to kill."

"No."

"He could have gone out," Carey said. "Gone out and called. Don't you know that? He didn't have to go through the reception room. Didn't you know that?"

Bill Weigand let himself look interested. He said he had known it.

"And," he said, "apparently you know the place, Mr. Carey. You've been there? To see Mott?"

The girl started to speak, but did not; it was pressure from Carey's hands on her shoulders that stopped her, Bill thought.

"Suppose I was?" Carey said. His tone challenged.

"I'd be interested," Bill said, and his tone was matter-of-fact. "Today, Mr. Carey? About noon?" Bill shook his head. "I told you not to be heroic," he said. "Come off it, Mr. Carey."

"Not today," Carey said. "Get it through your thick cop's skull it wasn't either of us. Or can't you?"

Bill Weigand merely smiled and shook his head.

"Twice I was there," Carey said. "About a month— six weeks—ago with Peg. To see if he wouldn't get some sense; quit pushing us around. And last week."

"Why last week?"

"To tell him he'd better quit it," Carey said. "To tell him if he didn't lay off I'd—" He stopped.

"Right," Bill said. "Go on, Carey."

"Hell," Carey said. "Kick his teeth in. I don't remember the words." He looked angrily at Bill. "And meant it," he said. "Whatever I said. Only she—Peg— calmed me down. Said we'd get along whatever he did, that he wasn't worth trouble. And you say she killed him!"

There was contempt in Carey's voice as he made the last statement. Bill Weigand did not appear to be impressed. He did not answer that.

"Pushing you around, he said. "How, Mr. Carey?"

"Getting her fired," Carey said, and stopped suddenly. "I'm making it easy for you," he said. "So what? He had money in a lot of shows. A lot of guys thought he might put money in theirs. So he goes around and says—hell, I don't know what he says. That he'd appreciate it if Mrs. Mott didn't get parts."

"Like that," Bill said.

"Something like that," Weldon Carey said. "He as good as told us that first time."

"Why?"

"Why'd he tell us? I don't know."

"Why did he do it?"

"Because she'd left him. To make her come back. How can you tell what makes a guy like Mott tick? A crummy heel who sits on his tail at a desk and gets to be a major while a bunch of guys are getting kicked apart. Better guys than—"

"Right," Bill said. "Skip that. Whatever he was, he's dead."

"He's a dead heel," Carey said. "O.K."

"Did he push you? Or just Mrs. Mott?"

"Both of us," Carey said. "I had a play coming on last fall. All set, options signed, casting started. Why do you think it was dropped? Why do you think they held it until the end of November, and then dropped it? Kicking in with option money every month? Because Mott told them to."

"You know that?" Weigand asked.

"Mott said it. He thought it was funny as hell. Said it would teach me to keep my hands off—the lousy bastard!" He looked at Bill Weigand and nodded. "Making it easy for you," he said. "Don't think I don't see it. Motive, and all. But it's as much for me as for Peg, you know."

"No," Bill said. "I'm afraid not, Mr. Carey. She hated him, he annoyed you. She was—had been—involved emotionally. She'd involved you in it, and you'd lost out. And—she gets the money, Mr. Carey.

And she was there. You had no motive to kill Mrs. Britton, to attack Leonard. And Mrs. Britton was killed, Leonard attacked. I don't think we want you, Carey."

"You don't want either of us," Carey said.

"I'm afraid I do, Mr. Carey," Bill said. He stood up. "You go," he said. "She—stays."

"It won't stick," Carey said. "You're a thick-skulled—" He let it trail off.

"If you want to do something, Mr. Carey, get her a lawyer," Bill said. "She'll be arraigned Monday in homicide court. She'll need somebody. I told her that."

"White of you," Carey said, with bitterness. "Damned white of you."

He turned suddenly to the girl, seemed to lift her out of the chair, held her in his arms with a kind of fury. Even his caresses are like blows, Bill Weigand thought. The poor, violent kid.

Carey let the girl go. He held her off and looked at her.

"You'll be all right, Peg," he said. "You know that?"

She seemed dutiful, like a little girl.

"I'll be all right," she said. "I'll be all right, Wel."

Weigand doubted it. He said nothing. Carey released the girl fully, turned, without saying anything more thrust himself out of the room. There were voices in the next room, Carey's loud, angry. Stein came to the door; he raised his eyebrows.

"Yes," Weigand said. "Let him go. For now. And Stein—take Mrs. Mott to the precinct and have her booked. Suspicion of homicide. The precinct, not downtown." He turned to the girl. "That'll keep the newspapers off you for a day," he said. "Talk to your lawyer before you talk to them. Maybe he'll want you to plead; maybe the district attorney will take a plea.

That's not up to me. Now, go with the sergeant, Mrs. Mott."

Peggy Mott stood up, held her head up. She's almost as tall as Stein, Weigand thought. The poor kid. She's had it. How she's had it! She moved toward the door. Suddenly, poignantly, the grace of her movements reminded Bill Weigand of Dorian. Blackly, at that moment, he disliked his job.

He sat down, picked up the telephone and, after a moment, began to report to Inspector O'Malley at O'Malley's home. O'Malley was pleased; O'Malley approved.

"We've wrapped it up," O'Malley said. "Nice going, Bill. Way I'd've done it myself. None of this fancy stuff; no Norths to make it screwy. Quick and simple." He paused. "Tell you what," he said, "I'll go down to headquarters and tell the newspaper boys myself, Bill. See that you get the credit. How's that?"

Not too good, Bill Weigand felt at the moment; not too probable, either. But he said, "Right, Inspector. I'll appreciate it."

He put the telephone back in its cradle. All wrapped up; wrapped up and tied together. Quick and simple, and no Norths in it, or almost no Norths. It was odd that he felt, obscurely, dissatisfied, even uneasy. It must be, he thought, because Pam North wouldn't approve, and, after Pam had talked to Dorian, Dorian wouldn't approve either. Well, it was too bad, but there was nothing to do about it. O'Malley couldn't be wrong always; the quick and easy couldn't be wrong always. This one was so simple it hit you in the face. Pam North—even Dorian—would have to accept that.

He was uneasy, but he did not expect anything to happen. He did not expect Stein to come back, his eyes glazed, a bruise seeming to grow on the right side of his jaw as he stood in the door, and swayed a little. But Bill was on his feet, around the desk, before Stein could speak, was saying, "What the hell, Lennie?"

Detective Sergeant Stein's voice was stiff; it seemed to be an effort for him to speak.

"Jumped me," he said. "This guy Carey—outside. I put the girl in a cab and was starting to get in and he jumped me. I was half in and he yanked me out and—" Stein motioned toward his jaw. "Knocked me flat," he said. "Damn near out. He ran around the cab and grabbed the girl. She yelled something—'No, Wel, no!'—something like that but after she was out she ran all right. The hacker tried to follow and they ditched him. Then he came back and told the boys downstairs. *Then* he told them!" He looked at Weigand, and swayed a little. "I'm sorry as hell, Bill," he said. "I certainly loused it up."

Bill said, "O.K., fella," to Leonard Stein. But it wasn't O.K. They would all get their tails burned for this, starting with Stein, not stopping with Stein. Quick and neat, wrapped up and tied in knots. That was Weldon Carey, that was them. Bill Weigand went back to his desk, used the telephone, curtly, starting the new chase. Then he telephoned O'Malley. "This is going to be fun," he thought, as he waited for Mrs. O'Malley to call her husband. "This is going to be fun and games."

It was.

8

One way to keep alive in the Pacific had been quite literally, to act before you thought. You did not wait for opportunity to knock; you moved to seize before opportunity had time to lift a hand. You made mistakes, but you kept alive.

If anyone had told Weldon Carey two minutes before he grabbed Peg Mott away from the police that he was going to do anything so reckless, so ruinously quixotic, he would have laughed. Being bitter, his laughter would have been bitter, and hard. He would have said, "Not a chance," have asked what kind of a sap he was supposed to be. He had not waited with any purpose outside the building which housed the Homicide Squad; he had merely walked out of the building and stood, in the darkness, huddled a little against the bitter wind, deciding which way to go and what to do. And then Peg had been brought out by the likable-looking detective he had seen inside, and the detective had, a great deal to Weldon Carey's surprise, beckoned to a taxicab down the block.

Sergeant Stein was, although Carey did not know it, acting in accordance with accepted, although not stip-

143

ulated, practice. Peg Mott was not a dangerous prisoner; she was being taken on a special trip, not as a
member of a group; squad cars, including the one Stein
had used earlier, might have other uses. Although she
was technically under arrest—or all but technically so;
that would await formal booking at the precinct—she
was not handcuffed, simply because Stein thought, as
Weigand would have thought, that it was absurdly
unnecessary. And Stein did not notice Carey, except
as a figure in a shadow, braced against the wind,
because in routine operations you did not plan against
the preposterous. So Stein was quite unprepared for
the preposterous when it occurred.

Carey watched the cab stop, watched Stein open the
door, and did not move, did not even think of moving.
He saw Stein, barely touching Peg's elbow, direct her
into the cab, and still he did not move. Then, just at the
instant Stein was stepping up, and hence was off
balance, Carey moved without thinking about it at all.
He grabbed Stein by a shoulder with his left hand,
yanked and, at the same time, swung with his right. It
was absurdly easy. He saw Stein stagger back, saw his
knees begin to bend, and ran around the cab—to put it
between him and the entrance to the building—
wrenched the door open and hauled at Peg. The driver
yelled before he moved, giving time.

Peg Mott said something, but Carey hardly heard it.
She didn't want to come, but he pulled at her, not
gently, and said, "Come on!" and, because things
were working that way, because it was absurdly easy,
she came. He grabbed her around the waist first, then
by the arm, and they ran down the street with the wind
behind them. It was precisely that easy. He heard the
taxi driver yelling and heard the motor start, and then
they dodged into what appeared to be an alley. Still,
Carey hadn't thought about it; he'd grabbed an opportunity (and his girl) and he had run for it. They were
out of an alley, on another street, still running and with

Peg gasping a little for breath, before he began really to think. Then he made them stop running.

Then Peg Mott spoke, in little breathless words, and said, "No—no, Wel—we've got—to go—go back. We can't—"

"It's too late for that," he said. "Come on."

She tried to stop. She said she was going back.

He let her stop.

"All right," he said. "We'll both go back. Maybe you're right."

But then she started on again, and he started with her.

"We can't, now," she said. "You know that. Unless you'll let me go alone. You hit the detective. You hurt him. They'd—"

She did not say what they would do, or anything more. But he could feel her trembling. At that, he thought, she was right enough. He'd stirred up a nest, all right. One that wouldn't quiet down in a hurry. They'd be pouring out of the nest, now; they'd be angry.

"Why did you?" she said. "What good can it do?"

There wasn't any answer to that, either; not any real answer. He hardly knew himself. There had been a picture of Peg locked up, in a cell, helpless. There had been a chance. That was all it came to. There wasn't any plan. But now, he thought, there had to be. And it had to be one based on going ahead. Maybe they'd had it, but they had to keep on, now, until that was proved. There was a subway station up the street and they went toward it. That was the first part of the plan.

Peg Mott went along with the feeling that she was walking into darkness. She had run with Weldon Carey because, after what he had done to Stein, he had to run, and clearly would not run without her. And now there did not seem to be any way to turn back which would not involve him in more trouble, worse trouble, than anything which had come yet. She went along, walking into darkness, and at the same time glad, brought to life again, by the pressure of Weldon's hand on her arm, by his presence. Although she felt that this was wrong, that there should be some other way, she did not hold back as they went down the stairs of the subway station, into the West Side local. They did not try to talk against the roar of the train. At the Sheridan Square station they got out of the train, and went up the steps and then, because Carey had a plan now, away from the square on Fourth Street, toward the west. The wind was against them now, trying to drive them back. He seemed to be thrusting them into it.

The wind snatched at her breath and Peg did not try to say anything, even to ask where they were going. She merely went on, head down, with Carey beside her. She staggered once when a gust struck her, and then he put an arm around her waist, holding her close, so that they were a unit thrusting against the wind. It was better, after that.

She did not know the street, beyond Eighth Avenue, into which they turned, and when they went into the door of what appeared to be an aged business building, she was thankful only that, inside, the air was still. It was no warmer, but it was still. They went up a flight of wooden stairs hugging one wall, and then up another flight. Then Carey knocked on a door, opening off a long corridor. He knocked and kept on knocking, and finally there were sounds of movement behind the door, and a man's voice began to swear, sleepily. Then the door opened suddenly, and a slim man in his late twenties stood in it, hugging a blue robe around him.

"Who the hell—" the man began, with anger, and then stopped. "So it's you," he said. "What the hell, Sergeant?"

"Hiya, Colonel," Carey said. "Wake you up?"

"You know bloody, god—" the man at the door said and then, for the first time, seemed to see Peg Mott. "Well," he said. "Well, well, Sergeant. What gives?"

"Look, Paul," Weldon Carey said. "We need a hand. How about it?"

"Then why the hell don't you come in?" the slender man said. "What are you waiting for?"

They went in. It was warmer inside, but it was not warm. There was a single light in the middle of a room which seemed tremendous, which did, Peg began to realize, include the whole floor of the building. Toward the front there was only dimness, against which the light from the dangling bulb made no progress. The other way there were curtains stretching across, cutting off an end of the enormous room.

"Come along back," the man said. "Wait a minute." He stopped. "Get some clothes on, Paula," he shouted. "Got visitors."

The voice which came back was clear, high. There seemed to be laughter in it. But the words were merely "Come along."

Carey seemed to hesitate a moment.

"Told you I was getting married, didn't I?" the slim man said. "Well, I got married. Come along."

They went back, the man Carey had called "colonel" holding the curtains apart for them. Warmth met them, faintly tinged with odors—the pungency of burning kerosene, of tobacco, of perfume. But most of all there was warmth.

There was warmth and rather remarkable space. The room the curtains cut off was still a big room, high-ceilinged, with a row of tall, narrow windows at the far end. There were curtains over the windows; there was a screen cutting off one corner, near the windows; there were several deep sofas and a number of chairs; scattered through the room there was enough furniture, and rather good furniture, for a largish apartment.

Peg Mott examined the room, unconsciously, because it was so surprising. She found that the "colonel" was looking at her, with faint amusement. But then he looked away and around the room and said, "Hey, Paula!"

A small girl, very slender, with deep red hair, came out from behind the screen. She was holding a blue robe around her with one hand and carrying a tray in the other. There were cups on the tray, a silver coffee pot, and a tall bottle. She put the tray down on a low table and came toward them and said, as if she had known them a long time, "Hello."

"This is Paula, Sergeant," the "colonel" said. "This is Weldon Carey, the guy I told you about. I don't know who this is." He motioned toward Peggy, and his whole face smiled.

"All right, Paul," Weldon Carey said. "This is Peggy Mott. Mrs. Tony Mott."

"Oh," the red-haired girl said, involuntarily.

"Yes, Mrs. Foster," Carey said. The challenge came back into his voice. "Mrs. Tony Mott."

"Why not," Paul Foster said. "Very handsome, too, Sergeant." He crossed to Peggy Mott and held out his hand. His smile was warming; the room was warming. And then Paula Foster came across the distance between them, with both hands out.

"Paul. Paula," Weldon Carey said. "What gives?"

Paul Foster turned, still smiling.

"Why we got married," he said. "Seemed too good to miss. Of course, she had all this fine furniture, too. That entered in."

"Only no place to put it," Paula Foster said, "so we got this."

"Very fine, too," Paul Foster said. "Homey. But plenty of room for expansion."

They were talking for time, Peggy thought; to give her time, themselves time. They kept at it. Obliquely, things were explained. Paul Foster had been a colonel—a lieutenant-colonel, at any rate—as surely as Weldon Carey had been a sergeant. "Air Force, naturally," Weldon pointed out, and looked at the other man with affection. "Dropped down on us one day." Foster had, literally, dropped down, bailing out of a fighter plane, coming to earth, hurt, near a group of Marines under Carey's orders. Carey had crawled out and brought him in, Foster said; the Marines had taken care of him and finally got him back. "Heroes," Foster said. "Particularly the sergeant here. And I was Army, remember. Must have been a temptation just to leave me there, you know."

The smile went all over his face again.

There was warmth in the room; they were trying to make it her warmth. It wasn't, couldn't be, Peggy Mott thought. Tell them, Carey; they won't want us after you tell them.

Carey told them.

"Hell of a note," Paul Foster said. "The cops must be crazy. Now what do we do?"

It was as easy as that; it was almost her warmth then, almost something she could share.

"First," Paula Foster said, "these kids get some coffee and cognac. Then they get some sleep." She looked at her husband, looking a good ways up. "Otherwise they'll catch cold," she pointed out. "And anything's better without a cold. No matter what it is."

They had coffee, with considerable cognac. Warmth came then, creeping—bodily warmth, a kind of drowsy acceptance. She was only half aware as the Fosters improvised, working together. She hardly realized, until morning, that she had slept beside the red-haired girl in a sofa turned into a bed, and that the two men—after long conversation which came to her dimly—had slept, less comfortably, on other sofas which did not turn into beds.

The Sunday newspapers had cats in them. Jerry North moved, suddenly, halfway across the room and removed Gin from the book section of the *Times*. He returned, clutching the book section of the *Times*, and

Sherry leaped from the couch, landed, somehow, under the amusement section of the *Herald Tribune*. The amusement section of the *Herald Tribune* began to travel, erratically, across the room. Jerry rescued that.

Martini, who had been watching her offspring with pleased approval, took a dim view of their dispossession. She looked up at Jerry, lashed her tail, and said "Yah!" The younger cats stopped and stared at her. Gin leaped, landing on her back, rolled her over. The two cats, locked, apparently, in a death struggle, rolled into the *Times'* Review of the Week.

"The long, lazy Sunday mornings before the fire," Jerry said, to nobody. "The rest, the relaxation. No, Sherry!"

Pam North appeared at the door of the kitchen and said that breakfast was almost ready. "I decided to make biscuits," she said. "I thought biscuits would be nice for a change. And, anyway, Martha doesn't seem to have got any bread. Are biscuits all right?"

Jerry said that biscuits were fine.

"Drop biscuits," Pam said. "I think they're better, don't you?"

"Fine," Jerry said.

Pam withdrew from the kitchen door, but she continued to talk.

"I don't know," she said. "More mellow, somehow. Drop biscuits, that is. And not so formal, of course."

"What?" Jerry said.

Pam came back to the kitchen door.

"Drop biscuits," she said. "What did you think?"

"Fine," Jerry said.

"Better texture," Pam said. "And, I'll have to admit, easier. I don't deny that."

"No," Jerry said.

There was a little pause, then, and Jerry was conscious that he was being looked at, waited for. He looked up.

"To be perfectly honest, I put too much milk in,"

Pam said, when he was looking at her. "And they have to be drop biscuits, or reconstituted. And then I'd probably have to measure. All right?"

"Fine," Jerry said. He grinned at her, suddenly.

"Damn," Pam North said. "You knew all the time I'd put too much milk in. Didn't you?"

Jerry nodded, still grinning.

"I never get away with anything," Pam said. "Boiled eggs? There's the telephone."

The last was a formality. The telephone was ringing almost in Jerry North's lap.

"Who'd be calling at this hour Sunday morning?" Pam said, with interest. Jerry said, "Hello? Yes?"

"Before breakfast," Pam said and Jerry, distracted by two points of view, compromised and said, "What?"

"Never mind," Pam said, and the man at the other end of a telephone wire said, "Paul Foster. You don't know me, Mr. North."

Jerry said, "Ummm?"

"About the Mott case," Paul Foster said. He had a light, oddly gay, voice.

Jerry said, "Ummm?"

"Who is it?" Pam said. "I just put the biscuits in. But they're almost done."

Jerry shook his head at her. He jerked it toward the front of the apartment, indicating the extension telephone in the study.

"All right," Pam said, "but remember there isn't any bread."

"I'm sorry," Jerry said into the telephone. "Something was going on. Will you say that again?"

"We want to engage you," Paul Foster said. "Retain you. Whatever the word is."

"Retain me?" Jerry said.

"You and Mrs. North," Foster said. "To find out what's at the bottom of it. Because Peggy didn't do it, you know."

"What on earth?" Jerry said. And then a new voice came in, strong in Jerry's ear. It was Pam's voice and it said, "He means he wants to hire us, Jerry. Don't you, Mr.—ah—?"

"Foster," the man said. "Mrs. North. Good. Hire you is better. To find out who killed Mott."

"Look," Jerry said, brushing off a cat which was resenting his withdrawal from the world of cats. "Look, we're not detectives. Where did you ever get that idea?"

"Officially," Pam said. "Which means for money," she explained. "Although sometimes I wonder—" The last seemed to be to herself.

Paul Foster said, "Oh." He seemed surprised and a little confused.

"Anyway," Pam said, "how do you know she didn't?"

"I've talked to her," Paul Foster said. "She says she didn't."

"For God's sake!" Jerry said. "Why wouldn't she?"

"And," Pam said, "where is she? Does she know the police are looking for her? And why did you call us, anyway?"

Paul Foster hesitated, momentarily.

"If I told you where she is, you'd tell the police?" he asked, then. Jerry came in; he was a little explosive; he said, "Damn right we would."

"Then, obviously—" Foster said. "Yes, Mrs. North, she knows the police want to talk to her."

"Then it's very simple," Mrs. North pointed out. "She ought to go to Bill Weigand—he's a detective lieutenant, you know—and let them talk to her. Why not, if she didn't do it?"

There was a longer pause, this time. Then Paul Foster, with an odd hesitancy in his voice, said it was not as simple as that. "There's more than's in the papers," he said. "It's—I'm afraid it's got loused up a bit. That's why we thought of you. Car—" He stopped abruptly. "A friend of hers telephoned a man named Leonard this morning, to ask him about something and—"

"What she said, really said, in that paper," Pam North said. "We know about that, Mr. Foster. A man named Weldon Carey called Professor Leonard. Go on."

"Leonard said he wouldn't talk. He said he'd told you all he knew, anyway. He said you—well, knew this Weigand. But that if you didn't agree with the police you'd, that is—"

"Listen," Jerry said, "if we know where Mrs. Mott is, we'll tell the police. You can count on that. I hope you haven't got any other idea, Mr. Foster." Jerry's voice was not friendly.

"If we thought Mrs. Mott didn't do it, we'd tell Bill that," Pam North said. "We might even try to persuade him. That's all." She paused briefly, but seemed to be holding the line open by an effort of will. They waited. "I still don't see where you come into this, Mr. Foster," she said. There was curiosity in her voice. Jerry heard it; identified it; unconsciously sighed.

"Pam—" he began. But he seemed to have, somehow, lost control of the conversation.

"Can't I come around to your place and explain?" Foster said. "That's all we—I—want. Just to have you listen and, if you want to, give us advice."

"I can do that now," Jerry said. "Go—" He stopped, realizing that he was not being listened to.

"All right," Pam said. "I don't see why not. When?"

"Now," Foster said, and his voice was, again, oddly gay.

"Pam," Jerry said. "We haven't—"

"Say in half an hour," Pam told Mr. Foster. "That'll give us time to have breakfast. All right, Jerry?"

"I guess—" Jerry began. His voice was unhappy.

"Good," Pam said. "In half an hour. Oh—the biscuits! Goodbye."

She hung up and so, apparently, did Mr. Foster. Jerry North took the telephone down from his ear, shook his head at it, and put it in its cradle. Pam came out of the front room, very rapidly. She did not pause, avoided a cat with what was half a dance step, and went on to the kitchen. Jerry heard the oven door open; heard Pam North say "Oh!" Then she came to the kitchen door, shaking her head.

"I don't know," she said. "Maybe we can eat a little of the insides. Of course, I could make pancakes, I suppose. Only with Mr. Foster coming so soon—?" She ended, her voice enquiring. They ate the insides of the biscuits, and bacon and boiled eggs. The cats, shouldering one another only slightly, finished the egg remaining in the cups. Pam watched them, considering. "After all," she said, "I guess they're as sanitary as we are, really. Unless you don't like cats."

Paul Foster came. He was slim, a little above medium height; he had a smile which lighted up his face. And a red-haired girl, hatless, seemingly wrapped around and around in a heavy cloth coat, came with him. "Paula," Paul Foster said, and the smile absorbed his face. "We know it's funny. But we decided to get married anyway."

Paula Foster, unwrapped, was very small. She was also very appealing. She looked at Pam quickly, and seemed pleased with what she saw. She looked at Jerry North. They both looked at Jerry North. Paul Foster looked around the room.

"I don't blame you," he said. "We've barged in. We're trying to drag you in. If you really want us to, we'll clear out."

He waited. Pam North waited, looking at her husband.

"No," Jerry said. "We'll listen, Mr. Foster. Now that you are here."

The Norths listened. They heard all of it. Jerry shook his head.

"Carey was a damn fool," he said. "You realize that?"

"He was," Foster said. "In some respects he is. But—he's a hell of a guy. Maybe he's a little bit mixed up, still. A lot of us are, you know. But he's a hell of a guy."

The police, Jerry pointed out, would not think so. Foster smiled and agreed with that.

"And eventually," Jerry said, "the police will catch up with them. You realize that, Foster? And that they're doing themselves no good?"

Foster agreed with that, in principle. He did not smile.

"But the damage is done, for the moment," he said. "And—something may turn up. Carey was a fool; nothing drastic was going to happen to the girl in jail. I realize that. But nothing drastic's going to happen, now, if she stays out of it for a day or two. Until she gets a lawyer, anyway. Then, of course, she'll have to surrender. The lawyer will make her. Say—tomorrow."

"I warn you," Jerry North said, "if I find out where she is, I'll turn her in. I ought to turn you in, now, you know. You're aiding and abetting, or whatever it is."

"By force?" Foster said, and his smile went over his face. "You don't know where we live, you know. If you call your policeman friend, you're going to force us to wait for him?"

"Stalemate," Pam North said. "Deadlock."

Jerry shook his head. He said it wasn't. He said they could give names to the police, descriptions. Paul Foster nodded to that.

"And they'll find us," he said. "I don't doubt that. By tomorrow, perhaps. But we only want until tomorrow. What do you gain?"

"Jerry," Pam said, "doesn't it make sense?"

Jerry North thought it didn't. He shook his head. He said, "Well, all right. What do you want us to do?"

"See the girl," Paul Foster said. "Listen to her."

"No," Jerry said. "Not unless she'll promise to give herself up."

"Under these conditions," Foster said. "We bring her here. You'll be in the same spot you're in now. If you telephone, we'll leave—and you'll be no better off. And you might persuade her to give herself up. All I want is for you two to listen to her first." He was earnest, now. "I've nothing against the police," he said. "Carey has, I guess. I haven't. But it's open and shut for them. Even if your friend doesn't think so, what can he do? And—if it's shut, if it's wrapped up, in their minds, they quit looking anywhere else. Well, I think somebody ought to look somewhere else. Because I'd swear the girl didn't do it, however it looks. I don't know her, but I've listened to her. I do know Carey. And Carey is certain she didn't do it. And Carey's not a fool, North. Not on things like that. Important things. I'm betting on Carey."

There was a considerable pause. The Fosters, Pam, looked at Jerry and waited.

"The fact is," Jerry said, finally, "you want us to bet on Carey too. But we don't know him, so it boils down to this—you want us to bet on *you*. On the two of you."

"Well?" Foster said, and now he smiled again.

"I suppose she's downstairs in a cab," Jerry said. "I suppose the idea's to shoot her at us before we change our minds?"

Foster didn't reply to that.

"You understand," Jerry said, "that I'll do my damnedest to get her to turn herself in?"

"Sure," Foster said. "Well?"

"Oh for God's sake," Jerry said. "Bring her up. Bring them both up."

*   *   *

Bill Weigand sat in his office and drank coffee without character out of a thick, mug-like cup. He had been there all night; he had slept for an hour or two on a couch and slept badly; his mind was filled with a kind of dull anger, a kind of resentment. There were lines deep in his thin face. The telephone rang and he picked it up and said, "Weigand speaking" and listened. His face did not change. He said, "Sorry, sir. Nothing." He listened again and said "Right." He put the telephone back in its cradle. He returned to the papers on his desk, which were a monument—a monument still in the progress of growth—to the efficiency of the New York Police Department. They represented efficiency, tirelessness; they also represented, Bill Weigand thought wearily, a certain ponderousness, and the momentum of ponderousness.

The machinery started when a certain thing happened. This time it had started, of itself, when André Maillaux had called the police, said Tony Mott was dead by violence. Bill Weigand was part of the machine, Mullins was part of it, Stein was part of it; even Inspector O'Malley was part of it. At any given time, they—and others like them—were apt to be the visible part of the machine. It would be easy to think that they were the machine. Most people, who thought about it at all, probably thought that. Those who read newspaper accounts might easily have a picture of Inspector O'Malley, looking a little like Sherlock Holmes, tirelessly interviewing suspects, poking into dark corners, now and then assisted by a subordinate named William Weigand, Lieutenant of Detectives. Because the major part of the machine was, to the public, anonymous, it probably seemed not to exist.

But it existed and functioned; it consisted of men, but it was, in the aggregate of their efforts, tireless. It consisted of medical experts, toxicologists; of varying specialists at the police laboratory; of men who knew fingerprints, and dust; of men who could tell all there was to tell, and find out all there was to find out, about fabrics and wood and metals. These technicians had gone to work, almost automatically, when a light glowed on a police switchboard and an operator heard André Maillaux's excited voice. Less automatically, after Weigand pressed certain buttons—it was a machine which pressed its own buttons—other parts of the machine started. While the medical men, and the other experts, worked to find out all that matter would reveal about Tony Mott's death, these other parts of the machine worked to find out all that could be found out about Tony Mott's life before his death.

Detectives—Smith and Jones and Robertson, Sibloni, Isaacson, Troblotsky and Murphy—went from place to place and asked questions and listened and wrote down the answers. Whom had Tony Mott known, who had liked him and who had disliked him? Had he loved this woman and hated this one, had this man a grudge against him because he had lost money through Tony Mott, and this man because he had lost love through Tony Mott? Was he suing somebody, or being sued? Had a finger in this pie, where someone did not want his fingers? Had he been in a good mood when he got up the morning of his death? Had someone threatened him five years ago?

Nothing, almost nothing, was too small for the machine, too irrelevant. The machine's raw material was Tony Mott, in his entirety, in all his relationships. The machine's product was information, piling on the desk of Bill Weigand, who became the machine's calculator.

The point was, Bill thought, looking at his desk, that the machine did not stop as automatically as it started. The night before, when he had decided that it was wrapped up, with Peggy Mott wrapped in the middle of it, Bill Weigand had pressed certain buttons which stopped the machine. After that, it sought no new raw material. But it seemed still to be full of material which it continued to process. It ground this material into information and deposited it on Weigand's desk.

Dossiers, for example, continued to arrive. There was one of a man who believed that Mott had defrauded him three years before, and had gone to court about it. There was one of a man who had taken a swing at Mott in a night club, for reasons about which there was variety of opinion. There were several of young women who had known Mott and loved him or hated him, or been married to him or tried to get married to him. There was one of the chef at the Restaurant Maillaux, who was said to have muttered darkly over some criticism Mott was supposed to have made of his Breast of Capon André. Weigand read with tired eyes and a tired mind. He did not see that it now had any particular importance; it was merely that the machine took time to grind to a stop.

"SNODGRASS," he read. "William. Maître d'hôtel; Associate M. from early days; admits tried to invest when M. needed money; said M. willing until Mott showed interest; Snodgrass then frozen out. Some gossip he resented this and showed resentment Mott. Snod. denies this. Gives age as 43, probably older; born London, naturalized Am. Cit.; married, lives Bronx; recently reported planning open restaurant of his own; says only had thought of it, not decided. Arrived restaurant about 10 a.m. Sat.; says did not see Mott alive. Could have without being seen; see attached."

"Snodgrass," Bill thought, and smiled, faintly. An unexpected name for the suave William. Bill saw attached, which was a sketch map of the office area at the Restaurant Maillaux. It told him nothing he had not known; access to the whole area could be had, from the restaurant, from the street (through the storeroom), in a variety of ways. William could have got to the office at any time without passing the receptionist. So could André. So could Tom, Dick and Harry. Bill sighed. "Tom, Dick and Harry"—those inevitable possibilities. The possibilities the defense, any defense, always played upon. The seven million or so in New York, the thousands who knew who Tony Mott was, the hundreds who knew him, well and not so well. How did the police know it was not one of these? A Tom? A Dick? A Harry? Why had they narrowed it to outraged innocence here on trial before this distinguished, perceptive jury? Was it not absurd? A hundred had opportunity as good, might have had a motive better. It was going to happen that way this time, when they put Peggy Mott on trial. (After they caught Peggy Mott again.) The district attorney would have his troubles. The layout of the office was going to be no help.

When they caught Peggy Mott again. Bill Weigand ground out a cigarette, almost instantly lighted another, got up from his desk and walked to the window. Looked out it a moment at a wall and another window, walked back to his desk. Angry impatience boiled up in him and subsided. The machine was functioning; it would turn her up. He could only wait and try not to simmer; wait and hope the newspapers did not get wind of the escape. O'Malley was hot enough already. He rumbled of departmental charges against Stein, against Weigand himself. Presumably O'Malley would calm down—if the news didn't leak, if the girl and her dark, annoying knight were turned up soon enough. Bill would fight for Stein; probably, with luck, win out. It wouldn't happen again to Stein, whose sensitive face was sombre, and also a little swollen. It was one of those things. It was also, admittedly, a hell of a note.

Bill Weigand went back to the dossiers. He had come to the women, now, and there were a good many. A tomcat, Tony Mott. An agile goat. "STOCKTON, Mary." "FRAWLEY, Katerine." "WOODS, Adelaide." "D'ALIA, Dolores." (There was fiction, for you. There was a name chosen to become well known, to fall smoothly from many lips. Bill Weigand could not remember that he had ever heard of Dolores D'Alia; apparently it had not worked.) "FARNSWORTH, Anita." (There was another, in all probability.)

He skimmed the dossiers. FRAWLEY, Katerine, had married Mott and it had lasted three months. WOODS, Adelaide, had told the newspapers she was going to marry Mott and Mott had said it was the first he had heard of it. FARNSWORTH, Anita—

She had been unlucky; it appeared she had been more earnest, more deeply involved, than Katerine Frawley, than Adelaide Woods. She had not married Mott and had not told anyone she planned to. But, three years before, she had been much with him; Winchell had said she was "that way" and apparently she was. She had been a young actress, for a time a protégée of Mott's. And then, rather publicly, in a restaurant, when he had been drinking, he had said to her, "Scram, baby. We're washed up." And then he had laughed, and several others had laughed. And Anita Farnsworth had disappeared, very suddenly, from the people who had known her, very completely. The machine ground at her disappearance and cleared it up. She had had a "nervous breakdown." The words were quoted in the dossier. She had been taken by relatives to a private sanitarium; she was still there. The physician in charge was hopeful; possibly, Bill Weigand thought, he was always hopeful. That would be part of his job. The kid had been unlucky. And Tony Mott had been—well, Tony Mott. There was no point in calling him names. That had been taken care of.

Bill found he was reading the dossier again, more carefully, wondering about it—wondering what the story sketched here, in terse words, in abbreviations, had been in its entirety. "Farnsworth, Anita, age about 23—" And then he stopped, suddenly, and read what his eyes had slid over a few moments before. "(Real name Leonard; changed for stage purposes.)" Bill Weigand looked at the words; the name repeated itself over and over in his mind.

Leonard. Leonard. Leonard. Coincidence? It could be, obviously. The long arm, reaching out—phooey! Bill Weigand did not believe it. He looked at the dossier, or seemed to, but he did not see it. He saw Professor Leonard, of Dyckman; tall and rather angular, in his middle forties. He could have had a daughter of twenty-three. Or, for that matter, a sister—a pretty girl named Anita who had been slapped down and laughed at, and who hadn't been able to take it. Bill Weigand lifted his head and looked at the wall opposite, and did not see it, and the fingers of his right hand tapped on his desk. Wrapped up, finished off. Was it, after all? He got Mullins in, told him to sit on it.

"O.K., Loot," Mullins said. He looked at Weigand and nodded. "Shuteye," he said. "That's what you need, all right. No use killing yourself, Loot."

But Wiegand shook his head.

"There's a guy I want to talk to," he said. "A guy named Leonard. Remember Leonard?"

Mullins looked momentarily puzzled. Then he nodded, and said, "O.K."

"Just the same," he said, reasonably, "you gotta sleep sometime, Loot. You know that."

Bill Weigand said, "Right," but there was no conviction in the word.

9

Pamela North would never have denied that, in almost all things, she was partisan. Sometimes her mind guided her; almost as often her mind was by-passed, now and then over its indignant objections. Her partisanship was catholic. Beginning with Jerry, it included a sometimes bewildering diversity of persons and objects. Franklin Delano Roosevelt she had been for, partly on a basis of conviction. But, in the end contradictorily, she had been also a partisan of Al Smith and, in a more moderate fashion, of Jim Farley. As far as she could ever determine, when she tried to analyze such matters, she thought General Eisenhower was a great man because he had a sunny, encompassing smile. She was also a partisan of cats, holidays in hot places, martini cocktails, the poetry of Conrad Aiken, trains, Beatrice Lillie, overcooked bacon and Maxwell Anderson. She was, further and in general, for all people who seemed to be having a tough time, whether they deserved it or not.

About Peggy Mott and Weldon Carey she had hoped to retain an open mind. But when they came into the apartment, when they stood there—the girl, for all the poise of her body, the assurance of her grace, so uncertain, so evidently afraid; the black-haired young man, for all his truculence, so uneasy and baffled— Pam North's hope vanished. Her first thought was, almost in words, "How ridiculous of Bill!" Her mind tugged at her, saying "Wait now. Wait!" Pam turned her back on her mind.

The girl was beautiful; the man stood close to her, as if to surround her, protect her from danger. He did not touch her, but he seemed to have her in his arms. Pam looked at the girl, saw that she was beautiful, and looked instantly at Jerry. Jerry was also looking at the girl, which was proper and inevitable. Pam smiled, without showing it, and wondered how firm Jerry was going to be now. And Paul Foster, coming in behind them, said, "Well, here they are."

Pamela North crossed the room to the girl, with her hand out, and said she was Pamela North. Her smile said more, and the girl answered it with an uncertain smile of her own. Weldon Carey nodded, and looked dark and angry, and Pam told them to sit down, realizing as she spoke that it would be a little difficult.

"Really, Jerry," she said, "we do need a larger apartment. See?"

They did. Two Norths, two Fosters, Peggy Mott and Weldon Carey, even without three cats and the Sunday newspapers, filled the small white and yellow living room. Jerry said he saw. Pam sat down where she had been sitting and Peggy Mott sat in another chair. The Fosters sat side by side on the sofa. Weldon Carey did not sit anywhere, but stood, facing Jerry North. He said, "Well?" There was still truculence, hiding embarrassment. Then Martini, unexpectedly to everyone, reared herself against his right leg, hooking gingerly with claws and explained, in a throaty growl which was supposed, by her, to be an ingratiating murmur, that she would like to be taken up. Carey looked down at her, and suddenly smiled and said, "Hullo. What do you want?" Martini repeated her request and, for emphasis, extended her claws so that they delicately touched skin under the trousers. Carey said, "Hey!"

"She does that to Jerry," Pam said. "She wants to sit on his shoulders, only now yours. She doesn't usually, except Jerry."

Carey looked at her, apparently started to say "What?" and changed it into "Oh." He bent, scooped up the small cat, held her out to look at her, and put her on his shoulders. She extended herself and swished her tail.

Somehow, Jerry North felt, the situation was slipping away from him. It was a feeling to which he was not unaccustomed. Irrelevance, that was what was the matter with things, Jerry thought, as he often thought. But on the other hand, irrelevance frequently seemed the underlying structure of almost everything. Chekov, he thought, and was momentarily baffled. It was even in your own mind.

"Well?" Carey repeated, but less truculently. With a cat on his shoulders, he seemed to have lost the conviction that events would be clarified by the direct approach. Martini, turning to investigate the source of this new sound, breathed into Carey's left ear.

"Take her down, Jerry," Pam said. "She's disconcerting. Put her somewhere."

Jerry took her down, put her somewhere. The young cats trotted after, their tails in the air. Jerry returned. Now Weldon Carey was sitting on the arm of Peggy Mott's chair. His left arm was along the back of the chair, as if around the girl.

"We've barged in," Weldon said. He had regained some, but not all, of his attack. "They made us—the Colonel here, Mrs. Foster. It was decent of you to let us." He said the last as a formality. Jerry took it as one and ignored it. He looked at Peggy Mott.

"You've got good friends," Jerry said. "Persuasive friends." She looked up at him.

"Weldon's," she said. "I know I oughtn't to be here, Mr. North." She looked at Pam and smiled again, uncertainly again, including her.

"Obviously," Pam said, "you ought to be in jail. Jerry and I both think that. He thinks you ought to give yourself up."

Peggy Mott looked at Weldon Carey and nodded. "See?" she said. "Oh—Wel—"

"Is that the point?" Weldon said, looking at Jerry. "The main point? She had nothing to do with it, you know."

"Not the main point," Jerry said. "The immediate point. Weigand's a friend of ours. Even if he weren't, we don't help—fugitives." He looked down at Weldon Carey. "For God's sake," he said, "Bill Weigand's a fair guy."

"He's a cop," Weldon said. "He thinks Peggy killed this bastard Mott. He'll try to third-degree it out of her."

"Not Bill," Pam said. "But let it go for a moment. Mrs. Mott, can you prove you didn't?"

"I can say I didn't," Peggy said. She looked for a long moment at Pam North. "Is it any good?"

What remarkable eyes she has, Pam thought. They must be inches long.

"Yes," Pam said. She was surprised, momentarily, at hearing herself speak the word. "You know why?" she said then, and now she included all of them. "Because nobody could be as guilty as she looks. You see, Jerry?"

"Listen," Jerry said. "I—"

"Everything in one direction," Pam said. "Too perfect. Instead of this way and that way, but mostly this way—all this way. It's—organized."

"Pam!" Jerry said. "Wait a minute." He ran a hand

through his hair. He spoke slowly, carefully. "Suppose we admit she didn't do it," he said. "For the sake of argument. Leave that open. But what you say is that she didn't do it *because* all the evidence points toward her. All the logic. What you say is that—that *logic* is wrong. You can't say that."

"Why?" Pam North said. "If it's too logical?"

Jerry shook his head, quickly, involuntarily. He looked at Weldon Carey, but Weldon was looking at Peggy Mott. Jerry's eyes sought Foster's, and Foster was smiling. "My sympathies, sir," Foster said. Then Jerry smiled.

"If it's easier," Pam said, "I'll put it this way. I think it's been planned. Planned too perfectly. I think things aren't usually so—so neat—unless somebody is making them that way. Look—"

She paused.

"The police find only one person with a motive," she said. "That person has, in effect, announced in advance that she had a motive—anyway, that she hated somebody, presumably the man who was killed. She was there, and we don't know that anybody else was. A man who could testify against her and not against anybody else, so far as we know, is stabbed. A girl—the little mink, poor thing—can testify that this person was there. The mink wasn't dangerous to anybody else, so far as we know. And she gets killed. And then, after hiding out all day, and finally getting caught, this girl—you, Peggy—has somebody knock out a policeman so she can get away. And all this time, there's nothing against anybody else; no suspicion pointing to anybody else. Well?"

"But—" Jerry started.

"She didn't *have* anybody knock—" Weldon began.

"It's too easy," Pam North said. "That's what's the matter with it. It's—it's the way Inspector O'Malley thinks things are. But they aren't that way, because if you stir things up there are always pieces left over. Things that don't fit. When things are natural. Like vegetables.''

"What?" Jerry said.

"Weeds," Pam explained. "Things that don't belong. It's just an example, Jerry." She paused and looked at her husband. "I wonder, sometimes, why you're always so difficult about examples," she said. "They're just put in to make things clearer."

"Oh," Jerry said.

"Anyway," Pam said, "what we have to do is to disorder things again. Because somebody has made them orderly. Don't you all see?"

Peggy Mott was leaning forward a little, her eyes on Pam.

"But," she said, "that means you think—you don't think I did it! You're—"

She stopped, because she couldn't go on.

"For God's sake," Carey said, "don't cry!" He took his arm from the back of the chair and put it around Peggy's shoulders and held her close and looked down at her with an amazing expression of tenderness on a face not built for tenderness. "Stop it!" he told her, in a voice which sounded angry, and pulled her toward him. "Peg!"

"For heaven's sake," Pam said, with, obviously, incredulity in her voice. "What's this all about, if we don't start with that?"

"But—" Jerry started, in a faintly agonized tone and then abruptly broke it off because, he was astonished to discover, he had never, during years of agreeing with Pam, agreed with her more completely than at this moment. It was an entirely upsetting discovery. . . .

That far they had got within the first twenty minutes. Now, after another hour and more, it did not seem that they had got much further. This might be, Jerry North thought, biting a lead pencil absently, because they had been forced back to logic. They had got their premise, so far as he could remember, by magic. But it was more difficult from there on.

Peggy Mott had not killed her husband. Ergo, she had not attacked Leonard, because she would have had no reason. She had not killed Elaine Britton. Ergo, someone else had done these things, since they had been done. And this, at first, seemed to open it to its widest.

"Anybody," Pam said. "The people we can think of, the people who seem to be concerned. But then—anybody. People we've never heard of."

Unexpectedly, it was Paula Foster who helped them there; helped them after she had, for some time, seemed to be only a spectator. But she had been thinking, apparently, and now she said, "No." Everyone looked at the small, red-haired girl, who seemed surprised that she had spoken.

"The real murderer," she said, "has arranged to make Peggy appear guilty. Now, he couldn't have made her write that silly paper. We'll have to count that out, as merely a lucky break he had. So the first thing he had to do was to get her to the office, to Mott's office, at the right time. Now, you went there, Peggy, because somebody—you thought it was your husband—telephoned you and asked you to come."

Peggy said, "Yes."

"But you're not sure it was your husband? The man who called?"

"Not now," Peggy said. "But only because now it doesn't seem to fit. I thought it was, then."

"That's it," the red-haired girl said. "Apparently it couldn't have been. That's what the police think, isn't it?" This last was to Jerry North, who shrugged. Then he nodded.

"Not 'couldn't have been,' exactly," he said. "Probably wasn't. He didn't call out through the switchboard after he got there around ten-thirty. He could have gone out, of course—but he would have had to go out of the restaurant, because all calls made in it clear through the switchboard. And the operator is sure he didn't call from anywhere. Well—the police can't see any reason why, if he wanted to call his wife, he should have gone out into the street, on a cold day, and found a telephone booth. Neither can I."

"Then," Paula Foster said, "somebody else called, pretending to be Mott, to get Peggy there. The murderer."

"Oh," Pam North said, "of course! How—how *stupid* we were!"

They looked at her, but she nodded toward Paula Foster.

"This person—this murderer—had to know one thing to make it work. He had to know that Mott was there. And he knew it because he was there himself. So we start with—who was there?"

But now Jerry North was shaking his head.

"No," he said. "It's not that easy. Two telephone calls came in for Mott. Both of the people who called knew he was there, because they talked to him. One of them was Elaine Britton, if she told the truth. The other could be anybody."

"But," Foster said, "the telephone operator. Didn't she ask who called?"

"Bill says not," Jerry said. "She was busy taking reservations, and just plugged through. She says Mott answered. She thinks one caller was a man and the other a woman, for what it's worth. If she's right, the man's unaccounted for."

Jerry paused, reflected, and continued.

"So," he said, feeling his way, "we have the people at the restaurant—and there may have been fifty. I don't know. A hundred, counting waiters and bus boys and everything. And a man who may have been anybody. We don't seem to have got much of anywhere.

Except that the person who called you, Mrs. Mott, was a man."

The girl looked at him blankly for a moment. Then she said, "Oh, of course."

But there was hesitancy in her voice, and they all looked at her and waited.

"Only," she said, "Cecily Breakwell is such a good mimic and the conversation was so short and all, that—oh, I'm sure it wasn't Cecily."

But they would not let her be sure of anything, and Cecily Breakwell's name went on the list, which was not as long as they would have liked. André Maillaux, himself. William. (Peggy could supply the last name— Snodgrass.) William Snodgrass. Cecily. And fifty (or a hundred?) people who worked in the restaurant, from waiter captains to dishwashers. And a man, entirely unknown, "anybody," who had telephoned Mott during the morning, knew he was there, and might have come into his office from the street, unseen, as easily as Peggy Mott had. ("Only you didn't, as it turned out," Pam said.) The trouble with opportunity was that everybody had it, and that physical facts pointed nowhere in particular.

"Except at me," Peggy said. She looked around at them. "Maybe it's no good," she said. "No good at all. I hadn't realized—" Weldon Carey broke in. He told her to shut up. He was very angry, and held her closer. Pam North pointed out, rather gently, that her innocence was what they started with. She said that if there was too much opportunity to go around, they would have to begin somewhere else. Everybody seemed to understand her perfectly.

"Of course," Jerry said, "the knife narrows it." He considered. "Not much," he added. "It suggests that it was someone connected with the restaurant—somebody who knew Mott had a knife on his desk—but it doesn't prove anything."

But this suggestion did encourage them to start with those who "belonged" in the restaurant; this, and the lack of anywhere else to start. ("Because, otherwise, we'll have to take in everyone who has a telephone," Pam North said. "And even then, there'd be booths." Jerry said, "Pam!")

They started with Maillaux himself, and with the question, "Why?"

"You knew them best," Paula Foster told Peggy. "I suppose you did, anyway. Can you think of any reason? Did Maillaux have it in for Mott? Had Mott injured him? Or did Mott threaten him in any way?"

Peggy thought and shook her head. On the contrary, Mott, and Mott's money, were things Maillaux wanted to preserve. Mott's money had rescued the restaurant from, perhaps, bankruptcy; Mott himself had brought in patrons. Maillaux had every cause to be grateful, to value Mott.

"Unless," Pam said, "all the golden eggs had been laid, of course."

Peggy shook her head at that, and the soft, pale hair swayed around it. She didn't think they had. "But I don't know," she said. "I don't really know."

Foster said he shouldn't suppose so.

"They've spent a lot of money, certainly," he said. "It's beginning to come back. But probably there's still more going into the business than coming out; after all, they've only been reopened a few months. Mott's checkbook would still be a handy thing to have around."

"Mott himself apparently was a handy thing to have around, if you come to that," Jerry said. "There wasn't any personal quarrel? About women, for example?"

Peggy shook her head again. She knew of none. She said it didn't sound like Maillaux.

There was a short, rather discouraged, pause. Then Jerry said, "Well. Snodgrass? William?"

They looked at Peggy again and again she had to shake her head. Then she paused.

"Tony did tell me once that William had saved some money and wanted to buy into the restaurant," she said. "I suppose he might have been resentful when Maillaux took Tony's money instead. But it doesn't seem very strong."

They agreed it didn't. They went to Cecily Breakwell. It seemed to Pam North, remembering the small frivolity that was Cecily, an incongruous place to go. Unless she was in love with Tony Mott, had been given encouragement, had been thrown over. There was always that. "I simply don't know," Peggy said. "I thought it was all—all poor Elaine, now. But I don't know."

It was speculation, insubstantial. The fact that Cecily was a mimic, wanted to give impersonations and was working toward that as a goal was hardly more substantial.

"Look," Carey said, suddenly. "I know the Breakwell kid. She couldn't plan that far ahead. We're wasting time. We want somebody who had a real grudge against Mott—who hated him." He paused and looked around. "As a matter of fact," he said, and his voice was unexpectedly quiet, "I hated him as much as anyone. I hated him down to the ground." He paused. "Under it," he added.

They all looked at him; Peggy looked up at him.

"No," he said. "But I could have. I'd have enjoyed it. The cops will turn that up. Because of Peggy and—well, he kept my play off Broadway." He nodded. "Maybe it doesn't sound like much," he said. "But—it's where I live. Where I lived, anyway. He knew it, all right. The—" he broke off, smiled faintly. "Anyway," he said, "he's particularly the kind of louse I don't like. Or was."

"Corollary premise," Pam said, "you didn't do it. Or why are we wasting all this time?"

There was no answer to that, or to the implication they were wasting time.

"Maybe he criticized a chef," Jerry North said. "Maybe he slapped a bus boy. Maybe—quite possibly, as a matter of fact—he did some other girl dirt. We just don't know enough." He looked at Peggy Mott and his expression was not happy. "And the police know too much," he said.

"I can't do any more than say it again," Peggy said, and did not look at any of them. "I can keep on saying it again. I didn't kill Tony. I didn't—"

"Stop it, Peg," Weldon Carey said. "We all know that." He looked around at them, and the truculence was back, the challenge. "Anybody who doesn't know that?"

There seemed to be no answer to that, no answer which would meet the demand in the voice of the black-haired man. Nobody made an answer. And for a time, nobody said anything at all, and then it was Pam who spoke.

"You know," she said, "I keep thinking about Mr. Leonard, somehow. Because, after all, he started the whole thing, didn't he? But there doesn't seem to be any reason."

John Leonard's apartment, which was not far from the University, was larger than one would have expected. If Leonard lived in it alone, Bill Weigand thought as Leonard let him in, he must rattle. Leonard looked at Weigand, looking down a little, and raised his eyebrows. Weigand named himself, described himself, and Leonard said. "Oh. That paper the girl wrote, I suppose?" he said, and welcomed Weigand in. "I told the Norths what I remembered. Didn't they tell you?"

"Oh yes," Bill said. He looked at the sling which supported Leonard's arm. "How're you feeling?" he said.

"Fair," Leonard said. He regarded Weigand. "If it's about that," he said, "I still don't know a thing. Somebody waited for me. In ambush. And stabbed me, very slightly. As I told your friends, the other detectives, I fainted when I tried to chase whoever it was. I'm afraid I'm not helpful."

It would be hard to be, under the circumstances, Weigand assured him. He said they were working on it. "Of course," he said, "you see the obvious answer, Mr. Leonard?"

Leonard said he was afraid he did. There was a pause, and Leonard said, "Well," without any particular inflection. Then he asked if he could get Weigand a drink. Bill Weigand shook his head and said no.

"Mr. Leonard," Bill said, "a point has come up, about which I'm bound to ask you a few questions. A new point—new to me, anyway."

"Yes?"

"Do you know, did you know, a girl named Anita? She called herself Anita Farnsworth. That wasn't her real name."

Bill Weigand stopped and waited, watching the man sitting across from him, the man who looked, Bill thought, so exactly as a professor ought to look. And he saw that Leonard hesitated, closed his eyes for an instant. Leonard opened his eyes and looked at Weigand and smiled, very gingerly.

"So," he said, "it came out. Yes, I knew Anita. My sister, Lieutenant. The girl Mott—hurt."

"Hurt badly," Weigand said. "Inexcusably. I realize that, Mr. Leonard. But—"

He let Leonard finish the sentence in his own mind. Leonard shrugged his rather bony shoulders.

"Oh, I'm not surprised," he said. "I expected it, in a way. I was fond of Anita, Mott hurt her, cruelly and, as you say, inexcusably. As a result, you presume, I hated Mott and might have killed him." His eyes narrowed slightly. "Which means, I suppose, that you are not satisfied that Peggy—Mrs. Mott—was the one? Otherwise—"

Bill Weigand said that they were bound to consider everything, whenever it came up, however it came up. He was mild. He pointed out that all he had indicated was that the incident of Leonard's sister required amplification.

"I'm glad, anyway, that you haven't settled on Peggy," Leonard said. "I'd hate to see anyone like that—spoiled. Destroyed."

"Right," Bill said. "So would anybody. To get back to your sister. Where is she now?"

"In a sanitarium."

"And?"

Leonard shrugged. He said nobody knew; that nobody could know.

"She may recover," he said. "She may not. You gathered that nervous breakdown—they called it that—was an euphemism?" Bill nodded. "Now," Leonard went on, "she's usually in a depression. Now and then she comes out of it and is, rather mildly, excited. She came up against what we call a block and—couldn't surmount it. Couldn't find a way out, poor kid."

"Mott was the block," Weigand said.

"Her love for Mott. His rejection of her love. Yes. Call it Mott if you like."

"And, naturally, loving your sister, you hated Mott for what he had done?"

Leonard looked at Weigand, his eyes narrowed again, but his expression was almost amused. It was as if he were going to upset something and was enjoying, in advance, the small, flickering triumph.

"One would think that, naturally," he said. "And, certainly, I disapproved of him. I disapprove of all people like Mott. But hate him? No. In a way, I was almost sorry for him. You see why?"

Bill Weigand said he didn't.

"Every now and then," Leonard said, "you read about some man's hitting another man, or merely pushing him away suddenly and that way killing him. Say the man falls and hits his head, because he's awkward and unsteady. Say the man who is pushed or hit has a weak heart, and a shock which would be nothing to a well man finishes this man off. Which man are you sorry for, Lieutenant?"

"Both," Bill said.

"Exactly," Leonard told him. "Even if the man who hits or pushes is an ugly customer, even if the attack has been unprovoked. The results are still—disproportionate. Unfairly disproportionate. A scuffle turns into—well, into the big thing. The aggressor is, in a sense, as much a victim, as helplessly a victim, as the man he kills. Maybe it gets him in trouble, maybe it only haunts him. But—how would you say it?—it's something he hasn't asked for, hasn't deserved. It's just his bad luck that he didn't push another man. Or, that someone else didn't hit, or push, the man who was killed. You see what I'm driving at?"

Bill said he saw what Leonard was driving at. He waited for Leonard to go on, thinking this tall, angular professor was a subtle man, and might be driving at a number of things. It would be interesting to see how far he drove.

"My sister had this—weakness," Leonard said. "As surely as if she had been unsteady on her feet, as if her heart had been weak. It didn't show, none of us knew it. There was no reason why Mott should have known it." He looked beyond Weigand for a moment. "None of us precisely understands that sort of thing," he said. "The psychiatrists don't, altogether. A kind of mental unsteadiness, a kind of weakness. Not of what we usually mean by the mind, the logical faculty, the ability to learn. Anita had those, rather unusually. It's a—well, a kind of weakness of the being, of the ego. If, philosophically, we can say—" He broke off, looked at

Bill Weigand, shook his head in deprecation. "My hobby horse," he said. "I go astray, professorially. The only point that is apposite is that Anita had this weakness, we didn't know it—and any one of a dozen things, a hundred things for all we know, might have broken her. It happened to be Mott, her love for Mott. And Mott pushed, as, because he was callous, unimaginative, he might have pushed anyone. Naturally, I think his action was reprehensible. But the results were disproportionate."

"You saw this then?" Bill said.

Leonard shook his long head and said, "Oh, no."

"Not at once," he said. "I was very fond of the kid. She was the family baby, of course. That may have had something to do with it, incidentally. Our parents' age when she was born, the sheltering she may have had as the baby. But no one knows. No, I wasn't so detached at the start. Perhaps I hated Mott then, wanted him hurt." He paused, looked at Bill and smiled. "But," he said, "he wasn't hurt then, was he? And now I feel only as I've said."

Bill said it was interesting. He said, "Of course, if it hadn't been Mott, this incident, she might have escaped altogether? Outgrown this—weakness?"

Leonard shrugged bony shoulders. He did not look directly at Bill Weigand. He said nobody could know about that.

"A possibility," Bill said. "You realize that?"

Leonard nodded. He said there were many possibilities. Then, as if he had thought more carefully, he made a negative motion of his head.

"Actually," he said, "I doubt it very much. From her condition now. The weakness must have been very great. I was out to see her a week or so ago. She didn't recognize me."

"Then the chances—?" Bill said.

"All right," Leonard said. "Perhaps I was palliating her condition there at first. One does—I don't know why. I don't think there's much chance. I did for a time, but this last visit—" He did not finish that. Bill waited, wondering if he would finish it, if he realized what might be made of what he had said. Apparently he did not. He looked at Bill Weigand with an expression which said the whole matter was finished off, disposed of. He asked if Bill were sure he wouldn't have a drink.

"Thanks," Bill said. "No." He watched Leonard's face become, again and suddenly, attentive. Bill realized that there must have been something in his voice.

"Did you telephone Mott yesterday morning?" Bill said. He spoke quickly, hurrying it.

"Did I—what—I—" Leonard had not expected that. Bill did not repeat the question.

"What makes you think I did," Leonard asked.

Bill shook his head. "Just, did you?" he said. "It ought to be easy, Mr. Leonard."

You reached in a dark room, pushed where there ought to be a door, and a door opened. It was surprising, gratifying. There was no reason why Leonard should appreciate how surprising it was.

"You find things out," Leonard said. "Yes."

"Why?"

Leonard waited a moment before he answered. He seemed to be pulling it together in his own mind.

"This term paper Peggy Mott wrote," Leonard said, and spoke slowly, still pulling it together. "The Norths told you about it, I think?" Bill nodded. "It worried me," Leonard said. "More than I admitted, because—well, I knew more than I admitted, I suppose. I'd talked to Mrs. Mott a few times, run into her at the coffee bar in the book shop, that sort of thing. I didn't connect her with Tony Mott at first; she was just a 'Miss' Mott, as far as I knew. And—well, I took her to dinner once or twice. It's not supposed to happen, as between male members of the faculty and female students. I don't mean that anything did happen, you understand." He looked directly at Weigand. Bill thought he had rather unusually red lips.

"She's a very pretty girl, of course," Leonard said, as if he were explaining something. "But I merely took her to dinner once or twice. I found out who she was, and something about her and Mott. That was before they had actually separated. Last spring some time. This last fall, in one way and another, I picked up other things. One does, you know. You couldn't miss her and Carey, for example. And I heard—I've forgotten who told me—that she and Mott were separated and that Mott was—behaving badly. Call it putting obstacles in their way, hers and Carey's. You know?"

Bill nodded.

"Then I get this paper," Leonard said. "This—this hymn of hate. Under the circumstances, it worried me. Normally, it mightn't have. Students write rather remarkable things, sometimes. But I was worried, knowing something about the Motts, and I suppose that's why, actually, I took it up with the Norths, asked them to pass it on to you. I thought that would—well, eliminate my sense of responsibility. You understand?"

Bill nodded again.

"Well, it didn't completely," Leonard said. "It—the sense of being responsible—kept coming back, nagging at me. So I called Mott up and—well, warned him. It seems silly, now."

"It worked?" Weigand asked.

Leonard shrugged.

"In a way," he said. "Obviously not very effectively if—" He broke off. "It got me over my conscience," he went on. "As a matter of fact, Mott just laughed at me. But that didn't matter. I'd warned him. I didn't expect him to be much concerned. Obviously, I had nothing definite to warn him against except— well, Peggy's state of mind. I even felt rather foolish, old maidish, warning him at all, after I'd started." He stopped, and waited.

"About what time was this?" Bill asked him. "This call?"

"Eleven. Eleven-fifteen."

"You didn't identify yourself to anyone? The switchboard operator?"

Leonard shook his head. He stopped shaking it and looked hard at Weigand.

"By the way," he said, "how *did* you get on to it?"

Bill shook his head this time, indicating it did not matter. It would be naive to mention a push in the dark at a door which only might exist.

"You didn't think of mentioning it to us?" Bill asked.

Leonard shook his head.

"Look, Lieutenant," he said, "why stick my neck out?" His tone indicated quotation marks around the phrase.

"Considering Anita," Bill Weigand filled in.

"Obviously," Leonard said. "Even a sheltered university professor, Lieutenant—" He did not finish it, or need to.

It was reasonable. An innocent man, however conscious of innocence, would prefer not to arouse unwarranted suspicion; would avoid "sticking his neck out," even if not particularly afraid for his neck. Still—Bill Weigand considered what he had learned, while Leonard waited. The telephone conversation, even if its content were actually as described by Leonard, served one other and obvious purpose. It established for Leonard that Mott was at his office. It would have been easy enough for Leonard to have established, further, that Mott planned to remain there for an hour or so. Leonard might have offered to drop down and show Mott his wife's "hymn of hate." Once at the office, Leonard might have sung his own.

"By the way, Mr. Leonard," Bill said, "have you eaten at the Maillaux place?"

Leonard seemed surprised by this. He nodded at once. He said, "Often," telling Bill what he wanted to know. Leonard would not, if he had been there often, need to fumble through a search for Mott's office. But—

"Recently?" Bill asked.

This time Leonard shook his head.

"Not so much recently," he said. "Once or twice since they remodelled. A little too rich for my blood, now. And for my salary. Not that it wasn't always. But they used to make it up to you, in the old days—no hurry, not so many people climbing over you, just rather remarkable food."

"Not that way now?" Bill said.

"For my taste, no. Just another first-rate place now. But I wouldn't tell old André that."

"No," Bill said. "Naturally."

Leonard was at ease, now, comfortably talking irrelevancies. It was not the time, Bill decided, to press for more. He thanked Leonard, again refused a proffered drink, went out and down to his car. He drove by his apartment, Dorian was surrounded by Sunday newspapers, smoking but not in flames. She came out of them eagerly, looked at Bill's face and was depressed. "You've got to go back?" she said. Bill nodded. "We were going to the Norths for drinks and somewhere to eat," she said. "Is that out?" Bill didn't know; he would call her. He showered and shaved, changed and looked longingly at his bed; held Dorian briefly and said again he would call her. He went on to the office, and found that Mullins was still sitting on it, and that it was quiet.

"Amateurs are hard to catch, Loot," Mullins said. "A couple of pros, now, you'd know where to look. Amateurs'll go anywhere." He was mildly resentful. "With pros you know where you are," Mullins said.

"The Norths telephoned." The connection in Mullins' mind was so obvious, so immediate, that Bill grinned suddenly.

"Yeah," Mullins said, "talk as if they had something, Mr. North did. But he didn't say what."

Bill Weigand made agreeing noises, but he had only half listened. Probably Jerry was checking on their cocktail engagement. Bill sent Mullins to lunch and sat on it himself.

He was no longer so impatient at the slowness of the machine in turning up Peggy Mott and Weldon Carey. It occurred to him that he was no longer, in any real sense, ready for them. This would be a blow to Inspector O'Malley.

10

Bill Weigand's mind was tired; he drank coffee, put
spurs to his mind, and it responded sluggishly. His
mind told him, dully, that things were in balance; that
there was no obvious way to unbalance them. Leonard
equalled Peggy Mott; Peggy Mott equalled Leonard.
That was the size of it, the rough size of it.

There was more against Peggy, and it was cleaner.
But there was enough against Leonard to mar the case
against the girl. The elemental clarity which it had
seemed to have, the clarity of which O'Malley so
much approved, was irretrievably ruined. Ruined sub-
jectively, because Bill himself was no longer sure;
ruined objectively, because as it stood he doubted
whether the district attorney would take it. Not, particularly, with Peggy looking as she did; not with the
sympathy with which, authentically enough, she
would be regarded, and which any clever lawyer
would artfully augment. The district attorney would
not want to take it to a jury, knowing that the defense
would present an alternative. They lacked, by much,
enough to convict Leonard of anything. But there was

enough against him, unexplained, to prevent their conviction of Peggy, once the defense got hold of it. And the defense would get hold of it. Bill Weigand's tired mind went, slower and slower, around in this trap.

A jury would be looking for a chance to let Peggy off. That was inevitable. Bill Weigand, drumming his desk with the fingers of his right hand, wondered irritably whether he were not as impressionable as a jury. It was possible he was creating difficulties. Wearily, he went back to Leonard, trying to break the balance.

Leonard denied hating Mott, and was convincing enough. His attitude could be as reasoned, as dispassionate as he described it. But, obviously, it did not have to be. Leonard, for all Weigand could be certain of, was a violent man at bottom, an emotional one. The lower part of his face, the full red lips, suggested the possibility. He might have felt for a long time as he said he felt about Mott; then have visited his young sister, whom clearly he loved, and realized, with a new hopelessness, what had happened to her. "She didn't recognize me." She was evidently deteriorating. The deterioration might be enough to come as a new shock, engender a new bitterness.

He had telephoned Mott on the morning of the day Mott died; he could have gone to the office afterward. He could have killed Mott. He could have faked the attack on himself. (Bill had always counted that as a possibility.) Could he have killed Elaine Britton? Bill rummaged through reports. Setting Elaine's murder at the latest hour, he could, apparently. He had been bandaged, sent home, some time after five o'clock the afternoon before. Nobody had taken him home, was sure he arrived there. He could as easily have gone to Central Park West. Why? There was no telling, at the moment; perhaps Elaine Britton had seen him, too. It was not certain.

We didn't go far enough, Bill thought. It was too easy; it was handed us on a platter.

If Peggy Mott was not guilty, it had been handed them on a platter, Bill realized. They had bungled; they had merely been too innocent, too naive. The apparent facts were sufficiently substantial but they had not gone far enough underneath to see what was holding them up. If Peggy Mott was innocent, the real murderer was holding them up. He had, to some degree, created them. Mrs. Peggy Mott had been very neatly, very expertly, framed. Or she was a killer. In no case, was the evidence against her accidental, or the result of misinterpretation.

And, Bill thought with his tired mind, Leonard was the one who first brought her into it. He was the one who started it. Bill checked over, one by one, the things which must have been done if Peggy Mott were a victim, not a killer. Nobody could have made her write the essay on hatred. He stopped himself. Conceivably, of course, someone could have suggested it to her; said something like, "I know how you feel. Write it. Get it out of your mind." For all Bill Weigand knew, that might be sound psychology. It was interesting that Leonard was a psychologist.

But it was not necessary to suppose that Peggy Mott had been worked upon and proved suggestible. Things did not need to be that perfect. It was more likely, if you wanted to build a case against Leonard, that he had seized an opportunity he had not created. Getting the essay from the girl, he had seen a way to use it. He had got in touch with the Norths, planted suspicion, paved the way. He had, if this was correct, two victims: one primary, the other cynically chosen for purposes of his own safety. (And the essay might have been the germ of the whole plan, of the murder itself.) His next step would have been to pick a place and a time. Hence his telephone call to Mott, at Mott's office; hence, presumably, an appointment with Mott for, say, eleven forty-five. With that done, he would telephone Peggy Mott, pretend to be Mott—a little mimicry would be required, but Leonard, as a university lecturer, was a trained speaker—and make an appointment with her, at the office, for noon. (If she were not at her apartment when he called, the whole thing could be postponed. But she had been.)

So far it added. Too well, Bill thought, a little gloomily. He was building up a hard case, tearing down an easy one. O'Malley would disapprove. Bill himself disapproved. But it began to look as if, going into court with their case against Peggy Mott and this case against Leonard not broken down, they would as Leonard had said, be sticking their necks out.

Bill kept on adding. So, minutes before Peggy was due for her appointment, Leonard showed up for his. Presumably he had taken his own weapon, opportunistically switched to the knife which apparently had lain ready on Mott's desk. He killed Mott. Presumably he had entered from the street, not through the restaurant, and had gone out the same way. Obviously, he might have been seen. (Had he been? Another thing to dig for.) But you cannot murder without taking certain chances. (He had had to take a chance that Peggy would show up for her appointment before Mott's body was found, but that was not so crucial. Involving the girl was merely a special safeguard, not his only safety. And if he timed it right, his chances were excellent to involve her.)

After that, Leonard must have waited for the newspapers. They said nothing about Peggy Mott's presence at the scene, which merely made it certain that she had not found, *and reported,* the body. That would have been encouraging; knowing that a background of suspicion against her was already in existence, the girl would have been apt to do what she said she had done: look and run. Leonard would still not know whether she had actually gone to the office. But he would have enough to go ahead on, and, when the later editions of the afternoon papers reported, guardedly, that Mott's pretty wife was being sought for questioning, he would have felt he had more.

Then what had he done? Reported the theft of the essay from his office, leaving the police to draw the obvious inference. Faked an attack on himself, to make the inference even more obvious. (Who else but Peggy Mott had anything to gain by theft or attack?) So far you could make it hang together. But then came the murder of Elaine Britton, and that did not fit. Did the case against Leonard fail on that point? Bill looked at it and began to suspect that it did. At first glance, it fitted perfectly—an additional, ruthlessly created, piece of evidence against Peggy Mott. But, Leonard could not have known that, because he did not know that Elaine Britton had put Peggy at the scene. At least, Bill Weigand did not see how Leonard could have known that since it had not been published. (The fact of Elaine's murder had been printed that morning, and printed large. But the police had not connected it with Mott's murder and the newspapers, hurried to make editions, had not independently dug a connection up. They would have it by now, but there were no papers until the first editions of the mornings.) It would be difficult to fit the murder of the slim show-girl into the plot against Peggy.

But—and Bill's fingers tapped more briskly on the desk—there was always another possibility. Elaine had seen Peggy going into the building next to the restaurant, on her way to Mott's office. Might she not also have seen Leonard coming out? If she had, if she recognized him, perhaps tried to cash in on what she had seen, Leonard had a valid motive for killing her. (Just as Peggy Mott had.) This, obviously, was speculation; it was also entirely possible. The whole thing, the whole case against Leonard, was entirely possible.

But, looking at it, Bill realized that it was no more

than that. It was merely possible. It was strong enough to weaken the case against Peggy Mott, but it was not strong enough to stand on its own feet against John Leonard. It was weak on facts, but facts might be found to fit it. They would have to look for them, certainly. But there was, Bill decided, a more fundamental weakness. The case as it stood forced the conclusion that John Leonard was two entirely different men with radically different emotional responses. Motive and method did not accord; they were even violently disparate.

Bill Weigand was, he realized, asking himself to believe that Professor John Leonard was emotional to the point of instability, and at the same time calculating as a chess master. Even tired as it was, Bill's mind boggled. Leonard had killed the man who had done an injury to his sister, killed him years after the event and under the compulsion of an emotion engendered by the recent sight of the sister in a condition worse than he had expected—a condition, it might be assumed, which put a period to hope. A flare of bitterness might be expected, under those conditions, against the man who had caused that condition. It was conceivable, given a man of a certain sort, that that bitterness might have carried over into action.

But the action would, almost certainly, have been violent, unbalanced, like the emotion which occasioned it. The action as Weigand postulated it, and as the facts presented it, had been precisely the reverse. It had been shrewd, contrived and, as it concerned Peggy Mott, entirely merciless. (And Leonard was, Bill thought, rather fond of Peggy than otherwise.) If Leonard had done both things, he was two men, in which event he was, almost by definition, psychopathic. Bill tried to think Leonard was that, and failed.

He had argued himself into it and through it, out on the other side. But that did not alter the fact that it was still there, and that as long as it was still there the

district attorney—and Bill himself, for that matter—
would be very reluctant to proceed against the pretty
widow of Tony Mott.

Bill Weigand shook his head. I need a fresh mind for
this, he thought. He wished he knew where he could
get one. Or I need fresh facts. And then, as that
thought came to him, his eyebrows drew together, and
lines formed between them. It began to look as if that
might, indeed, be the whole trouble.

What had happened, Bill thought now, was what
now and then did happen, and was difficult to guard
against. A problem had been presented and, almost
simultaneously, a solution which appeared to be in all
respects neat and adequate. Under such circumstances it was desirable, as always, to keep an open
mind, but it was very difficult. The digging you would
do, the police machine would do, was still done, but
almost unavoidably in perfunctory fashion. The machine had its answer, the machine's heart was not in
further research. The machine was, after all, humanly
susceptible.

With Peggy Mott so obviously meeting all the re-
quirements—with her motives abundant, her opportunity demonstrated, her flight in itself almost convict-
ing—they had merely not been as thorough as usual.
Part of it, Bill thought, was his fault; part of it was
nobody's fault. It was almost by chance that the
evidence against Leonard, the hypothesis against
Leonard, had been noticed at all. To a man who prided
himself upon thoroughness, upon the way he did his
job, that thought was disquieting. If there was a case,
even this much of a case, against Leonard, if he had
come upon it by accident, what might there be in other
corners, so far only partially explored?

Bill wondered if he were creating difficulties where
there were none: if a tired mind were inventing phan-
toms. Nine times out of ten, perhaps ninety-nine out of

a hundred, the obvious was the true. O'Malley had had a long and reasonably successful career merely by playing on those odds. You could not very well miss, granted you were bright enough to see the obvious. Justice might miscarry here and there, but justice would in any case. Not for the first time, Bill Weigand wished he could adjust his behavior to this evident logic. But it was no good.

"All I can do," he had told Dorian once, "is to convince myself. I can't act on anything less, and I can't hold out for anything more. I don't know any other way to play it. I've got to use the mind I've got and try not to cheat it. Right?" They had been relaxed in front of a fire, with drinks. They talked most freely then, quite often about themselves, saying more than they would often have said, but not often anything they did not mean.

What it came to now was that his mind was not satisfied. The case against Peggy Mott remained good and probably—nine to one the probabilities ran—it was true. But Bill Weigand was no longer certain in his own mind. If O'Malley had been in the habit of using the word, he would have told Bill Weigand that he was being squeamish. Bill could not see any help for that.

The practical outcome of all this was that Bill no longer wanted very badly to have Peggy Mott, and her angry rescuer, brought in. If she was picked up now, her presence would raise an issue—an issue with O'Malley, eventually with the press—for which Bill decided he was not ready. Perhaps it was just as well, he thought—and was interrupted by Mullins, who appeared at the door with a rather odd expression on his face. Bill Weigand said, "Yes?"

"The Norths are here," Mullins said, and it occurred to Bill that Mullins' tone was somewhat dazed. "They've—ah—got people with them." Mullins' voice reflected his own awe of his understatement.

"They've—" He waved a hand, then, and Pam North came in, and after her came Peggy Mott. Bill Weigand merely looked at them and waited, and a small, vivid girl with red hair came in after Peggy Mott. Then Weldon Carey came in, thrusting toward Weigand, wearing his shoulder chip proudly, and after him a slender youngish man with what appeared to be an amused smile, and then Jerry. Mullins stood aside to let them in and then looked past them at Weigand and slowly shook his head.

"That's all, Mullins," Pam North said. "Just the six of us. Hello, Bill."

"Only six?" Bill Weigand said. "Close the door, Mullins. Stay in."

"O.K., Loot," Mullins said. He looked at the crowded office. "O.K.," he said again, doubtfully.

"Bill," Pam said, "Mrs. Mott wants to give herself up, but you're wrong just the same. We've gone over it and over it, and she didn't."

"All right, Pam," Bill said. He looked at Peggy Mott. He looked at Weldon Carey. "You've made trouble," he said to both of them. His voice, however, was mild. "What was the idea?" This last was to Carey.

"So what?" Carey said. "She's back."

"I'd like to let Sergeant Stein answer that," Bill said. "I really would, Carey."

"Any time," Carey said, and was angry.

"I can't," Bill said. "But I'd like to. Stein was a paratrooper, Carey. He knows some very interesting tricks."

"I—" Carey began, but Bill Weigand shook his head and, rather surprisingly, Carey did not continue. Bill said, and his voice still was quiet, that they might go into that later.

"Let's," Pam said. "Bill, you didn't hear me. Mrs. Mott didn't do it."

"No?" Bill said. "Who did, Pam?"

"Somebody else," Pam said. "We haven't quite worked it out, but it wasn't Peggy."

"Why?" Bill said, and was told by Pam North to look at Peggy Mott. Bill looked at her. He looked back at Pam.

"Can't you see?" Pam North asked him, with something like indignation in her voice. "*Look* at her, Bill! Listen to her!"

"I have," Bill said. He turned to Peggy Mott. When he spoke next his voice was without any particular expression. "I listened to her for quite a time," he said. "She lied and got caught in it. She ran down rat holes."

Watching the blond girl with long eyes, Bill saw the eyes go blank. He had not expected that; he saw her shudder, almost imperceptibly, and had not expected that, either.

"The holes are all stopped up," the girl said, not as if she were speaking to anyone. "I—" She swayed, this time perceptibly. Instantly Carey was beside her, an arm around her, and almost as quickly, and very gently, almost reluctantly, she moved out of the circle of the arm. "All right, Wel," she said, softly. Then she looked at Bill and her eyes were no longer blank.

"I came back," she said. "The Norths said I had to. But I think—I think I would have come back anyway, Lieutenant." She looked at him for a moment without speaking. "I didn't lie about what counted," she said. "I know I—I ran down rat holes. But not when it counted."

"Of course she didn't," Pam said. "Anybody would have." It was momentarily unclear, but Pam did not wait. "Bill," she said, "don't you see? It's too perfect. That's what's the matter. If it were true—if it just *happened*—it'd be fuzzy. Everything is. But this isn't, so somebody arranged it. Don't you see how logical it is?"

Bill Weigand found he was smiling at Pam North;

that his mind, for some reason, was no longer so weary as it had been. His mind was panting slightly, but it was no longer really tired.

Bill transferred his gaze, and his faint smile, to Jerry North.

"You know what she means," Jerry said. "That is— well, near enough. She knows it doesn't prove anything. But—"

"But," Pam repeated. "That's it, Bill. But. You have to get around 'but,' Bill. The more you think about it, the more you see that. We all did." She made a small gesture which encompassed Jerry, the Fosters, Carey and Peggy Mott.

"The deputation," Foster said, suddenly, and smiled widely. "My name's Foster, Lieutenant. This is my wife." He indicated Paula.

"Thanks," Bill said. "I'd begun to wonder. And— where do you and Mrs. Foster fit in?"

Foster continued to smile. He explained where they fitted in.

"Harboring," Foster said. "Probably that isn't the word, Lieutenant. We took Carey and Mrs. Mott in, knowing they were fugitives. Accessories after the fact?"

Bill Weigand waved it off, abstractedly. Unexpectedly, Foster sobered. He said, "Sorry, sir." Bill waved that off, also. Pam North seemed about to say something, and to be stopped by the expression on Weigand's face, or by the gentle tapping of the fingers of his right hand on the desk in front of him. It occurred to Pam that, from Bill's point of view, something had gone wrong. That was puzzling, because the most obvious thing was surely something which had gone right. They had persuaded Peggy Mott and Carey to come in. Bill should, she thought, be pleased with them. But she thought he was not. Which could only mean—

"Mrs. Mott," Bill said, "I'm not going to hold you.

I'm not clearing you, you understand. But I'm not holding you. There are two conditions. If you'll agree to them, I'll let you go for the time being."

Peggy Mott looked surprised, and Carey continued to direct an angry, suspicious gaze at Weigand. The girl nodded.

"First," Bill said, "you don't try to hide. You don't leave the city, you show up at your apartment tonight by ten o'clock and you stay in it. I'll take steps to find out whether you do or not. If you don't, I'll turn the town upside down to find you, and when I do I'll lodge a homicide charge against you. You understand that?"

Peggy Mott nodded again.

"That goes for you, Carey," Bill said. "I'd still like to give you to Stein, and I may yet. Or I can see you serve a stretch for resisting. I may yet. But now you can go—and you'll be in your apartment by ten o'clock tonight, and I'll check up on you." Bill looked directly at the glaring young man. "Do you want to play it that way?" he asked.

Carey seemed to hesitate for a moment. "You can't—" he started, and looked at Peggy Mott. "All right," he said. "I'll play it that way. For now."

"Right," Bill said. "Now—and this goes for all of you." He looked from one to the other. "All of you forget that you came in here. Forget that Mrs. Mott gave herself up; forget that you saw her today." Carey seemed to thrust himself forward. "No, Carey, I'm not framing her," Weigand said. "Obviously, if it comes to that, all of you'll see that she gets credit for having come in. If charges are made—and you all understand they probably will be—you can talk your heads off. Until then—nothing. You agree?"

One by one, nodding, they agreed.

"Right," Bill said. "That's all, then." He nodded toward the door, toward Mullins at the door. And, by the slightest of gestures, imperceptible to a person who was not looking for it, he indicated Peggy and

Weldon Carey. Mullins slightly closed his eyes, re-opened them.

Carey put his arm around the girl again, and she did not, this time, move out of its circle. The two of them, close together, went through the door first, and Paula Foster smiled at Weigand and went after them. Her husband raised his right hand in what was almost a salute and followed, and Jerry said, "Come on, Pam."

Pam looked at Bill Weigand and her eyebrows went up.

"Timing," Bill said. "Bad, Pam."

Pam North said, "Oh." Then she said, "Bill—" and Bill Weigand shook his head at her and said, "Later." She said, "Oh," again and then, "Are you and Dorian coming down this evening?"

"Unless something—" Bill said, and threw it away.

"About six then," Pam said. "We thought you wanted her."

"Right," Bill said. "So did I. Perhaps I do."

"But you're not sure any more?" She looked at him. "Good," she said. "I think you're right, Bill."

Bill Weigand did not say anything to that, and watched them go. Beside Mullins, Pam North paused. "You come with Bill and Dorian," she said, "if they do?" Mullins looked at Bill Weigand, who nodded. "Sure, Mrs. North," Mullins said. "O.K."

They went, then, and Mullins went after them, momentarily, and returned. Bill looked up at him, and Mullins nodded. "They got company," Mullins said. "Mrs. Mott and this guy Carey. Listen, Loot—does he get away with it?"

"I don't know, yet," he said. "We may have to leave it up to Stein."

Mullins reflected and said, "Yeah. Only this Carey needs—" He let it rest. He looked puzzled. "Listen, Loot," he said. "I didn't get it. Should I of?"

"Have," Bill said. "Did you ever hear of enough rope, Sergeant?"

"Oh," Mullins said, "that."

"For everybody," Bill said. "By the way, we'd better cancel the pick-up for the girl. And Carey."

Mullins said, "O.K., Loot," and started out. "And then come back," Bill said. "I want to talk to you about a guy named Leonard, Mullins. And maybe we'll think of a couple of other guys to talk about. Right?"

"O-o-oh?" Mullins said, and seemed enlightened. He went out.

11

Bill Weigand was late at the Norths. Dorian came, a
few minutes after six and said that Bill was coming;
that he had telephoned her and asked her to go on
ahead and said he might be a little late. The young cats
sat in front of Dorian Weigand and adored her, with
purrs. Martini sat a little distance off and considered
everything, without committing herself. Jerry North
suggested that there was no use waiting for Bill, and
Dorian and Pam agreed and watched, with anticipation, while he stirred. One of the cats jumped to the
chest which served as a bar and offered to help,
smelled gin and crinkled its nose. It left.

"Don't be silly," Pam told the little cat. "You were
named after it." She regarded it. "And you cast a
damper," she said. "You're a prohibitionist." The cat,
apparently regarding this as an endearment, jumped to
Pam's lap and tried to rub noses. Pam held it for a
moment and put it down, just as Martini spoke in a
low, harsh voice. "Jealous," Pam explained. "It's all
got very complicated. Did Bill say anything?"

"No," Dorian said. "Just that he was coming."

Dorian curled in the big chair, looked at the fire. The

198

three of them drank slowly, relaxed, watching the cats play. It was six-thirty, or a little later, when the doorbell rang.

Bill Weigand looked very tired as he stood in the doorway; his eyes moved quickly until they found Dorian. Then his gaze stopped moving, having come home, having found her there. Pam North, watching, thought he had never quite got over the feeling that, if he left Dorian, she might vanish. It was not unreasonable, Pam thought. After all, there had been a time, and a very bad time for a while, when Dorian had vanished, and been hard to find.*

Pam saw Dorian nod, smile, to prove that she was surely there. Then Pam looked back at Bill Weigand's face and did not need Dorian's "No, Bill?" and his shaken head to realize that this one wasn't over. It was a long way from over, she thought, looking at Bill's tired face.

"Mullins?" Jerry said, practically, moving toward the chest which served as bar. "Coming," Bill said. "Parking the car." Almost at once the doorbell rang again, and Mullins appeared, looking as he always did. Jerry made another round of drinks, and until he had almost emptied his glass, Bill Weigand merely sat. Then he looked at the Norths, smiled and said, "Right. Ask it."

"All right," Pam said. "Why, Bill?"

Bill turned to Dorian.

"They brought Peggy Mott in," he said. "I turned her loose." Dorian nodded and he turned back to Pam North. "Because I'm not sure we want her," he said, paused and added, "yet." He finished his drink. "Among us," he said, "I'm not sure of anything." The words seemed to make him more tired, his face showed it. He spoke to his empty glass, as Jerry got up

---

* During the investigation of *Untidy Murder* (J. B. Lippincott Company, 1947).

and went to the bar. "It looked so damn simple," Bill told the glass.

"Too simple," Pam North said. "The too-perfect murder."

"As you said," Bill agreed. "But you see—you don't have to be right, Pam. I do, in the end. That's the catch. I can't just say 'too perfect' and close my eyes." He nodded, slowly. "Nine to one," he said, "it was Peggy Mott. Only—"

"Only the one," Pam said. "Your trouble is, you're honest." She looked at Dorian. "Isn't he?" Dorian said, lightly. "An inconvenience, sometimes."

Bill looked at her and his lips curved. But they went back almost at once to a tired line.

"A great inconvenience, if that's the trouble," he said. "But there's a practical point. We can't leave loopholes. That's really the reason I turned her loose. And Carey because the two things go together. If we finally charge her, we'll charge him, too. But first—"

The telephone rang.

"For me, probably," Bill said. "Right?"

Jerry North nodded and Bill said, "Weigand speaking" into the telephone. He listened for several minutes, making only encouraging sounds. Then he said "Right," and hung up.

"There'll be more," he said. "We're going over the whole thing again, in a way. Doing what we should have done earlier, I suppose. There was a lot of dope about Mott. Business affairs, girl affairs. The highlights, from Stein." He paused, looked with pleasure at his refilled glass, and drank. "Nothing spectacular," he said. "Grist." He did not continue and they all drank, companionably. Mullins speared the cherry in his old-fashioned and the cherry vanished into Mullins. Jerry made a new old-fashioned.

"Leonard's sister was involved with Mott," Bill said. "She got a dirty deal." He told them part of it.

"That opened it up?" Jerry North said, and Bill nodded.

"Cracked it," he said. "Made me go over it. It was accident I happened on that. So—"

He did not need to develop it. They all nodded.

"So—we start over," Bill said. "Get it clean, if we can. Find out—"

The telephone rang again. Again Bill answered it. Again he listened and ended with "Right." He put the telephone back and said, "More grist" and did not amplify. "It will go on all night, probably," he said. "And with nothing coming of it." He was morose.

"Take time out, Bill," Dorian said. "Drink your drink. Watch the cats. Suggest some place for dinner."

"Not me," Bill said. "I'm resting."

"Charles'," Mullins said. He seemed surprised it needed saying; more surprised when Pam shook her head at him. "Not on Sundays," she said. "So many places aren't." Mullins said, "Oh." The news appeared to depress him.

"Sundays are so difficult," Pam said. "Why do they all want to be difficult on the same day?"

"People out of town," Jerry told her. "A dull day."

"Out of town?" Pam said. "In this weather? When you could stay home and curl up with a warm radiator?"

Jerry said he didn't know. He said all he knew was what the restaurants appeared to think. Pam said she could make an omelet.

"Several omelets," she said. "Only there wouldn't be anything else."

"We go out," Jerry told her. He suggested several places; Dorian suggested several places. Each place was languidly approved and, so, dismissed. They had another drink.

"Look," Pam said, "maybe Maillaux's is open. Would that be too—"

"Yes," Dorian said. "Much."

"Anyway," Mullins said, "the food's not worth it."

They all looked at him. Bill came out of what was apparently a deep reverie and looked at him.

"Look," Jerry said, "it's supposed to be very superior—very special."

"O.K.," Mullins said. "I don't like it. I was there two, three weeks ago—on the Simpkins case, Loot, remember?—and it cost a lot and so what? Four guys serve you, and so what? This steak I got—"

"Oh," Pam North said. "Well, steak. I don't suppose M. Maillaux really feels much about steak. After all, steak isn't French, Sergeant."

"O.K.," Mullins said, comfortably. "O.K., Mrs. North. You get something à la something, and I'll get steak. All the same, a restaurant ought to be able to do a steak." He nodded. "Anybody ought to be able to do a steak," he said. "This steak I got—"

He shrugged the steak away.

"So Maillaux's is out," Pam said. "Anyway, the prices are ridiculous. Luchow's?"

Everybody agreed that Luchow's was fine. Nobody made any move to go toward Luchow's. Jerry made more drinks.

"Of course," Dorian said, "we could just stay here and drink dinner. Only—"

"I can't," Bill said. "Mullins can't. We—"

The telephone rang. Bill listened as before, said "Right" as before, returned the instrument and resumed his drink.

"Grist," Pam said. "Gritty grist."

Everyone looked at her. She had the expression of one who is looking at himself.

"Maybe we had better get something to eat," Pam said. "Do we all think Luchow's? Or do we think the Algonquin?"

"Either," Dorian said, and seemed about to stand

up. Her eyes were on Bill. "I want to feed him," she said, nodding at Bill. "I—"

The telephone rang again. Bill Weigand said "Damn" and picked it up. He listened and his eyes narrowed slightly. He did not listen long, and his "Right," this time, had a new quality. He looked at the others, and his face had lost some of its weariness.

"The Mott girl and Carey have just gone to Maillaux's," he said. "I think we join them." He looked around at the others and nodded his head slowly. "I think we join them," he repeated. He smiled at Mullins. "Maybe the steak—" he started, and then seemed to abandon it. He stood up. "Right?" he said.

You went into the foyer and left hats and coats at the check stand; to your right, beyond a wide arch, was the bar. From either foyer or bar, depending on the immediacy of your thirst, you could go down three steps to the level of the restaurant proper, encounter William or M. Maillaux himself, be greeted—with graduated enthusiasm—and turned over to Henri or Armand, the greater captains. You were passed on, then, lingeringly if of sufficient importance. (Early diners from out of town were passed on politely, but rather as if they were hot.) You reached, in time, your own presiding captain, waiter, bus boy, sommelier, hot bread purveyor and, on occasion, page boy. Maillaux's, empty of customers, was still comfortably filled.

The Norths and the Weigands, with Mullins behind them, amiably disapproving, went into the foyer and the three men turned toward the check stand. The slight girl waiting there began her professionally welcoming smile, saw Weigand and Mullins and abandoned the smile. Then, almost quickly enough, she resumed it.

Cecily Breakwell was not, it occurred to Bill

Weigand, glad to see them. He found this interesting, but not self-explanatory. It might well mean nothing; he doubted if anyone at Maillaux's, who recognized Mullins and himself, would be particularly glad to see them.

Cecily said, "Good evening, Lieutenant," nodded to Mullins and said, "Thank you, sir," to Jerry North. She removed coats from the counter of the stand, retired with them into the depths, returned with identifying checks. "I work here Sunday nights, too," she said. "During the lunch period other days, but in the evenings on Sundays." She seemed rather in a hurry to explain, Bill thought. But that might well be no more than nervousness. Bill said "Right," vaguely, and he and Jerry North and Mullins rejoined Pam and Dorian.

They had turned, as if by reflex, toward the bar and then Pam, who was in the lead, checked herself and turned back toward the others, at the same time making a little motion of her head toward the bar. She said, "Look," and they looked. John Leonard was there, by himself, long, a little hunched on a bar stool, his back to them. Pam North formed words with her lips, almost soundlessly. "Did you know?" she asked with her lips.

Bill Weigand watched her, guessed. He shook his head. They went on to the bar, moved down it toward the end nearest the main room of the restaurant, and found places in a row. The restaurant did not seem to be crowded. They sat and Leonard leaned forward and looked down the bar at them. He said, "Hi," in an unprofessorial tone. It occurred to Pam that he had had even more drinks than they had had. She nudged Jerry and said, in an inclusive tone, "There's Mr. Leonard, Jerry." She nodded at Leonard then, and so did Jerry. Leonard got up and walked down the bar toward them, moving with slightly too much care.

"Hunting?" he said, addressing them generally. He

did not give them opportunity to answer. "I thought you didn't drink, Lieutenant. Now where did I get that idea?"

He stood above the five at the bar, leaning down a little, looking down the bar at them. He enunciated very clearly, in his speaker's voice. He did not wait for Bill to answer.

"Or just with me," he said. "Is that the rule, Lieutenant? Stipulated by the Emily Post of the department?"

He seemed amused, but there was an edge under his amusement. This time he did wait for Bill Weigand to answer.

"I'm a sundowner," Bill said. "Nothing to do with you, Mr. Leonard. I drink in the evenings."

Leonard bowed, not quite burlesquing it. He said he stood rebuked. "Join us?" Jerry North said, and Leonard shook his head. "Waiting," he told them. "A friend. Good hunting." He bowed again, went back up the bar to his stool; sat hunched over a drink and appeared to forget them. Pam North looked at Bill, her eyes challenging him.

"You're not, particularly," she said. "At least, I've known—"

Bill Weigand looked at her without any particular expression. Then he raised his eyebrows.

"It is Emily Post," Pam said, with an air of discovery. "Then—you do."

"Are you two talking about something?" Jerry North said. "And if you are, what? Four martinis, one old-fashioned. One of us ought to see about a table."

"No rules," Bill said, to Pam. He stood up and told Jerry he would see about a table. He hesitated a moment. "Don't make too much of it, Pam," he advised, and went to the turn of the bar and down the three steps to William Snodgrass, resplendent, correct, beside a restraining velvet rope. From the bar they could see William bow.

From where they sat, they could look out over the main room of the restaurant—a room which was commodious without appearing large, which had banquettes around the walls, which was lighted artfully. It did not seem crowded, and there was no one, so far as they could see, waiting admission at the ropes. There was an atmosphere which Pam could not at once identify. Then she decided it was an atmosphere of leisure. This surprised her a little.

"You know," she said to Jerry, "I thought it would be different. More—I don't know—keyed up. You know?"

"Sunday night," Jerry said, lifting his glass.

"Well—" Pam said, and lifted hers.

Bill came back to them, nodded and sat in front of his drink. Whenever they were ready, he said, William was ready.

"Was he glad to see you?" Dorian asked, and Bill shook his head and said, "Not particularly, I imagine. Rather surprised." He sipped his drink. "Which is natural," he said. "They'd all like to forget the whole thing. I—remind them."

There was movement up the bar, beyond a young couple who leaned their heads close together over their drinks, making a circle against the world. John Leonard rose to his considerable height, looked down at them and bowed, and went out into the foyer.

"Tired of waiting?" Pam said. "Going home?"

"Or going to telephone," Jerry said. "Or—"

Pam looked at Bill, her gaze urging response. Bill merely smiled and shook his head, and went back to his drink. He could be irritating, Pam thought. She looked at the back of his head, as he turned toward Dorian, who sat between him and Mullins. It occurred to Pam, suddenly, that Bill might be up to something. It was odd that he had not had a drink with Leonard that afternoon. And it was, to a degree, true that Bill Weigand did not like to drink with people he might, subsequently, have to arrest. She thought it was a preference, rather than a rule, and hence nothing to build too high upon. But it was interesting.

It was interesting that they had come there, on Bill's suggestion—almost, it seemed, on Bill's orders—after he had heard that Peggy Mott and Weldon Carey were there. It was interesting, also, that they did not seem to be there. At least, they were not immediately in sight. They were not at the bar, unless— She checked the bar. No, they had not come in; they were not at the bar itself, or at any of the little tables she could see from where she sat. And it was interesting that Bill, who had seemed so tired when he first came that evening, so much at a loss, no longer seemed particularly tired. Of course, Pam thought, the drinks helped, and seeing Dorian helped. But there must have been something more. She tried to think what it had been.

There might, obviously, have been something in the "grist" which had come in over the telephone. That was the most likely. It might have been something that, with or without the grist, had happened in Bill's mind: some new light that logic had shed, suddenly, on facts already known. It might have been something which had happened at their apartment. Thinking this, she tried to remember what had happened. Bill had come in, they had debated where to eat—with Bill taking little part—they had had drinks. The telephone had rung and been answered by Bill, and he had listened to reports about which he had told them nothing. (If it was something in one of those, I didn't miss anything, Pam thought; I can't be blamed.) Bill had heard, presumably from a detective who was trailing Peggy and Weldon Carey, that the two had gone to the Restaurant Maillaux. Was that it? Did that fact, merely as a fact, have significance? Pam worried the idea, finishing her drink. If it had, it escaped her.

Then, here at the restaurant, there had been the presence of Cecily Breakwell at the check stand and the presence of John Leonard at the bar. The first did not seem either remarkable, or important; the second, while unexpected, seemed without any particular significance. Those things were all she could think of. And yet, somewhere, at some time, since he had come into their apartment, Bill Weigand's attitude had changed.

Pam North looked at the back of Bill Weigand's head as if she expected to see through it. It was annoying, it was— She regarded her glass, making her mind work.

"Pam," Jerry said. "Hey—Pam. Come back. We're going to eat."

She looked up. The others had slid from their stools, were grouped to advance on the restaurant. Jerry put a hand on her shoulder. "Wake up, lady," he said. "Wake up."

Everybody's so cheerful, Pam thought. It's as if they *all* knew something. She got up and went into the group, and they moved on William, who bowed and smiled, took down the restraining rope, and passed them on to Henri. As they walked through the restaurant, seeming to pick up attendants as they went, like a convoy acquiring protective craft, Pam looked around, seeking Peggy Mott and Peggy's angry companion. She did not see them.

They sat and were hovered over; menus, enormous and in French, seemed to descend from all directions into their hands. Henri remained, supervising; a secondary captain brooded close, a bus boy darted in and out, a waiter stood expectant. The Norths and the Weigands worked through the menu, translating anxiously in their minds. Mullins put his menu down and the lesser captain moved in, while Henri, without moving, seemed somehow also to advance.

"Can I just get a steak?" Mullins said. "Just a steak, rare?"

"But of course," the lesser captain said. "But certainly, m'sieu."

The lesser captain repeated, "Steak, rare," and wrote it down on a tablet. Henri nodded approvingly; the waiter beamed and nodded too.

"And," the lesser captain continued, his attention still raptly on Mullins, "to begin, m'sieu? The oysters? The potage?"

"Steak," Mullins said. "O.K."

"The potatoes?" the lesser captain said, beaming at Mullins, obviously charmed by Mullins' decision. "The green vegetable?"

"O.K.," Mullins said. "French fries. All right. Some peas, I guess."

"M'sieu," the waiter said, with acceptance, admiration, and finality all in the word. He saw that Dorian had laid her menu down. The spotlight shifted, focussed on Dorian.

"Madame?" the lesser captain said. He was breathless. Dorian ordered, Pam ordered (what she believed to be breast of squab turkey under glass) and, sharing the spotlight, Jerry and Bill told the high priests of *la grande cuisine* what royalty would deign to eat. The emergency passed, things quieted. The sommelier offered, and was declined; the hot bread passer passed and was welcomed.

"They're not here," Pam said to Bill, sitting next her on her right. "You said they'd come here." She was somehow accusing; she felt somehow accusing.

Bill smiled and explained. They had only started, when he heard. They had parted after they left the office of the Homicide Squad, met again—each with his assigned detective in attendance—and had a cocktail uptown. Then they had gone out of the bar, their detectives converging, inconspicuously merging. Carey had flagged down a cab and Peggy Mott's detective was near enough to hear him say, "Maillaux's restaurant." Thinking this might be of special interest, Peggy's detective had remained to telephone Weigand. Carey's adherent had followed in another taxicab. "Just to keep them honest," Bill said, "they ought to be here pretty soon."

Pam North realized then that Bill had arranged the seating so that he could watch the entrance. He was watching it.

"Pretty soon," he said. "Now, in fact. There they come."

There they came, and Bill's eyes were not the only ones on the rather tall, slender girl who stood so easily and so confidently, with the dark man on her left and a little behind her. Peggy Mott knew that people looked at her, Pam thought. She had learned to know it, and not show she knew it.

"No wonder you let her go," Dorian said, from beyond her husband. Bill took an instant to smile at her, and continued to watch the girl. His eyes seemed to have narrowed, Pam thought. Oh, dear, Pam thought, is it going to be her after all? Is he sure about her again?

M. Maillaux himself had replaced William at the rope. It was he who advanced upon the two who were waiting. From this distance, from Maillaux's back, and from his movements, his gestures, he seemed all the welcoming host. It was clear that he said something, that Peggy Mott smiled, that Carey answered him. Then M. Maillaux himself led them off, toward the left, toward a banquette. He walked plumply ahead of them and his hands summoned, out of the air, a captain and a captain's aides. And M. Maillaux himself hovered, evidently still talking, until Peggy Mott and Weldon Carey picked up menus and disappeared behind them. Only then did M. Maillaux turn away and now, that he was facing them, an expression of rather special affability was on his features.

"They're popular," Pam said to Bill. "Isn't that a rather special welcome?"

Bill nodded. He said it seemed to be.

"Pleased she's out of it?" Pam said. "Since he must guess she is. Since she comes here openly."

"It looks that way," Bill agreed, and now he turned his eyes away from the two on the banquette and looked around the room.

"You know," he said, "in spite of all the fuss they make over you, this is rather a pleasant place. Don't you think so? Relaxing, once you're past the—the reception committee?"

"Yes," Pam said. She looked at him with calculated intentness. "It's certainly relaxed you," she said. She paused. "Or something else," she added.

He raised eyebrows at her.

"Or you're holding out," she said. "Not that there's any reason why you shouldn't, if you want to. Only—"

He shook his head. He said, "No."

"Well," Pam said, "don't tell me there isn't something." She looked at him suspiciously. "A hunch," she said. "You've gone and got a hunch!"

He did not answer this. His eyes were again on the steps which led down from foyer and bar. He nodded in that direction.

A slender man, smiling, was coming down the steps behind a small, vivid girl with red hair. The Fosters had arrived; William greeted them and there seemed to be hesitation. It was presently resolved; the Fosters, preceded by a lesser captain, moved down the restaurant. Bill Weigand continued to regard them. Pam could see his face only from an angle, but she thought his eyebrows had drawn together as they sometimes did when he was puzzled. She looked at his right hand. Yes, the fingers were tapping gently on the tablecloth.

He expected Peggy and Carey, Pam thought; he

wasn't surprised at finding Leonard; he didn't expect the Fosters.

The Fosters, connected with the lesser captain by an invisible tow-rope, approached. Some tables away they recognized the Norths, Weigand. Foster's pleasant face, on which there seemed always to be an expression of gentle amusement, went into a new smile, this time personalized, one of greeting. The Fosters reached the table and stopped; the invisible tow-rope lengthened and seemed about to break. Then the captain realized he had lost his tow and stopped, looked back, and began to hover. Jerry, Bill and Mullins stood up and Mrs. Foster said, "Please." They remained standing.

Foster appeared to feel he should say something, explain something. But he hesitated, his smile meanwhile disarming.

"Really," he said then, "it must look as if we were following you around, trying to—what? Horn in?"

There were deprecating sounds.

"Actually, I suppose there's something in it," Paul Foster said. "I don't mean we did follow you; we didn't think about your being here. But—well, we'd heard so much about the restaurant, I suppose we just got curious, you know." There was a rising inflection on the last word.

"Why not?" Bill Weigand said. "It's a public restaurant." His voice was amused.

"Well—" Foster said. "Well—nice meeting you. Come on, Paula."

He and Paula went on. The towing captain was relieved. Bill looked after them.

"Just curiosity?" Pam said, after he was seated again. He said, "Why not?" and looked at her quizzically.

"All right," Pam said. "There is something going on. About to go on. You know it perfectly well. It's like—like people coming into a theater. Members of the audience, people in the cast—isn't it?"

Bill Weigand said only that he saw what she meant. It was not enough, but then food began to arrive.

Potage Maillaux distracted Pam North. It was delicious, but it was more than that. It was delicious in a new way; it was at once unexpected and reassuring, flavors not quite new, so that it was not necessary to wonder about them, be uneasy about them, and yet not, in this combination, by Pam North, ever experienced before. Cheese, certainly, clarified stock (chicken?) undoubtedly. These things could be identified. But it would have been absurd to say that *potage Maillaux* was a cheese soup, just as it had always, to Pam, seemed absurd to describe Vichyssoise as "leek and potato soup." It was, obviously; now and then it too evidently was. But the essentials, added together, did not make the essential soup. *Potage Maillaux,* unquestionably, contained ingredients more familiar than ambrosia. It would be ridiculous to contend that there was not in it, somewhere, a drop or two of onion juice. Homely things, familiar things—cream, no doubt, sherry, perhaps?—had gone into it. But they did not come out of it, out of its fragrance, its flavor. Pam took another spoonful and looked at Jerry, who was also eating *potage Maillaux*.

"Good," Jerry said.

"Jerry! It's incredible," Pam said. "Good indeed. What does good mean?"

"Means it's good," Jerry said, and swallowed. He dipped his spoon. "Incidentally," he said, "good is an absolute term." He raised the full spoon. "Except to a copy writer," he said, and put the spoon to his lips. He swallowed. "Of course," he said, "you can always use a 'very' if you want to be extravagant."

"You can use 'um-m-m good,'" Dorian Weigand said, also out of the depths of *potage Maillaux*. They all looked at Bill, who was looking, with regret, at an empty cup.

"The thing you say," Bill told them, "is 'ah-h-h!' You hold it, you raise your hand—so—with the fingers—so—and you say, 'Ah-h-h.' Means you like the soup. It's better if you're wearing a chef's cap, of course."

"I still like just 'good,' " Jerry said, scraping. Pam looked at Mullins, commiseratingly, and Mullins said, "O.K., let's see 'em do a steak." Then attendants swooped, a cart approached, breathing flame, and the lesser captain dished, with an expression of worship. He handed plates to the waiter who served, somehow giving the impression he was on his knees. The Norths and the Weigands tasted, beamed and regarded Mullins. Slowly, Mullins lifted steak; with care he regarded it. Then he put it to the hazard, and chewed. And, slowly, with a subexpression of surprise, Mullins beamed.

"O.K." Mullins said. "O.*K.*"

It was an interlude, peaceful and almost quiet. Nobody said anything for a considerable time. There was no tension anywhere, for those moments. Pam North forgot to wonder what Bill Weigand was up to; Jerry's mind freed itself from that lurking unease, so common to it when things were assuming a shape which presaged that Pam would get into trouble. It was Sunday evening; it was delicious food after the proper number of drinks. The air was free from the vibrations of approaching crime. They would finish dinner, perhaps with a cognac, Jerry thought; they would go peacefully home in a taxicab to warmth, a fire, the sleepy purring of silken cats. It was all conspicuous waste, and very comforting.

"Everything goes well?" a voice said. "Lieutenant? Madame North? M'sieu?" Jerry came out of it, with the feeling that he had been about to go to sleep. M. Maillaux was in attendance.

M. André Maillaux, seen at close range, was none the worse for wear. He exuded tactful greeting, restrained confidence. Possibly, Pam thought, there was something about his eyes—a weariness? A strain? But the voice was firm and round; he was all the host. She watched his eyes, alert, travel over their table, checking its accoutrements. She saw them hesitate at Dorian's almost empty butter plate, admired the inconspicuous gesture by which he summoned a bus boy, indicating the plate. He did all this while still attentive; was attentive while still dignified.

"You are well served, yes?" M. Maillaux said. He directed attention toward Mullins. "The knife, she is sharp?" he said. "The steak—?"

"O.K.," Mullins said.

"I am pleased," M. Maillaux said. "Things go well." He continued to beam.

He is more foreign than I thought, Pam told herself. More French. The clothes, the accent—I had not remembered they were so characteristic.

"Everything's delicious, M. Maillaux," Pam said. "Everything. The soup is marvelous."

"The *potage*," M. Maillaux said. "Ah-h-h—the *potage* is indeed good. I am delighted, madame. A speciality *de la maison,* you perceive. Of my family, madame."

He was evidently proud. He was not averse to continuing.

"Your family?" Pam said.

"But yes, madame. The recipe, you perceive. My grandfather, as a young man—he created *potage Maillaux,* you perceive. In Paris, *naturellement*. My father, my uncle, always it has been a secret in the family. Always we have been proud of *potage Maillaux*. You know the Restaurant Maillaux in Paris, madame?"

"Ah-h-h," Pam said.

"My uncle's, you perceive," André Maillaux said. "Before the war— Ah-h-h!"

"U-m-m," Pam said.

"Here I attempt the same," Maillaux said. "It is difficult, yes. It is not Paris, you perceive. And now my poor Tony!" His smile faded. He shook his head sadly. "A loss irretrievable," he said. He turned to Weigand. "You have not yet discovered, Lieutenant?"

"No," Weigand said, "Not yet."

"A tragedy," Maillaux said. "For me, catastrophe." He looked very sad. "Who will come now to Maillaux's? Now we have only the good food, the wine. It is not enough, no?"

"Oh, I'm sure it will be, M. Maillaux," Pam North said. "Such wonderful food!"

Maillaux brightened a little.

"The food, yes," he said. "The food, certainly. That we can achieve. But is it sufficient, Madame North? And the time to prepare, you perceive. People are impatient, no?"

He looked earnestly at Pam North, who did not know the answer and made a sound which she hoped was encouraging. It seemed to be.

"We must attempt," he said. "When this—this tragedy—is finish. Already—" He broke off. "You will come again, I hope, Madame North?"

"Of course," Pam said.

"So tragic," Maillaux said. It seemed to haunt him. "Poor Tony. It is unbelievable."

"And the girl," Pam said. "Mrs. Britton."

"Mrs. Britton?" he said. "Ah yes, the poor Elaine. So sad, Madame North."

He doesn't take that part of it very hard, Pam thought. I'd have guessed he would. She was momentarily puzzled that she would have guessed that, and then the point cleared. The little mink—the poor little mink—had been attractive, no doubt approachable. And M. Maillaux was French. The connection was tenuous, but serviceable.

"She I knew only a little," M. Maillaux said. "You

perceive, madame? A—a friend of the poor Tony. But it is very sad, of a certainty."

Poor little mink, Pam thought again. I hope somebody minded more. But she merely nodded to M. Maillaux.

He had turned a little toward Bill Weigand, in any case, and Bill was looking up at him.

"You no longer seek Mrs. Mott, I perceive," Maillaux said. "She is—what do you say—in the clear?"

"Why do you think that?" Bill Weigand said.

Maillaux looked surprised.

"But," he said, "she is here. Surely, Lieutenant, you have perceived that—"

"Oh," Bill said. "Yes, I noticed she was here, M. Maillaux."

"With a friend," Maillaux said. "A young man. Very dark?"

"Yes," Bill said. "I noticed him."

"And you do not arrest her," Maillaux said, and nodded. "It is so I think she is exonerated, Lieutenant. No?"

"As I said, we've not closed the case," Bill said. "Nobody is—exonerated. But we are not ready to arrest anybody."

Maillaux nodded. He said, "So?"

"Mrs. Mott is certainly a—" Bill said, and stopped as if, Pam thought, he felt he was saying too much. "However, she is not under arrest, M. Maillaux. As you see."

"I am so glad," Maillaux said. "I should not like to think a woman so—what shall I say—so *exquise* would do such a thing. But I was disturbed, you perceive. She did not love Tony. And there was so much money. And then the little Elaine, who had become the good friend of poor Tony. You perceive, Lieutenant?"

He seemed anxious to explain, Pam thought. She could appreciate his probable feeling. One felt so about Peggy Mott. One felt defensive of her, one did not want to suspect her. But the facts— The grist, Pam thought, the gritty grist.

"I am aware there is a case against Mrs. Mott, M. Maillaux," Bill said. He nodded. "Very much aware of it," he added. "All I can tell you, again, is that—well, that we're not ready yet. You understand?"

Maillaux nodded.

"It is not complete?" he said.

Bill Weigand said, "Right."

Maillaux seemed saddened. He shook his head. Then, with an evident effort, he became again the host.

"These things," he said, "we should forget them, no? For the digestion. Now—you will have the dessert? The *bombe glacée Maillaux?* The cherries flame? The *crêpes?*" He smiled around at them, fully the host again. "Ah-h-h!" he said. "The *crêpes!*"

They ordered *crêpes Suzette*. The waiter brought the pancakes, the ingredients and the table with its spirit lamp. M. Maillaux remained, observant. The lesser captain came and compounded, pouring liqueurs, squeezing orange. He built the pretty bonfire on the pancakes and apportioned them, pouring the flickering sauce. He beamed, Maillaux beamed. And, unexpectedly, John Leonard came down from the bar, walking almost too steadily among the tables, and joined them. He stood above them, looked down.

"The moth," Pam North said. "To the flame. I thought you'd left, Mr. Leonard."

"Left?" Leonard said. "No, I haven't left. Still waiting for my friend. Got lost somewhere, my friend has, I'm afraid."

"Join us," Jerry said. "Have a drink with us."

Leonard shook his head.

"The lieutenant wouldn't approve," he said. "Emily Post. Anyway, I'm waiting for a friend. Got lost somewhere, I'm afraid." He nodded. He was not drunk,

Pam thought. On the other hand, it would be venture-some to call him sober.

"Sit down," Bill said. "Sit down. Have a drink."

"No," Leonard said. "Can't do that. But I wanted to ask you something, Lieutenant." He stood up, dignified. "May I ask you something?"

"Right," Bill said. "Ask away, Professor."

"I will," Leonard said. "Did you know that Peggy Mott's here? In the restaurant?"

"Yes," Bill said, nodding. "I saw her, Mr. Leonard."

"That's Carey with her," Leonard said. "Weldon Carey. You knew that?"

"Yes."

"All right," Leonard said. "You know she's here."

Bill nodded again.

"So far as I can see, no handcuffs," Leonard said. "On Peggy. On Carey. No minions of the law." He paused and shook his head. "The sort of thing Handleigh says," Leonard told them. "Minions. Could I be intoxicated?"

"No," Bill said.

"Thank you, Lieutenant," Leonard said. "Or did you mean, no minions?"

"Both."

Leonard said, "Oh." Then he said:

"And that, I take it, means that you no longer think she killed her husband? You're no longer looking for her?"

"Obviously, I'm not looking for her," Bill said. "At any rate, not to arrest her. Now."

Leonard looked at Bill Weigand intently. He was obviously trying to go beyond the words.

"She's clear, then? In your mind?" Leonard said, after a little pause.

"Now, Mr. Leonard," Bill said. "You want to know a lot, don't you?"

"Why not?" Leonard said. "You come to me and ask a lot of questions. Imply a lot of things. And then I find you no longer want the obvious person—the girl who hated the man who got killed, who gets his money. Why wouldn't I be interested?"

"Why?" Bill said.

"Off with the old suspicion, on with the new," Leonard said. "Is that it, Lieutenant?"

"Oh, that," Bill said. "Should it be? And did I say, off with the old?"

"But—" Leonard said.

Weigand looked at him more intently. He shook his head at Leonard.

"For your information, Mr. Leonard," Bill said, "nobody is entirely in the clear. Including yourself. But we don't always arrest suspects—immediately. Including yourself, obviously." He let it sink in. "Don't jump to conclusions, Mr. Leonard," Bill said. "Right?"

Leonard again studied Bill Weigand's face.

"Then—?" he said.

"Any conclusions," Bill told him. "One way, or another way."

"You can't keep me from guessing," Leonard told him, and Bill shrugged.

"Why should I?" he said. "Guess away, Mr. Leonard." He sighed faintly. "Half the town is, probably," he said. "Why not you? Sit down and have a drink."

"Enough rope," Leonard said. "No, I'll go back and wait for my friend. Unless?" He looked at his wrists. Bill Weigand told him to wait for his friend. He went off toward the bar.

Pam North was looking at Bill Weigand. "Isn't it—" she began, and Bill shook his head at her. He motioned faintly with his head, and she saw that André Maillaux was only a little way off, talking to a waiter. She did not understand the warning, entirely, although she obeyed it. What difference would it make if Maillaux heard her say it was interesting that Leonard was so interested in Peggy Mott's continued freedom, that he had gone out of his way, almost, to review for Weigand the evidence against the girl? Could it be that Bill had expected her to say something else, something Maillaux should not overhear? And—could it be that Bill had missed Leonard's odd, intent interest? Leonard was worried for his own sake, his own safety. That's obvious, Pam thought; how can Bill have missed it? And M. Maillaux is, just as obviously, worried about Peggy Mott, worried about the facts against her. Pam shook her head.

Enough rope, she thought; it's true he's giving somebody enough rope. He's waiting for something to happen, for somebody to do something. And then, looking at Bill, remembering how he had spoken, first to Maillaux, then to Leonard, Pam had an unhappy conviction that she knew who was getting the rope. Because, although he seemed to have tried not to, he had given it away in his words to both the men.

He's back where he started, Pam thought. He thinks it's Peggy Mott. Only—this time he's sure. This time he hasn't any doubts. She looked at Bill, who was looking at her, smiling faintly, abstracted. She knew him that well, she thought. He knows where he's going, now. Only—he's going wrong. It has to be that he's going wrong.

Pam, eating *crêpes Suzette* without tasting them, looked across the room at Peggy and Weldon Carey. They seemed secure, she thought. Almost happy. It would be so very—so very upsetting if Bill Weigand wasn't going wrong.

It was then that Pam North realized, for the first time fully realized, that they were all there in accordance with some plan; that they were there waiting for something to happen. The plan was Bill's, and now, remembering what he had said, studying his expression, she was convinced she knew at whom the plan was directed, She did not know what the plan was; she did not know what Bill Weigand expected to happen. But he had let Peggy Mott go, and Carey with her, because he believed that, free, they would lead him to something; that their freedom would force an issue. It is true, she thought, that he hasn't enough evidence— enough evidence to exclude all other possibilities. He is waiting for them to give it to him. He has set the stage. Now he is waiting.

She looked at him, saw that his eyes, as hers had been, were on the couple across the restaurant. He was watching them, waiting for them to move, to do whatever it was he had arranged for them to do, or whatever some inescapable logic of events, to which he had somehow become privy, was forcing them to do. She looked at Peggy and Weldon Carey again, and tried to work it out.

But they were, so far as she could determine, merely finishing dinner. There was nothing in that to account for the intent look on Bill Weigand's face; for her own tightening nerves, her own conviction that it was almost time. There was nothing in anything that was happening, or had happened within the past hour, to account for the way she felt now. It was obscure, baffling.

She was in a restaurant, in which perhaps sixty or seventy men and women were dining, at leisure, well and at considerable expense. The atmosphere was one of relaxation, of contentment. Of all places, Pam thought, this was one of the ones least likely to create, of itself, that odd stretching of the nerves, that kind of impatient irritability, which she now felt. She could see Maillaux patrolling his restaurant, stopping at a table to speak to patrons, as he had stopped at theirs to speak to them, bowing and smiling and moving on, watching a captain who was slicing, with almost ludicrous care, a ham fixed by prongs to a wheeled table, pointing to an empty table and sending a bus boy scurrying. There was nothing in what Maillaux was doing to create tension. There was nothing in what Peggy Mott was doing, or the man with her.

William, the immaculate, the maître d'hôtel, was at his station near the ropes, and he was merely standing, easily, greeting the final trickle of the evening's trade. He bowed to a couple as she watched, went a few steps with them and assigned them to one of the greater captains. He smiled and bowed to someone at a table near the ropes, and went back to wait. There was nothing in any movement of his, any attitude of his, to suggest that he could be involved in this—this thing, this action—for which Bill Weigand was waiting.

The two at the table across the room, Maillaux, William—the sense of tension she felt did not seem to emanate from any of them. And they, surely, would be in the center of it; if Bill was right, Peggy Mott and Weldon Carey would *be* the center of it. Unless Leonard—she looked around, seeking John Leonard. At first she did not see him, and for a moment she had a quick hope that his absence was what Bill had been waiting for; that it was Leonard, rather than Peggy Mott, who was to be at the center of things.

Because I still don't believe it, Pam thought; I still don't believe it was Peggy. I think it's too easy that way, too—made up. She looked at Bill again and the hope lost quickness. She knew that expression. Bill Weigand was sure, was very sure. He was merely waiting for a thing he knew to be inevitable.

Leonard appeared, then, at the top of the short stairway leading to the bar. He stood there, very tall, peering at the restaurant, looking for something. He shook his head after a moment and went back. Pam looked quickly at Bill Weigand, and thought he had also been watching Leonard. But Leonard had done nothing.

It was all, outwardly, so matter-of-fact, so free of—threat. Pam, her nerves growing still tighter, felt that she was somehow shut away from it, or lifted somehow above it. It was as if she were watching the gathering of a storm of which she alone had cognizance; as if all these others, the actors and the spectators, were moving in a dream of ignorance, of imperviousness, while the storm gathered—while the air drew itself together and held heavily still. She wanted to shout a warning; to do something which would break this slowly gathering spell.

"Pam," Jerry said. "Hey, Pam!" His voice was casual, reflecting no tension such as hers. He was smiling at her. She heard herself speak, heard herself say, "Yes, Jerry?" and watched him shake his head. "Just 'hey,' " he said. "You'd gone off."

"No," she said. "No, I'm around." She realized, then, that Dorian and Jerry, and Mullins, had been talking idly; that a waiter was pouring coffee for them, that, here as elsewhere in the restaurant, things went on matter-of-factly. It was only around Bill that there was that tension, that charge, and she was the only one aware of it. For an instant it occurred to her that all she felt was subjective, lacked any outer reality. Then she saw that Dorian, now, was also watching Bill Weigand, and that her gaze was intent, as if she, too, were trying to break into Bill's mind. It's reached her, now, Pam thought.

Then Bill spoke. He turned his eyes, his attention, back toward the others, and spoke to Mullins.

"Sergeant," he said, "d'you want to give them a ring? See if anything's turned up. They know where we are, of course, but—"

"Yeah," Mullins said. "O.K., Loot. Sure."

Mullins did not feel it, Pam thought. But then she saw his almost imperceptible nod, thought it was an answer to some signal Weigand had given him, and looked quickly at Bill. But Bill's expression, now, was merely easy and relaxed, as his voice had been. Mullins got up and went among the tables toward the foyer of the restaurant. They watched him.

"You expect something?" Jerry said, and Bill Weigand shook his head. He said something about routine; he seemed to prove his indifference by taking up his coffee cup and drinking from it. "You know," Jerry said, "I could do with a brandy. Anybody else?"

Pam was suddenly, briefly, furious. All hell was about to break loose, and Jerry wanted a brandy. Oh, damn! Pam thought. What's the matter with everybody?

Then they saw Mullins coming back through the restaurant, and he was moving quickly. When he was still some distance away, he raised his right hand in a gesture, commanding Bill Weigand's attention. Bill Weigand got up, unhurriedly.

"There's something—" Mullins said, when he was near enough. He looked around at the Norths, at Dorian, and seemed to decide not to go on. "One of the boys—"

"Right," Bill said. "I was expecting it." He seemed suddenly morose. "Just let me settle down a minute," he said, "and something—" He did not finish.

"Bill," Dorian said. "What a shame! You'll be back?"

Bill Weigand shrugged, and seemed to consider. Then he nodded. He said he would try the telephone; if that wasn't good enough he'd come back and tell her.

"Sit tight," he said, including the Norths, this time. "Probably it's nothing much."

He joined Mullins and they went off together. Pam saw that Peggy Mott and Carey were watching them; thought that M. Maillaux was aware of their going; knew that William must inevitably see them as they passed. The Fosters? She turned to look back, seeking the Fosters. She did not see them; apparently they had eaten more quickly and gone on.

And now Bill was going. But I was right, Pam thought, I'm sure I was right. Did it miss? Fail to go off? Or—or is this the start of it?

"Jerry," she said, "I'll take a brandy."

She was aware that something in her voice surprised Jerry North, and that he was looking at her oddly. I must have sounded as if I needed one, Pam thought. Whatever's the matter with me?

12

"O.K., Loot?" Mullins said. "What you wanted?"

"Right," Bill told him. "Just what I wanted."

"Look," Mullins said. "What was I supposed to mean? Back there?" He moved his head toward the restaurant.

"God knows," Bill told him. "However—we're out. Very publicly."

"All set, then?" Mullins said. Bill nodded.

"It's set," he said. "Now—we'll see whether it goes off. Only—" He paused and Mullins waited. Bill picked up his hat and coat, handed out Mullins' hat and coat; put money on the counter. The girl was not Cecily Breakwell, this time; Cecily was nowhere visible.

Bill turned away from the coatroom, started to join Mullins nearer the door and hesitated. He stood for a moment and then nodded to himself, half smiling. He turned back and said, "Sheet of paper?" to the girl at the stand. She had a sheet of paper. Using the counter as a desk, Bill wrote briefly, folded the paper and wrote a name on the back of it. A page boy, watching, showed anticipation and appeared at Bill's elbow.

227

"Oh," Bill said. "Yes, will you?" He moved back, with the page, to a position from which they could see into the restaurant. Weigand pointed; gave the page half a dollar and then rejoined Mullins.

Mullins had been watching, now he nodded.

"Now it ought to be all set," Bill said. "Unless Pam—" He did not finish immediately and Mullins, after a moment, said, "Yeah?"

"Oh," Bill said. "Pam North. She's—on to it, Mullins. She knows something's up."

"That Mrs. North," Mullins said, and Bill, smiling a little—and looking a little worried—said "Right."

"You know, Loot," Mullins said, and pushed the outer door open, "Mrs. North, she goes off on tangents. Did you ever notice?"

Bill Weigand joined Mullins on the sidewalk and shook his head.

"No," he said. "It looks like it, sometimes. I used to think that. But what she really does, Mullins, is to cut across tangents. Often without even appearing to notice them. It's equally confusing, sometimes, but it's different. See what I mean?"

Mullins shook his head.

"Nope," he said. "To me, she's sorta screwy. Nice, you understand, but sorta screwy. I always feel she's leaving things out."

Bill agreed with that. They declined the offer of the doorman to get them a cab, and turned right and started up the street.

"And," Mullins said, "she never looks where she's going, Loot." Bill nodded to that.

"Because she sees it so clearly, probably," he said.

"It's a good way to get hurt," Mullins said. "You know that, Loot?"

Bill had known it for years, and had felt he should do something, and had never quite succeeded. But this time, he thought, Pam's safe out of it—she and Dorian.

This time neither of them gets in a jam. This time I'll tell them about it when it's all over.

Mullins and Weigand walked on up the street.

The sense of sitting still, untouched, in the center of tension remained with Pam North. The brandy did not help, she hardly knew that she was drinking it. But when she put it down, she touched the base of the glass against her coffee cup, and the sharp, small sound was almost shattering. She jumped, felt herself jumping. Dorian was looking at her, now. Dorian said Pam was jumpy.

"No," Pam said, "I don't think so. Oh, perhaps, a little. Why did Bill go, do you think?"

"To call the office," Dorian said. She made it sound simple.

"I think—" Pam said. "Never mind."

"Relax," Jerry said. "Take a deep breath, Pam." He was smiling at her. He shook his head, slightly, when he had her attention. "Take a deep breath and forget it for an hour," he said. "For five minutes."

"All right," Pam said. She took a deep breath and tried to relax. She looked around the restaurant and thought, nothing is happening; nothing is going to happen. I'm just sitting here jittering about nothing. Jerry's right; it isn't ours anymore. We've passed it on. We're just onlookers. And anyway—

She saw M. Maillaux across the room. As she watched, he stopped again at the table where Peggy Mott sat with Weldon Carey. He leaned toward them and seemed to say something and Pam saw Peggy smile and shake her head. Maillaux was there only a moment; then he went on toward the front of the restaurant, his head moving, his eyes, she thought, seeing everything.

Peggy and Weldon had finished eating, now. They had coffee cups in front of them, and cigarettes in their hands, and they seemed contented and at ease. Pam picked up her own small, silver coffee pot and shook it, and when it sloshed promisingly, poured coffee into her cup. Jerry nodded at her and smiled approval, and she smiled back. But she watched the door, still, for Mullins and Bill, who ought to be coming back soon.

She had not, at first, wanted to go to the Restaurant Maillaux, but Weldon had insisted. She had wanted to go to some small place, some hidden place and it had been that desire of hers—that desire to make herself small, to draw shelter around her—which had, apparently, been what had made Weldon so insistent. He had been abrupt, he had said, "The hell we will!" It was then he had, evidently thinking of the action most unlike that she desired to take, said, "Hell, we'll go to Maillaux's." He had not said, "We'll show them," but that had been in his voice. He was wearing his chip again, and there was no arguing with him. And she had not, in any case, felt up to arguing.

And then, once at the restaurant, she had, unexpectedly, almost enjoyed herself. She had not seen Weigand at first, and she had never known that the man a few tables away, by himself, was there because she and Weldon were there. (Carey had suspected it; he had not been surprised. He had looked at the man challengingly and got a blank gaze back and had then, uncharacteristically, shrugged it off.) She had seen the Fosters come in, and been glad, although she could not think why, that the Fosters had not joined them. The two of them were enough; somehow, although they were in no small, hidden place, she felt the reassurance, the protection, she had hoped to find in such a place. She and Weldon could make a little corner for themselves, even here. Why, she thought, we can do it anywhere! It must be right, then. It did not even matter that Carey was so often angry.

And, in the restaurant, he had not been. He had

seemed to feel the same relaxation she felt; their moods joined. It became, without either of them having planned it so, worked to make it so, an interlude utterly carefree. Weldon had talked, for the most part, and she had listened. He had talked about things which were not of their immediate concern, except as they were things which concerned everyone. And, although many of the things he said were essentially somber, even frightening—so much one could talk about was both, that winter—he spoke with a kind of gaiety. It was as if, in their small, momentarily safe, corner, they had for a little time escaped to a place where even members of the human race could breathe freely, without foreboding. It was as if they cut this small interlude out of time itself.

That had lasted through dinner, which was delicious; the two visits, one early, one when they were finishing their coffee, M. Maillaux made to their table had not broken the spell. The first time he was merely the attentive host, impersonal. The second time, and this seemed to have been an afterthought, he had come to suggest that, after "this is all over" but as soon as was convenient, she and he confer about the restaurant. "I have a proposal, you perceive," he said, and beamed down at her. It was almost the first time she had realized that now, with Tony dead, she was Maillaux's partner in the ownership of this large, quietly glittering, place. But even that did not, for the time, break in upon them in their miraculous, protected corner.

And then, when it had begun to seem that the interlude would continue, unbroken, to a natural ending which would be part of it, the page boy had come. She had been looking out over the restaurant, hardly seeing it, listening to Weldon, and she had seen the boy coming in their direction. She had watched him, idly, as one watches something moving when the mind is somewhere else, and had not realized until he was actually there that their table was his goal. Then she had taken the folded slip of paper, still almost automatically, and had opened it without fear. Weldon stopped talking and it was as much that as anything, which shook her out of peace.

Then she read what was written on the unfolded paper and it all came back—the fear came back, the sense of struggle. She sat, for a second, rereading the brief message; then, for another second, she stared at the paper without seeing it.

"Peg!" Weldon Carey said. "What is it?"

I can't let him know, she thought, and her thoughts raced. (As the rat had raced, seeking an unstopped hole.) I can't let him be caught again; I can't have him hurt by it.

She turned so that she half-faced him, and she smiled. The smile said it was nothing before her words said it was nothing. She had never tried to act for Weldon before, but she tried now.

"Nothing," she repeated, and made the smile hold, made the word come easily, unstrained, out of a throat suddenly constricted, dried out. "M. Maillaux wants me to give him a moment." She managed to make the word "give" sound as if she were quoting it from the letter. "In his office." She smiled. "After all," she pointed out, "I'm a kind of partner now. Or will be, I suppose."

"For God's sake!" Weldon said. "Why now, Peg?"

But he seemed to accept what she said, without question. It did not seem absurd to him, made up. It was merely, he seemed to feel, badly timed.

It was easier to smile, now; to act. It was going over. She could raise her shoulders just a little, let them fall; repeat the gesture in the expression of her face. She didn't know. But it was not important.

"Only a minute," she said. "I'd better see him, don't you think? You don't mind, Wel?"

"I guess not," Weldon said. His voice minded, but not too angrily. "You won't be long?"

"Oh no," she said. "Oh no, Wel."

He got up, pulled the table out for her, and she slid around it. Not long, her mind repeated, not long—not long, now. But she managed to keep the smile on her lips for Weldon Carey.

Knowing that he was watching her, wanting desperately to look back at him—to run back to him—she walked with her shoulders back, her body erect, as she had been taught to walk, toward the door ahead of her. She knew where the door was; Tony had showed it to her once when, in spite of what was between them, he had insisted that she praise the changes he had made. It was inconspicuous, leading from the restaurant into the office suite; it was convenient. It was convenient now—terribly convenient. Its nearness robbed her of time.

She walked, unhurriedly, and the words of the note, which had not been signed by M. Maillaux, went over and over in her mind.

"Mrs. Mott," the note had read. "Come at once to Maillaux's office." It had been signed with one word, "Weigand." The brevity of the note, the curtness of the signature, told their own story. Weigand did not need to temporize further, to be polite any longer. He had the right to order her, and he wrote out an order. Well—it was better than if he had sent one of his men for her. He had been thinking, probably of the restaurant, of avoiding a disturbance, rather than of her. Still, it was better this way. She could at least walk to it, with her head up.

She opened the door and went through it and, by an effort of will, closed it quietly behind her. She came into the office reception room, near the corner of the room. Farther along, in the same wall, was the door which opened into the coatroom; ahead of her was a corridor which led between the office, on her right, which had been Tony's and the smaller office, on her left, which was Maillaux's. This corridor joined, at the end farthest from her, a hall which ran the length of the building, at one end to a door onto the street and at the other a door to the kitchens. It was through that hall she had come the previous day, keeping her appointment with Tony.

She went across the empty reception room to Maillaux's office and knocked on the closed door. There was no answer, and she realized that she—or Weigand himself—had made a mistake about the offices. She went back across the reception room and knocked at the door of the office which had been Tony's. She heard, almost at once, "Come in, Mrs. Mott," and was opening the door before her mind formulated the thought that the voice was not the one she had expected to hear. She still kept on moving into the room and heard her own voice say, "Why—?" She heard fear in her voice.

Bill and Sergeant Mullins had not come back. But a page boy had come across the room from the restaurant foyer—a boy wearing a tightly fitting jacket, a tilted pill-box hat, a boy who almost, in the perfection of his costume, burlesqued a page—and headed with confidence for their table. Pam looked at him and, seeing her intentness, Jerry turned his head and Dorian twisted in her chair. The page boy stopped and, with an air of accomplishment, produced a folded note. He said, "Mrs. Weigand, please?" and Dorian held out her hand. Jerry tipped the expectant boy, who wheeled, military in his exactitude, and went off. Dorian read the note and held it out to Pam.

It was brief. It read: "Have to go to office after all and may be an hour or so. Get P & J to take you home with them and I'll collect you there." It was signed

"Bill." Pam read the note and handed it to Jerry, who read it and at once beckoned to the waiter.

"He sort of wishes me on you," Dorian noted. "I hope—?"

"Nonsense," Jerry said. He looked at the check, remained nonchalant—with some effort—and put bills on top of it.

"My," Pam said. "My!"

Jerry grinned at her and said, "All right now? You see, there wasn't anything to jitter about."

"Well—" Pam said.

But apparently Jerry was right. Apparently she had been imagining things—imagining a tension, a trap set. Apparently Bill was not, after all, ready yet. It was even, since she had been mistaken about that, possible that she had been mistaken, also, in her unhappy certainty that Bill had made up his mind, closing it, finally, against Peggy Mott's innocence.

Jerry North got back change on a tray, left most of it on the tray, smiled at them and said, "Well?"

"Let's," Pam said, and pushed back her chair. The three of them stood up, dropping napkins on the table, accepting bows from their retinue. They started to make their way toward the front of the restaurant, and Pam took one last look—for reassurance—at Peggy Mott and Weldon Carey. And then, as quickly as it had left, her sense of tension returned.

Weldon was just sitting down again at the table. But he was alone. And Peggy Mott, with a kind of stiffness in her movements, looking straight ahead, with her face set, was walking in front of the banquettes along the far wall. Pam stopped, involuntarily, and then, feeling Jerry's nearness behind her, went on. But she saw Peggy Mott go on, in front of the banquettes, until she came almost to the corner of the room. Then she turned to her right and opened a door and, without looking around—without looking back at Weldon Carey, who was watching her—went through the door and closed it behind her.

It was an ordinary movement and yet, to Pam, there was a kind of hopeless finality about it.

The door could, Pam thought, lead only to the restaurant offices. And Peggy Mott had been summoned there, had gone through the door and the door had shut behind her—*shut like a trap!*

Oh, Pam North thought. Oh! Oh, it's happening! I wish it weren't. I wish I—I could do something. Because it's wrong. *I know it's wrong.*

But I *don't* know it's wrong, she thought, and moved on toward the door. I just want it to be wrong; I'm—what does Jerry say?—thinking with my emotions. And, anyway, I can't do anything. There isn't anything I can do.

The thought brought a kind of numbness. She walked on, behind Dorian. She felt, somehow, as if the bottom had dropped out of things. I don't want it to be this way, Pam thought; I don't want it to be this way. But she realized, at the same time, that she was no longer convinced it was not this way. Bill would not move until he was certain; he never did. And when he was certain, he was almost always right.

Pam North saw Leonard again. He was standing, where he had several times stood before, at the top of the steps leading to the bar. When she first saw him, he was looking off toward his left and, after a second or two, Pam became sure that he, also, had been watching Peggy Mott go through the door, into the trap. It did not, at once, seem significant. Then Leonard turned his head, momentarily looked down at Dorian and the Norths, without appearing to see them, and turned back toward the bar. There was a quickness about his movement, now. It was a nervous quickness.

Dorian walked on toward the foyer and Pam North walked behind her, although she did not want to be doing this. It was wrong to be leaving, Pam thought;

there was an alternative action, a necessary action, they were leaving undone. They were walking away from something, deaf to it, blind to it, and Pam walked reluctantly. She felt, in addition to reluctance, to incompleteness, something against Dorian and Jerry which was almost resentment. It was as if they were, merely by being there, merely by accepting, without protest, this course of action, forcing her to do the wrong thing. She wanted to say, "No, it's wrong!" but the wrongness was too intangible for so direct and strong a statement. And, in any event, she did not know what would be right.

They had gone up the three steps to the foyer, now, and Jerry had moved a little away from Dorian and Pam. He was standing behind another man at the check stand, waiting to turn in the little disk which would lead to the recovery of his hat and coat. And then Dorian saw someone she knew and smiled at whoever it was and took a cordial, formal step toward this other person. For that instant, Pam was alone. She felt that the others had gone away. She thought of it, in that second, in those words—gone away. And then she knew what was wrong.

Bill had gone away. That was what was wrong. Bill had gone to the office; he was not at the restaurant. *But, although he was gone, the trap had been sprung.* And that was wrong. That was not the way it would happen, could happen. Bill had given up whatever he had expected to happen. But now it was happening. Then—*this was not the same thing.* If Peggy Mott had walked through the door into a trap, it was not a trap of Bill Weigand's setting. And that was frightening.

Pam acted, then. Afterward, she could not ever clearly explain why she had acted as she did. It was, in all logic, an absurd and dangerous way to act. That it did not, at the moment, seem so was, she tried to make clear, because of the tension she had been under, and because out of that tension there had grown this irrational resentment of Dorian and even of Jerry, this feeling that they were on the other side. ("Impulse," Jerry said to this. "It boils down to impulse," and looked at her and shook his head as if he were worried about her.) It was, of course, also true that at the precise moment Jerry and Dorian had, in a fashion, gone away.

Pam herself went away. She went very rapidly back into the restaurant, turned to her left, walked as quickly as she could without running toward the door through which Peggy Mott had gone. When she reached it, the door was unlocked and Pam opened it, unhesitatingly, and went through and closed the door behind her. Then, only then, she paused.

She had hurried into an empty room. It was as if, late for an appointment, she had hurried with all her might and then found, on arriving, that the other person was not there. There was certainly nobody in the room. It was lighted, not brightly; there were several chairs along a wall, between the door she had come in by and another door to her left; there was a desk facing the chairs and, beside it, a typewriter table with a covered typewriter on it. It was an office, a reception office, after quitting time, with the light left on for a cleaning woman. It was utterly commonplace, entirely an anticlimax.

Pam felt this only briefly. Then she realized it would not be happening in the reception room, but in one of the offices. The door to one of the offices was in front of her, a little to the left, behind the desk. There was another door in the wall to her right. She advanced, quietly now, into the middle of the room and stopped there, and held her breath. Then she heard a voice.

It came from behind the apparently solid door which had been to her right when she came in. At first she could not understand why she could hear the voice at all, even, as she did hear it, dimly. Then she saw that, in the lower panel of the door, there were two hooded slots. They were for ventilation, of course. It was through them that the voice seeped out of the room.

Very quietly, now, she moved over to the door. She could hear a little more plainly. She crouched to get nearer the slots and then, because it was simpler, she sat down on the floor. She felt defenseless, and a little absurd, sitting so, but it was the only convenient way.

She realized at once that there were two voices, a man's and a woman's. The man was speaking when she began to understand the words.

She came in on the middle of a sentence.

"—very simple," the man was saying. "The police have proved to be fools. It is impossible to predict what they will do."

There was no immediate answer, although the silence was that of an answer awaited. Pam tried to identify the voice and realized, with perplexity, with uneasiness, that she could not. It was not Bill Weigand's voice, or Mullins'. Of that she was certain. By that she was not surprised. There was no accent, hence it was not André Maillaux's. Then it ought to be John Leonard's; almost had to be his, unless, during all this, they had all been hopelessly lost. But she could not identify it as Leonard's. It might be, but she could not be sure.

"You want me to make it easy for them," the woman said. "You think that would be simple."

There was no doubt about this voice, no perplexity. The other person in the room was Peggy Mott. And in Peggy Mott's voice there was an odd kind of deadness; it was as if she were reading lines written for her, but reading them without understanding.

"I want you to make it very plain," the man said. "So plain, and so clear, that even they will not look any further. You understand?"

"You don't give me any reason," the girl said. "You ask this—ask me to write this. Why should I?"

"The reason—" the man said, and did not continue. "Don't be a fool."

"But you're a fool," the girl said. "It's you who—are a fool. Don't you see? What good will it do?"

Pam bent closer to the ventilating slots; she flogged her mind. The man—who is the man?

"Leave it to me," the man said. "Only write it. 'I killed Tony Mott.' I don't care what else you say. Write that much and sign your name."

"I won't," the girl said. "Don't you see I won't? Why should I?"

There was something strange and frightening in the deadness in Peggy Mott's voice—and in what she did not say! Pam waited, waited with an increasing, deepening anxiety, for the girl to say the one thing, "I didn't kill Tony." But she did not say it.

"Because you've no choice," the man said. "Don't you realize that?"

There was no answer in words. There might have been one in a gesture, in a shaken head.

"Time," the man said. "What else is there?"

That was not clear to Pam. If only she could see, as well as hear! Still the girl did not speak.

"Count on a mistake," the man said. "Hope for anything you want to. What do they say? While there's life. It's something everybody believes. Maybe something might happen."

"No," the girl said.

"Make it longer," the man said. "Explain. Extenuate, if you want to. It will give you time. Five minutes—half an hour—who knows?"

"It's not good enough," the girl said. "You see that."

"I do not lie to you," the man said. "I do not pretend it is very much. But people will do anything even for half an hour."

"No," the girl said. "It's still not good enough."

The man laughed, shortly. Pam could not identify the laughter, and sometimes it is more easy to identify a man from his laughter than from his voice in speech. When the man laughed, even the faint, the haunting, sense of familiarity the voice gave her vanished. *If I had heard him laugh before,* she thought. *Is it someone I've never heard?*

"While you say it, you're thinking of time," the man said. "Of the little hand going around on the watch—the sweep hand. 'Thirty seconds,' you say. 'While I speak. Half a minute, while he answers.' And you're still alive. While there's life—"

"Stop it!" the girl said. "I won't!"

Life had come back into her voice; awareness had come into it, and terror.

"Oh yes," the man said. "You will, you know. When the time runs out. Now!"

The last word was sharper, commanding.

"I killed Tony Mott," the man said. "Write that first. Then what you want to say. To explain. For Mr. Carey, if you want. So he will understand."

"No," the girl said. "There couldn't be a good enough explanation. Not for that. You still don't—you still—"

But now the girl's voice was faltering. Her will was faltering, her determination. Under what pressure Pam could not guess.

"For time," the man said. He was inexorable. "For a little time. For another revolving of the little hand. For—"

But it can't be, Pam thought. *It can't be. That isn't right! There wouldn't be any reason.* But even as she though this, she had no longer any doubt.

There was a longer pause behind the door.

It was the girl who ended the pause. And now her voice was strong again. It was no longer dead. Fear was in it, and hopelessness, and with them a kind of pride, almost exultation.

"No," the girl said. "I'll never do it. Never, do you hear? Never—never— You can't—"

And then suddenly, with horrible violence, the man began again. Words poured from his mouth as if he were spitting them out. They were vicious, furious words. They blurred together too rapidly for Pam's hurrying, baffled mind. Only the fury behind them, the almost inarticulate rage of the man, was clear. The man was beating the girl with words, using them like— *like knives!* And he was speaking French.

Pam North did not think and did not hesitate. She was on her feet, pushing at the door, throwing herself against it before she realized it was opening. She almost fell as the door opened.

Peggy Mott was standing in front of a chair which had been pushed sideways near the desk. She was standing, forced back a little, her face contorted and her lips half parted as if she were trying to scream.

Pam could see only the girl's back-tilted head, her contorted face, one side of her straining body. Between them, his back to the door—one of his hands reaching toward Peggy Mott's throat—was André Maillaux. For an instant, even after the sound of the opening door reached him, he could not seem to stop lashing at the girl with words. And then he whirled. It was incredible that so round a little man could move so quickly, that so round a face could be so twisted. And then he jumped toward Pam.

The instant seemed to freeze. Released, Peggy Mott was falling backward—was in an attitude of falling, but seemed not to move. For that frozen second, André Maillaux seemed caught, also, in suspension, as if the air had turned suddenly to an invisible jelly, holding him in the act of rushing toward Pam North, with a knife in his right hand.

Pam drew air into her lungs to scream and thought she heard a scream. Then, while she had still not screamed, had not moved, Maillaux staggered grotesquely and at the same time there was a great, sharp sound which filled the room. And, quite slowly, André Maillaux fell to the floor at Pam North's feet.

There was a door beyond the desk, opposite the one by which Pam had entered the room. Bill Weigand was standing in the door, with an automatic in his hand. His face was filled with anger.

Then a good many things happened very rapidly, as if hurrying to catch up, to obliterate, that vacuum there had been in time when Peggy Mott was falling and did not fall, when Maillaux was rushing toward Pam North to kill her, and not moving. Mullins appeared at the door with Bill Weigand, and he had Leonard—tall, thin, with a look of utter astonishment on his face—by the arm. And then behind Pam there was movement and somebody—Jerry—had her by the shoulders and was pulling her back against him and Dorian was saying, anxiously, in a voice much higher than belonged to her, "Bill! Bill!"

Maillaux was trying to get up and Mullins was beside him. Maillaux still held the knife, and Mullins ·icked at the hand which held it, and the knife slid, harmless, soundlessly, across the carpet. And then Pam North heard her own voice and was astonished, because she had not intended to speak.

"Why?" Pam said. "I don't see why."

Good heavens, Pam North thought, I'm talking aloud to myself again. I thought I'd got over that.

13

The small, white and yellow living room was as full as
it had been twelve hours before; it was fuller by one,
John Leonard, whose now relaxed length seemed to
take up a disproportionate amount of the little space.
Jerry had pulled up a straight chair and sat straddling
it, leaning on the back. Dorian was back in her chair by
the fire and curled in it again; Pam and Peggy Mott and
Weldon Carey sat in a row on the sofa. Carey had his
elbows on his knees, his hands supporting his head
and he seemed, even seated, to be thrusting forward,
driving at something. Then, quite gently, Peggy
touched the one of his hands which was nearer her and
he turned, suddenly, and smiled and leaned back.
They all looked at Bill Weigand, who looked at his
drink.

"No," he said, "I wasn't surprised. Not at the very
end."

"Well," Pam said, "I wasn't either. But you have
to expect something to be surprised when it isn't. By
that time I didn't really expect anything." She paused
and looked at Leonard. "Except maybe you a little,
Mr. Leonard," she said. "I'm sorry about that."

Leonard waved it off, not speaking.

"And I still don't see—" Pam said, and left it hanging.

"Mullins' steak," Bill said, and he seemed amused momentarily. "You missed Mullins' steak." He looked at Pam, who looked back as blankly as it was possible for Pam North to look. "Not the one he had," Bill said. "The one he remembered."

Pam looked momentarily enlightened and said, "Oh, that!" But then her face clouded and she shook her head. "I'm still not sure—" she said.

"Listen," Jerry said. He said it with emphasis, and everyone looked at him. "Listen. Maillaux killed his partner, Mott. He attacked Leonard here. He killed the other girl—Pam's mink, Elaine Britton. He tried, in the end, to make Peggy write a confession. From what Pam says, he was going to kill her after she signed it and—"

"And I knew it," Peggy said. "But—I almost did." They looked at her, now. "It was very strange," she said. "I almost did it just—just to gain minutes. The minutes it would take to write it. I could never see before why people—oh, let themselves be taken for rides, marched to gas chambers. It's just for minutes." She looked at Carey. "Well," she said, and her voice was strained and a little frightened. "Just for minutes. *Minutes!*"

It was the dark man, his face no longer angry, who this time put a hand over one of the girl's.

"Take it easy, Peg," he said.

"Maybe we'd better leave all this for now," Pam said. "Just forget it, for now. After all, it's all right. Maillaux gave himself away. And—**he talked**?" This was to Bill, who nodded.

"Somehow," Bill said, in a voice carefully without inflection, "M. Maillaux got the idea he was worse hurt than he was and thought he might as well tell the whole business."

"You wouldn't know how he got that idea, would you?" Carey said. He seemed mildly angry again. Bill looked at him, kept his face expressionless, and shook his head.

"No," Peggy Mott said, "I want to find out about it."

"Then," Jerry said. "Two things. We know what he did. I don't know how you tumbled to it, Bill. And I don't know why he did any of it. Or, anyway, I don't know what started him. And this business about Mullins' steak. What was that?"

"The steak he didn't like," Bill said, "was the tip-off."

Nobody saw it, they looked at him puzzled.

"At first," Bill said, "we had a perfect case against Mrs. Mott. We all saw that, including Mrs. Mott. Pam said it was too perfect but that was a—an esoteric objection."

"Nevertheless—" Pam said.

"Nevertheless, I considered it," Bill admitted. "I never denied that. I considered the possibility that someone was handing it to us on a platter and that, because it seemed so easy, it was possible we hadn't gone deeply enough. Then I talked to Mr. Leonard and—"

Leonard, who had been looking at the carpet, sighed, audibly.

"All right," Bill said, and smiled slightly. "I'll leave out the detail, Mr. Leonard. However—I had two cases, then. One interfering with the other. And so, because I wasn't sure enough, I held up on Mrs. Mott. And, I began to wonder whether there might be another case—or half a dozen more cases." He paused. "It was—disquieting," he said, mildly. "I went back over everybody. Went back over all we knew about them, looking for something we'd missed. I didn't find it, at first. I just lost certainty."

"Plowed the ground," Pam said.

They all looked at her.

"Loosened it," she amplified. "Then Mullins sowed seed on it. Right?"

"Mullins sowed seed," Bill agreed. "I saw why somebody else might have wanted to kill Mott. It was just a glimmer. Then, you two"—he nodded at Peggy Mott and Carey—"decided to go to the restaurant. And, I saw the pay-off coming up. For obvious reasons."

"Obvious?" Jerry said. It was part question, part cue. Dorian turned a little in her chair. "He likes this, you know," she said, conversationally. "Don't you, Bill?"

Bill grinned at her, not answering.

"Obvious?" Carey said. "How obvious?"

"If somebody other than Mrs. Mott had killed Mott, and the girl, he had certainly gone out of his way to arrange things so Mrs. Mott would appear guilty," Bill pointed out. "Arrange a frame for her. Now, this somebody finds that it hasn't worked. That, so far as he knows, Mrs. Mott's cleared or, at least, that we're not satisfied. So what will he do, in view of what he's done before? Obviously, he'll provide something new—something that *will* satisfy us. So it seemed like an idea to go along and see what this person would do." He paused and his face hardened momentarily. "See he didn't do too much," he said.

"You thought it was Maillaux by that time?" The question was Pam's.

Bill nodded, then hesitated.

"I thought so," he said. "I still only—well, thought so. It still might have been Leonard. And I still might be doing it all the hard way, refusing to accept the obvious. Mrs. Mott. But there wasn't any harm in finding out. In giving everybody enough rope. I pushed it along a little, too—hinted that we still

thought it was Mrs. Mott, hoping that the right person
would figure one more little thing planted against her
would finish things off."

"Me," Leonard said. "You hinted that to me." He
was morose.

"You," Bill said. He was cheerful. "You were still
in it, Mr. Leonard. I gave Maillaux the same hint. I'll
admit when you stumbled over Mullins in the corridor
while we were listening to Maillaux and Mrs. Mott, I
was a little confused."

"My own interests," Leonard said. "I wanted to
keep track of things. Also, I had had a couple of
drinks."

"Right," Bill said. "But, anyway, it was clear by
then. Clear what Maillaux was trying to do, hence
what he had done. It wasn't necessary to know then,
and I didn't know, that he'd got her to go to the office
by sending her a note supposed to be from me. And I
thought he'd killed Elaine—Pam's poor little mink—
merely because the person with an obvious motive to
kill her was Mrs. Mott."

"That wasn't it?" Pam said. She paused. "I ought to
have had a glimmer myself," she said. "She was so
anxious to see Maillaux when she went to the restaurant to say she had seen Peggy go in. In the foyer
when Jerry and I were waiting for a cab."

"Anxious?" Jerry said. "I didn't get that."

"Anyway," Pam said, "she asked for him, first off.
Why, Bill?"

"Because she was in a position to give us the
motive," Bill said. "Because she thought he might
make it worth her while not to give us the motive.
She—well, she tried again. Unfortunately for her."

"Bill," Dorian said. "Get back to the steak. Please
Bill. Tell us about the glimmer."

Bill looked at Dorian and smiled. He said, "Right."

"Maillaux comes from a family of restaurant
owners," he said. "And—not just people who happen

to own restaurants. People to whom running restaurants—great restaurants—is the most important thing in life, or just about. You have to get that picture—blow it up to size. The importance of running a restaurant which is really great. A restaurant epicures think of first when you mention eating, mention a city. Or, think of among the two or three you think of first. The great places, the *grande cuisine. Cordon bleu.* Do you see that—see that coming down through several generations of the Maillaux family? See the pride building up?"

He paused and looked at them.

"Try to," he advised. "Because that was what did it. Incredible pride. In a way, incredible honesty, too. For Maillaux, it wasn't the point, merely, that he operate a famous restaurant—one *everybody* knew about. It had to be more than famous; it had to be great in the eyes of the few people all over the world who know about food. Not just the food people all over the world are dying for lack of. Food in the epicure's sense."

"Anachronistic," Carey said. "Good God!"

"Right," Bill agreed. "But it still goes on. And that was Maillaux's league. And, until a year or so ago, he seemed to be getting to the top of it. Maillaux's was one of the great restaurants of New York, and that meant of the world. Then—I don't know precisely why, perhaps to keep up the standard, Maillaux's prices had to get too high for too many people—he got into financial difficulties. And—Tony Mott bought in. He did the place over and, *aimed at a new clientele.* The crowd which cares more about glitter, and service, and going to the right place, than about food. People who—well, I'll tell you what Maillaux said. 'Pigs,' Maillaux said. 'They smoke through dinner. You perceive? The palate—bah!' "

"But," Pam said. "Even so. I mean, he made money?"

Bill nodded. He said she didn't see what Maillaux was really like. Money he had to have, obviously. But—

"Mott knew the kind of crowd he wanted," Bill said. "He knew they 'smoked through dinner.' He didn't care and, it gave him a chance to improve the profits. He liked profits, didn't he, Mrs. Mott?"

"Very much," Peggy said. "Oh, very much."

"So, what was put into service-chi-chi—could come out of the kitchen," Bill said. "That was obvious, and nobody would know the difference. But—you have to see how this hit Maillaux. It was like—well, like making a Supreme Court justice into an ambulance chaser, a shyster. And, don't think that Maillaux would think the parallel extreme. He'd probably say, 'A Supreme Court justice, phooey!' "

"With a French accent," Pam said. "No—wait a minute. There in the office he didn't have one. Until he said 'revolving' when he meant 'revolution.' "

"He turned it on and off," Bill said. "He'd been here a long time. He had a good ear. But he spoke to customers as he realized they preferred. However—"

"Go ahead," Jerry said.

"Mott had control," Bill said. "He could call the turn. He did. Probably, although Maillaux doesn't admit this, the way the money came in kept Maillaux quiet for a time. Perhaps Maillaux thought he could get his own way back in the end. But apparently things got worse and—well, they fought about it. That's what Elaine had to tell us, incidentally. Mott had told her that Maillaux was acting up, and had laughed about it. She knew Maillaux. Maybe she guessed that, on such a point, he had a monomania. Maybe Mott did, but figured he could handle Maillaux. Well—he couldn't. Maillaux decided that—that he would be better off if he had Mott's money without Mott. Of course somebody would have inherited Mott's share—you, Mrs. Mott, if you didn't kill him—but Maillaux figured he could handle any ordinary person. And, no ordinary person would have the ability Mott had to get the kind of patronage Mott wanted. Anyway, Maillaux took a chance."

"With a knife," Pam said.

Bill nodded.

"Now you see where the steak came in," he said. "Mullins knows a good steak when he gets one. And—any good restaurant can give you a good steak. It isn't esoteric. It's something a place like Maillaux's would do, perfectly, without thinking about it one way or another. If it gave Mullins an indifferent steak—well, the kitchen was falling apart. And, if Maillaux didn't like that, and considering his history, his family's history—well, I got a glimmer. And played it that way."

There was a considerable pause. Jerry refilled glasses.

"Maillaux didn't move without planning," Bill said. "He wanted it to be perfect. Mrs. Mott was obviously the one to pin it on; her motive was ready-made. So he called her up, pretending to be Mott, and arranged for her to be on hand. Then, just before she was due, he went into Mott's office, picked up the steak knife, and stabbed Mott from behind. That was all he had to do except, a little later, go around and discover the body. If Mrs. Britton hadn't seen Mrs. Mott there, if nobody had seen her, Maillaux could have come to us himself and said *he* had seen her. That would start things going the way he wanted them to go. After that, he improvised. He was around when Miss Breakwell told about that paper you wrote, Mrs. Mott. He was there when you two"—Bill indicated the Norths—"came to tell me the paper had been stolen. That was a nice break for him. He made it better by his attack on Leonard, which wasn't, incidentally, intended to be more serious than it was. Maillaux himself wouldn't have missed; Mrs. Mott might have. And, although he decided he had to kill Mrs. Britton for his own protection, that was useful too, because Mrs. Mott had an obvious motive. Everything was perfect."

"Too perfect," Pam said. "Too good to be true."

There was another pause. Pam ended it.

"Look," she said, "you say he heard about the paper's being stolen. You mean, he didn't steal it?"

Bill smiled slowly. He nodded. He said, "Right."

"Did he, Mr. Carey?" Bill asked. "That's just something you did for him. Wasn't it?"

Carey leaned forward again, as if he were about to leap.

"Damn it all," he said. "What else would I—?"

His voice was angry.

"Suppose I did?" he said. "Are you going to make—"

Then, quite unexpectedly, he stopped. He stopped because the slim blond girl sitting beside him reached out and took his face in both her hands and turned the face toward her own.

"Shut up, Wel," she said. "Shut up, dear."

And then, apparently to see that he did, and still holding his face in both her hands, she leaned forward a little and kissed him on the lips. She did it quite simply, as if there were no one else in the room.

A MR. & MRS. NORTH MYSTERY

THE CLASSIEST COUPLE EVER TO SOLVE A CRIME— MR. AND MRS. NORTH

Pam and Jerry North, a charming, witty and sophisticated pair who like nothing better than a very dry martini and a very difficult murder.

Enjoy all these Mr. and Mrs. North Mysteries

DEATH TAKES A BOW 44337/$2.95
THE JUDGE IS REVERSED 44338/$2.95
MURDER BY THE BOOK 47333/$2.95
MURDER COMES FIRST 44335/$2.95
MURDER IN A HURRY 44336/$2.95
MURDER IS SERVED 47328/$2.95
MURDER WITHIN MURDER 44334/$2.95

FROM POCKET BOOKS